Praise for *Gag Reflex*

"Nash's ability is that she isn't constrained to a subjective point of view at all, but may perhaps embody the omniscience of a daimon, trapped in a physical form insufficient to its capacities." —*Heavy Feather Review*

"It's more relevant than ever...Nash does not shy away from detailing the horrors of an eating disorder, though any such physical descriptions are eclipsed by the sharp articulations of its psychological impacts and the low self-esteem it engenders." —*The Rumpus*

"Elle Nash writes like she recently climbed out of a black hole, simply to invent the knife." —*The Observer*

Praise for *Nudes*

"The overall effect of Nash's mastery of tension and efficiency is stories that compel you to read them, the way you might feel compelled to one more drink after you've had a few." —*Vagabond City*

"Transgressive and immediate: you feel these stories shoot through and wrap around you." —*Full Stop Magazine*

"Never a dull moment, Nash succeeds in capturing the full attention of her reader with the finesse of the most popular girl in school sharing everyone's secrets." —*BOMB Magazine*

Praise for *Animals Eat Each Other*

"Nash writes with psychological precision, capturing Lilith's volatile shifts between directionless frustration, self-destructiveness, ambivalence, and vulnerable need. A complex, impressive exploration of obsession and desire." —*Publishers Weekly* (**starred review**)

"Strands of emotional confusion and self-loathing run through *Animals Eat Each Other*, and Nash writes brilliantly and viscerally about the connections between physical and emotional intimacy. There is a superbly tactile flow to her beautiful, stripped-down prose that absolutely sucks the reader in, making this a disturbing and deeply moving piece of modern storytelling. Brilliant stuff." —**Doug Johnstone, The Big Issue**

"Elle Nash's *Animals East Each Other* is a desire map, a cartography of eros. Two women and a man weave their contradictions and obsessions and aches into one another until names, bodies, and selves dissolve and reconstitute in ways they could not have imagined. Mirrorings, doublings, triplings, and reproductions bring the right questions to the surface: who are we when we enter into love stories? Does anyone know? A heartbomb." —**Lidia Yuknavitch, author of *The Book of Joan***

Praise for *Gag Reflex*

"Nash's ability is that she isn't constrained to a subjective point of view at all, but may perhaps embody the omniscience of a daimon, trapped in a physical form insufficient to its capacities." —*Heavy Feather Review*

"It's more relevant than ever...Nash does not shy away from detailing the horrors of an eating disorder, though any such physical descriptions are eclipsed by the sharp articulations of its psychological impacts and the low self-esteem it engenders." —*The Rumpus*

"Elle Nash writes like she recently climbed out of a black hole, simply to invent the knife." —*The Observer*

Praise for *Nudes*

"The overall effect of Nash's mastery of tension and efficiency is stories that compel you to read them, the way you might feel compelled to one more drink after you've had a few." —*Vagabond City*

"Transgressive and immediate: you feel these stories shoot through and wrap around you. —*Full Stop Magazine*

"Never a dull moment, Nash succeeds in capturing the full attention of her reader with the finesse of the most popular girl in school sharing everyone's secrets." —*BOMB Magazine*

Praise for *Animals Eat Each Other*

"Nash writes with psychological precision, capturing Lilith's volatile shifts between directionless frustration, self-destructiveness, ambivalence, and vulnerable need. complex, impressive exploration of obsession and desire." —*Publishers Weekly* (**starred review**)

"Strands of emotional confusion and self-loathing run through *Animals Eat Each Other* and Nash writes brilliantly and viscerally about the connections between physical and emotional intimacy. There is a superbly tactile flow to her beautiful, stripped-down prose that absolutely sucks the reader in, making this a disturbing and deeply moving piece of modern storytelling. Brilliant stuff." —**Doug Johnstone, The Big Issue**

"Elle Nash's *Animals East Each Other* is a desire map, a cartography of eros. Two women and a man weave their contradictions and obsessions and aches into one another u names, bodies, and selves dissolve and reconstitute in ways they could not have imagined. Mirrorings, doublings, triplings, and reproductions bring the right questions to surface: who are we when we enter into love stories? Does anyone know? A heartbor —**Lidia Yuknavitch, author of *The Book of Joan***

Deliver Me

a novel

Elle Nash

The Unnamed Press
Los Angeles, CA

AN UNNAMED PRESS BOOK

Copyright © 2023 by Elle Nash

Published in North America by the Unnamed Press.

www.unnamedpress.com

Unnamed Press, and the colophon, are registered trademarks of Unnamed Media LLC.

Hardcover ISBN: 978-1-951213-71-8
EBook ISBN: 978-1-951213-85-5

LCCN: 2023015315

Cover design and typeset by Jaya Nicely

Manufactured in the United States of America by Sheridan

Distributed by Publishers Group West

First Edition

For L
For B
For Baby and Me

O Lord, deliver me from evil men. Preserve me from the violent.

—Psalm 140:1

Deliver Me

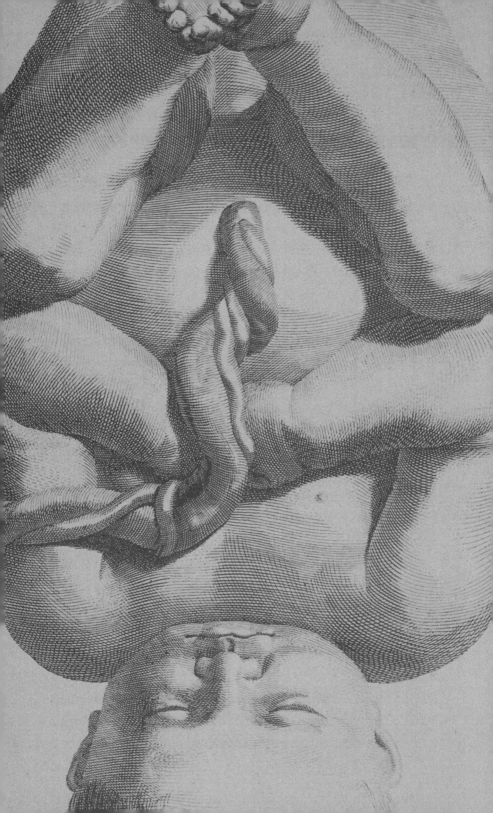

First
Trimester

XXXX

The factory is a fertile body, each breast a beginning. I make geometry of the meat and that keeps my mind in line—calming, comforting tenders and perfect fingers, my pneumatic scissors make sense of the mess. It's ten to four when I arrive on the floor in my sexless scrub top and Number Five is pissed. I slip on my disposable arm wraps, then tie my plastic apron behind my back. Everything that drops into our section is mostly peach with pale yellow lumps of fat. Thank God there is no blood. When I'm not at work, I remember moving the length of my fingers over each smooth breast, feeling for the catch of bone or a string of tendon against my latex glove. Number Five catches me missing a breast and shouts. I look up, then cut faster to catch up. Trembling flesh flops and tumbles down a conveyer belt at 140 birds or more a minute, and I cut, cut, throw the pieces into wide emerald vats to be sorted. It's hard to focus, and sanitizer fogs my eye protection. This morning the sky was July clear, and as I walked through the glass doors glittering with dawn light, I knew something was different, couldn't stop squeezing the skin of my stomach. In the locker room, I pressed my hands deep into my hips, searching for the nubs of my pelvis through the surrounding paunch of my sore, spongy fat.

During first break I swallow back the nausea worming up my throat. I step outside and walk past the rows of parked cars, the sun barely rising and the constellation fading out in the north. Momma calls it the Northern Cross. "God is watching over us," she would say, but when I moved out and got the internet I looked it up. It's not a cross but a swan in flight. The air outside is normally swollen with blood and animal waste, but today it smells earthy, like wild grass and fresh milk. The mild country across the highway is peppered with paste-colored double-wides, old barns, twined bundles of hay, our factory nestled neatly between that and a few acres of chicken farms—if you can call them that. Oblong, warehouse-sized huts with thousands of clucking broilers breathing in their shit. We're the kill station. The biggest poultry supplier to Missouri, Arkansas, and Oklahoma.

When first break is over, workers sort into their sections like marbles rolling toward one uneven end. Number Three shows up next to me.

"Good morning, Number Four."

I nod and cover my nose with my paper mask. My hunger prods, and pressure in the muscle of my jaw, below my tongue, makes me salivate. A bloat sits below my belly button, achy and full. I try to remember the last time I bled. Three weeks, maybe. It's never been regular, sometimes it takes months, but always I'm thinking, *She's here again. Inside me.* An alarm rings and the assembly line clunks on, first from the adjacent warehouse rooms, then ours. Air hisses through the hose of my scissors, and I ready the blades by schlicking them open and shut a few times. For the rest of the day I cut and cut and cut.

When I get home, Daddy is on the couch watching a show about women who undergo extreme plastic surgery and spend weeks in a hotel away from family, working with physical trainers to lose weight. Then they're revealed in their new, authentic forms. These women have never been ugly, the announcer says, they were just hiding their good looks. The plastic surgeries helped them unfold, like teasing open a flower bud. The TV light catches in the light of Daddy's whiskey. It's the bottom-shelf stuff; I can smell the sweetness from where I am. When I lean over and kiss the side of his mouth, the taste of acetone moves into mine. I drift a weak finger down along his pockmarked jawbone and it speed-bumps over the gnarled scar on his cheek.

"Eaten yet?" I ask.

"No," he says. "Texted Blake, no landscaping work today."

I scrub my hands and forearms at the kitchen sink and notice an inflamed cut near my thumb. On day one Momma asked if I feared being injured or losing a finger. She lives an hour away on some wooded land alongside a tiny ravine and calls nearly every day. Momma loves to call me, now that she is all alone. A daughter has to listen to her momma. Isn't that what the Bible says? Honoring your parents. It's the child who always must be dutiful, responsible, especially now that Momma's getting frail. And Momma has needs, and she doesn't want to be alone anymore. Momma wants grandchildren, and I'm the only one who can give them to her. Once I passed into my thirties she began to ask with increasing intensity, "When are you going to *get married* and *have children*, Dee-Dee?" I understand, because I want children, too. More than anything, I want a daughter for myself. So I can teach what I have learned, so I have someone to relate to. Someone I can see myself in. I move through most of my days thinking of Momma and pregnancy and of my future daughter, obsessing over the fat at my thighs and waist, which is already large and soft and shapely, willing my torso to grow, grow more. All day my thoughts blunder forward like *my momma, my momma, my momma.*

If I told Momma about my blessing now she'd repeat my name in her soft, sprawling tongue as if I weren't already yearning for her approval.

Dee-Dee, she'd say, then pause and rewet her lips, *until the church bells ring and that rice is raining down on you both, you shouldn't even think about having a child. It's not right. Not right now.*

Right in the eyes of God, she means. At this point she only has to imply it. Everything in this town and the state of Missouri is about what is right in the eyes of God. It's so hard to make her happy, and yet I know she's right, because some assurance from Daddy would make the daily slog of work so much easier. If we were married I would know we were a team, that he was going to take care of me; that someday, the killing would end.

Momma would then cluck her tongue and switch the topic: *Has he found a job yet?*

At the kitchen sink, I put the sponge's green side to my skin and scrub the scratch with antibacterial soap. There's red around a scab of yellow.

"Did you pay rent?" I ask Daddy.

He eases back into the couch and shakes his head. "We have to kite the check," he says. He chews on the inside of his cheek, and the thick scar that twists from his chin to the bed of his eye moves with it. I love its hard pink and trace the scar from bottom to top, as if his entire past were burrowed inside its trail.

"I'll ask for overtime," I say.

I rip off three paper towels from the roll and pat my wrists dry, but my hands still smell like the caustic stink of sanitizer. I won't tell Daddy about the baby, not yet. Not until I'm sure. I pick up a can of chili, but the muscles in my hand won't grip, and it keeps slipping around the can opener. Not much longer, then I can give up the factory.

"Daddy," I say.

He keeps his attention on the TV. A woman in a royal-blue dress stands onstage in front of a screen the size of a building. A shot of her

Before face frowns next to a live feed of her After face as she glides down the runway. The Before face is round, the lips thinner, skin paler and pockmarked, eye bags mooning up as her mouth forms a flat line. The new face flashes veneered teeth so bright they appear blue, tight eyelids, the skin even tighter over her brow bones, all forming a waxy tension that's pulled a decade from her face.

"Daddy," I say again, "I need your help."

His head turns. Even with the scar, he is the most beautiful man I'll ever love. I've only ever been with one other person.

"What?" he says, annoyed. "What's wrong with you?"

I walk into the living room, handing him the can with the opener affixed to it. I don't say what's wrong with me. He puts down his drink and takes the can. Daddy twists until the lid cracks in release and hands it back to me. The smell of cold meat permeates the air.

"Don't forget to feed the bugs," he says, turning back to the show.

"They're your bugs," I say.

Momma never allowed me to watch TV, and when I see Daddy's eyes gloss over I understand why. He is gone, lost inside the fantasy of the woman in the sequined dress, who looks into a beveled mirror at her new self. She cries, and a group of people rush the stage to embrace her. A mother and father, a husband, and two children crowd around her and cry, too, as though the woman has just returned from a kidnapping or death. She's been growing the new, better version of herself this entire time. The children, especially, are sobbing, twisting their faces to play to the camera and to the audience, all of whom stood up to applaud. Their mouths stretch in ecstasy, but you can see in their darting eyes: the kids are just mirroring what they think they're supposed to feel. *This is it,* their eyes say. *The mother we were meant to have.*

1996

Revival season at Faithful Floods Temple of God. Service was usually held in church, a building that was essentially two double-wides attached either way to a circular brick room in the center. When it was revival season we moved to tents in large fields out by the Wal-Mart. In the tent I clasped my hands together, fingers joined into a fist. The stiff cotton of Momma's dress brushed my arm as she stepped toward the stage, the scent of White Diamonds in her wake. Momma lived for this—she adored a deliverance, attended baptisms as often as sermons, to watch people sprawl on the carpet in tears for Christ.

My father touched her shoulder, and she shot him a look, pulling away. This was before the earth took him back, which is how I see it now. I don't believe in angels anymore. I always wonder if Momma regrets anything about the way she treated him. Momma doesn't talk about it. My father glanced at me and resumed clapping to the rhythm of the organ.

We had joined the congregation the first year we moved to Cassville, after my father got out of the army. For him, it was a renewed effort to make community, to please Momma, I'd always thought. Momma had been raised in the faith all her life. She craved the spectacle, like the rest of the congregation. A parishioner weeping and falling to the carpet. What they called the power of Christ. Wood stretched and popped as half the crowd stood from the antique folding chairs, their slew of hands and fingers stretched toward our sister Sloane onstage. Sloane, Sloane, I pushed my knuckles into my lower lip and pressed hard against my teeth. I don't know how I hadn't noticed her before. I was so young then, susceptible to the fears of God that settled inside good people and made them sick.

"Let's put hands on our sister," the pastor said. His open palms faced the light and the congregation's did, too, everyone moving closer to the stage. The timbre of his voice was sultry, like a song booming into Sloane's ears. She dropped to the ground, her shaggy hair set loose against the grass, light blue eyes sharpened by the stage lights. The women crowded around, touching her, praying, brunette victory rolls and floral skirts swaying to the reedy organ music. It was what the pastor wanted: No trousers, skirts only. No makeup, so you didn't stink of pride. The crowd prayed together until their voices melded into a single rumble while a stray shriek or two punctuated the edges.

My father put his palm on the space between my shoulders and nudged me forward. I walked past the women with their plain hair up in buns, past the men with sweat beading on their shaved necks. The second I put my hand out, palm up like the pastor's, Momma grabbed my wrist and pushed it toward the girl.

"Touch her," she hissed. "There's not much time left." I placed my palm on her calf. Sloane smelled like stone fruit. Peach-colored flush feathered her cheeks.

The pastor began to speak faster, louder. "Your relationship should be with the Living Word," he said. "Out there are the enemies. They prowl, try to keep us ignorant, control us, keep us from knowing the truth of this world."

His fingers pressed on her forehead, then pushed her hair back, leaving wet snarls plastered to her skin. Our hands held her in place; Sloane kicked and waved her arms, and a throaty moan rattled from her chest. We locked eyes. Her mouth curled into a smile, and she licked her teeth and winked. I thought I might've made it up, created a lie, when in truth she had let me into hers.

I looked back at my father, then to Momma. Both were totally entranced in the moment. Everyone pushed against Sloane, their oily faces hungry for their own taste of her deliverance.

Sloane's dress had bunched up around her hips, and the pastor held her waist down with his fingertips. Stray hairs glittered on her otherwise smooth knees. I played with the lace of her sock, tufted at her ankle, then released my hand from her leg, but something pushed me back toward her, jarring my head and neck forward, clattering my teeth. The pastor kept chanting, "Resist the adversary! There is not much time left!" I turned to see the pink membrane of Momma's lips, her red Avon lipstick bleeding into its edges. "O the adversary!" her mouth repeated. "Our sister needs your help, O Lord!" The sea of sweating cheeks, all chanting, "Resist! Submit to the Lord!" The words grew indistinguishable until Sloane closed her eyes and began to shake and snarl. Suddenly our world was normal again, and the lie went on as Sloane shuddered once, twice, then collapsed into the sea of hands.

XXXX

Meat chickens are not bred to make life. The internal mechanisms are all there—ovaries with their tiny clusters of eggs, the hormonal drive—but meat chickens don't live long enough to lay. They are bred to be eaten. Their breasts and bodies grow at an abnormal rate, tripling in weight in those first few days of life, and are sent to slaughter at five pounds. Each chicken on my line is only fifty days old. Every one must be processed by the end of the day. If even one person calls off work, the rest of us have to pick up the slack, we don't get to leave until the work is finished.

In each section of the warehouse, a massive digital counter on the wall marks the processing of an entire bird. It counts up red, until we hit our death goal. I use it to keep track of the time. There's no clock, and we have to keep our watches and phones in our lockers. A buzzer alerts everyone to breaks, lunch, and shift changes. If we manage to process 140 birds per minute, we know we're near break time when the death counter approaches twenty-six thousand. At fifty thousand, first shift is over and my day is done.

The deboning line comes with the bonus of not having to see the birds die. They begin their journey feathered and writhing, their feet in fork-shaped hangers attached to a long chain. The chain moves behind a steel wall, where the birds' heads are dipped into a trough of electrified water before they're reeled to the killing room, where their throats are dragged past an automatic cutter. Then they're scalded bald, hocked, and beheaded before getting disemboweled and moved to the deboning room. By the time the birds make it to me, they're so clean they don't look like anything that's ever been alive.

Once the line starts, no one talks. For the next four hours, my ears are filled with the whirring of ceiling fans, the spritz of sanitizer, and the slop of flesh into buckets until the lunch buzzer.

I weave through at least a hundred sweaty foreheads lined up for the building's two toilets to get lunch from my locker. The pneumatic scissors make my palm tingle. I stretch my fingers back to my wrist, pulling out the ache. Daddy is probably waking up, checking his phone for messages or calling around for work. I shoot him a text. Daddy doesn't text back, and part of me wants his attention so badly I consider telling him right away about the pregnancy. I open my lunch bag and pull out tuna salad on Wonder Bread. My mouth waters as I bite through it, soft on top and soggy in the middle. The tang of mayonnaise and salty flecks of fish separate onto my tongue.

"How did you find out you were pregnant with me?" I ask Momma over the phone.

"Oh"—she coughs—"I knew the instant I conceived you, honey." She drags from a cigarette and blows out. "I just knew, the way you know when you've got a tickle in your throat that you're about to get sick. With you, there was an ache in my bones. I told your father the day it happened, rest his soul. Why, Dee-Dee? Are you pregnant again? You can't think this one will succeed. You know you are living in sin and need to redeem yourself to the Lord."

"Daddy promised me a ring," I say. "He's saving up from his odd jobs."

"God judges all sexually immoral people, and that includes you, Dee-Dee."

My chapped lips stretch into a stinging grimace. She always pushes past me and into God.

"He wants the ring to be bought with honest money."

"The Lord blesses only those with a pure heart," Momma says.

I wipe crumbs from my face, from my shirt; place my hand on my abdomen over the new fragility. Then Momma mumbles something I don't hear. I'm too distracted by thoughts of a pregnancy test and what else I need to buy on the way home.

"Swollen?" she asks.

"What?"

"Are your hands still swollen? I can hear people in the background. I know you're at work, honey."

"I woke up this morning with my rings cutting off my circulation," I say. "Had to soak my hand in a bowl of ice water to get them off."

It's a lie, but I want her sympathy. I hold my palms out even though she can't see; they're red where I've been rubbing them.

"Sometimes aspirin works," she says. "You know, you should call Sloane soon."

"Momma," I say.

They've kept in touch ever since Sloane moved away years ago. I don't know why. Probably Momma wanted to pretend she had a daughter who did all the things she liked. Probably her and Sloane did pretend that—that they were family all these years—and they talked about how I wasn't very good, and how I was dating a criminal now, and how I'd never have a baby because the last five have died inside me. Probably Momma loved to tell Sloane she thought my womb was a coffin and about how I quit going to church, and how proud she was of Sloane for going back to God after all her mistakes. Sloane would have everything I couldn't: a good husband as hot as a movie star who didn't care about her teenage pregnancy; maybe she even got to keep it, all while he was funding her stay-at-home life.

"Sloane doesn't want to talk to me," I say.

Momma tuts. She tsks. She sucks on her cigarette. Momma says, "I know she would love to hear from you."

Every time I think of Sloane I go wet with envy. A gnawing hunger for her life, unnamable, as deep as sex. Sloane and her husband in bed, her nose pressed into his inky hair, the two so close they smell as one. Babies sleeping, soon to wake up and adore them. Scribbly drawings and colored handprints all over the fridge. Sloane for sure would have a life full to bursting. Whenever a girl in the church got married, we'd all gossip about who'd be next and how many months it'd be until the newly married couple announced their pregnancy. Before wedding season, Sunday school teachers had the preteens write letters to their future husbands, encouraging us to imagine being blessed by a man who would bring us closer to God. Some girls kept purity journals where they described all the ways they would serve these men. I prayed that God would surround me with an assortment of devout males laid out like a buffet: short men, tall men, feminine men with slim wrists and long torsos, silky hair, amber eyes. I prayed for jutting pectorals, beefy arms. Religious men to make me right. Rebellious men to make me slick and thirsty. Most of all, virile men. Someone who could make me a woman, give me the chance to grow—to become a doorway for something greater than myself. ("Before every great doorway is a doormat," Sloane loved to say.)

Within months of her wedding, the newlywed girl would become something else. Her skin would ripen; she would glisten. Her arms flushed pink; her hair grew longer, shinier. Her breasts swelled. We'd gossip, write our letters, dream about a man passionate for fucking and following Christ. We'd imagine our bellies inflated, too, hump our pillows at night. Then we'd sign the letters, *Yours in Christ, Your Future Wife*.

The buzzer rings harsh, and I tell Momma I got to go. Lunch is over. I check my phone once more and Daddy still hasn't messaged me. Amid the crumple of lunch bags and the scrape of chairs against concrete, I pet the fat beneath my belly button as if it's a blanket tucking in the multiplying cells—my manic, buoyant new life.

XXXX

Three weeks of pregnancy is too early to tell anyone, even the father. The highest risk of miscarriage exists between four and six weeks of pregnancy, and after that it drops by over 15 percent. I have researched these numbers countless times because it's when I lose every baby. By week eight, the rate falls to 3 percent, and I've made it to week eight only once. Pregnancy is a thing that *happens*, and we have little choice what happens, so we speak of it in passive terms: I've *been* pregnant. Over the last two years I've been pregnant five times, and each time a heart the size of the tip of a sharpened pencil thrums inside me as the embryo attempts to cross the threshold into that of a fetus. In Missouri, a fetus is protected life. One time the state prosecuted a woman, an addict, for miscarrying at eight weeks, and she almost went to jail for infanticide. Before the cluster of cells develops eyelids, the buds of toes and fingers, the shape of a human heart, it's considered a person. But somewhere along the way the heartbeat stops, and before I can get to a doctor, I bleed it out.

That first time I missed my period I bought a test from CVS and the faintest cross bloomed inside the window. Two days later I took another and the line appeared lighter. I shook Daddy awake, waving the uncapped stick in front of his eyes.

"A baby!" I said. "We're going to have a baby!"

He turned on the lamp on the nightstand and squinted at the stick. "Get that out of my face."

I grabbed his hands and put them to my cheeks, fever-hot and heavy. The rims of his eyes were a bright, burning pink. "I love you," I said to him. "I love you, I love you."

He lifted his groggy eyelids and cupped my chin.

"Our baby will have your wide ears and my upturned nose," I said. "Its hair will be brown, like mine, or maybe more serious and dark like yours."

Daddy rolled his eyes, and I traced my fingers down his scar.

"Don't fret," I said. I went to kiss him, and he turned his face, leaning back into his pillow.

A week before that first ultrasound, desperate meat chickens parted as I shuffled through the hut at work, their clucks and bawks shrill and constant. A ragged, peach-colored crew of them scattered from me, many of them missing feathers, skittering on ghostly feet. I searched for stragglers. Cleaning out the huts meant clearing up the dead or killing the sick ones. The sick were worthless to the factory. I never wanted to kill them. I wiped sweat from my forehead, queasy from the stink, my stomach cramping tighter and tougher. Pregnancy pains. Implantation, or my uterus expanding. Rows of feed funnels and large overhead fans repeated in a dizzying geometric blur from one end of the building to the other. It became hard to breathe. One hen stopped and sat in place as I stumbled through the flock. I dreaded this part. My hands shook. I pressed my stomach with one hand to hold in the pain and picked up the hen with the other, turning her over on her side. The hen's torso burned hot through my latex glove. The knuckles of her feet showed large, knobby abscesses—signs of infection. I held her legs in one hand and her head in the other. The bird's small pupil whirred shut, and I broke her neck the way management taught me:

grab at the base of its head, pull the neck away from the torso as fast as I could, then slam it down quick to snap the spine. She was gone. I tossed the hen behind me. Her wings flapped on autopilot, a small bowl of dust and shit kicking up, as if she were still alive.

The cramps got worse and I hunched over, holding back tears. A passing coworker locked eyes with me, and the smallest acknowledgment of my discomfort caused the wall to buckle. I burst into tears, which channeled muddy tracks through the dirt on my cheeks. The woman had walked away as I cried, and I wanted to ask her to come back so I could tell her I wasn't in pain, I wasn't losing my baby, anything to make it not real, but talking was not a choice. Management was strict with fraternization. It was considered time theft. We weren't allowed unscheduled bathroom breaks. When my shift was over I hobbled straight to the bathroom, where I removed my disposable jumpsuit and pulled down my underwear to find a dark clot of blood, mucusy and thin like a brown egg yolk. I wiped at it.

Daddy told me the miscarriage was nature's way of eliminating bad genes. It was retarded, he'd said, or it had extra fingers. Daddy knows a lot about breeding because he breeds exotic insects. Sometimes, Daddy said, Mantodea abandon their young only to find them and eat them alive.

"Am I diseased?" I asked. "Am I broken?"

"That's just nature," he'd said, tapping on one of the insect cages in our bedroom.

Momma told me to get a different job. But where was I going to go? I'd applied at Wal-Mart three times, and besides, I didn't want to drive over an hour to work every day. Momma had no answers. She just asked if I was going to church like I was supposed to be. I spent the whole evening in the tub until the water turned frigid and pink from the remaining tissue leaking from me. I broke into tears, my quiet heaves sending ripples through the water. Daddy didn't check on me once.

The second through fifth miscarriages were the same: the thin blue line, excitement, and, a few weeks later, crushing disappointment. Blood beneath me, from inside me, the same dark blood.

XXXX

In the family planning aisle at CVS there's only condoms and lube. Up and down other aisles are pads and tampons, vaginal washes, shaving cream in pink cans, and expensive razors. Clear plastic bottles full of blue and red pills, turquoise gelcaps, colloidal silver. Cartoon bandages. Not a single pregnancy test. I give up, anxious and a little damp, and grab a Redpop, Bugles, and a chocolate bar. An associate in a red vest is bent over in the candy aisle, checking inventory.

"Miss?" I ask. She straightens up. "Where are the pregnancy tests?"

"Oh," she says. "Behind the counter. With the cigarettes."

She pushes her acetate glasses up the bridge of her nose and takes me to the counter, unlocks a glass cabinet behind it.

"We have the generic kind, which are only two dollars, then there's the brand-name sticks—here's one with two in it for eight dollars; here's an electronic one, that's fourteen."

Fourteen dollars could go far.

"Eight dollars," I say. She pulls down the pastel-colored box and scans it with the rest of my items, removing the plastic antitheft sensor. I want her to say something—giddiness branches inside my chest, an itch to share—but she just wipes at the puffy gray skin beneath her eyes.

"Do you have children?" I ask. Her eyes flick up at the question.

"Will that be all?" she says.

"Yeah. Thanks."

When I walk through the front door, tests hidden in my purse, Daddy's on the couch watching a forensic cop show. Some boomer in sunglasses makes jokes to a younger associate while standing over a corpse.

"Did you see the new car?" I ask.

"Red Volvo?" Daddy says.

"Yeah, and it's parked in my spot. Gotta be a new tenant upstairs."

"Where'd you park?"

"Blake's spot was the only open one," I say. I open the Redpop with a snap and take a loud sip.

"He's gonna shit bricks," Daddy says. He reaches his hand out to me; at first I think it's a sign of affection but realize it's for the soda.

"Shit," I say. "I only got this one for me."

Daddy lets his arm fall in disappointment. "It's fine," he says.

I take it to mean it isn't fine. It's hard to discern when Daddy is being truthful and when he isn't, when he's joking or serious. Like me and Momma, anxiety underpins our relationship. I fear his leaving me, as though any mistake can end the whole thing. I don't know for sure where I got this idea, but it showed up one day like a rock in my shoe. I hand him the soda without a word.

"You gotta move your car," Daddy says, and takes a loud sip. "I don't want drama."

"I'll move it after dinner," I say.

The husk of our microwaved meal sits by a sink full of dishes. It's Daddy's night to wash them, but he's too absorbed by his TV show. In this scene, police officers are questioning their suspect, a young boy with autism. I sweep up crumbs from the floor and find ants crawling from under the sink toward the fridge. I watch their tiny marching bodies, which look like specks of dirt walking in a neat, thin row. Daddy keeps his special insects in our room: rare cockroaches, a stag beetle, and a massive praying mantis. Sometimes there are more and sometimes less. The room is also filled with dozens of shadowboxes of insects that have passed; insects he's preserved himself. He's more meticulous about their care than he is with anything else in the house. If one of them dies, he gets physically upset, ritualistically setting the body on foam with its most beautiful and vulnerable parts splayed for the world to see, before buying a new one mail order and growing it from larva. The beetles, they stay larvae for eight months before becoming adults.

Watching the perfect, ignorant symmetry of the ants pisses me off. I grab a bottle of Calgon "Take Me Away" body spray from my purse and spray the line a few times, floral droplets misting down, and get on all fours. The bugs scatter, scrambling around in satisfying circles. I lean in closer to see one ant's legs working the liquid off its antennae, touching the drops and circling, lost without the scent of its fellow workers. Anger gives way to curiosity. I mist them again, and again, until I make a puddle and watch as one of them swims around, then stops moving completely. A few struggle still. I get up, bored with their suffering. Daddy hasn't even noticed me crouched on the floor.

In the bathroom, I turn the fan on to drown out the crinkling plastic. I take the cap off one of the pregnancy tests and place it on the vinyl countertop. Feet shuffle across the ceiling. I sit on the toilet and spread my legs, placing the test between them, and aim a stream of piss.

An older woman, Ruby, had lived upstairs for several years, but she moved after falling behind in rent, leaving most of her furniture behind. Ruby had placed the key under her doormat before she drove off in a small Subaru packed to the brim with coolers, towels, a tennis racket (though I never once saw her take the tennis racket anywhere), and many plastic tubs. I snuck up there to look inside before the landlord found out she'd left. She'd trashed the place: cigarette butts pressed into the institutional carpet, dried spills, cereal bowls brown with crust. On the coffee table I found a shoebox filled with her old name tags: RUBY, HOUSEKEEPER; RUBY, MCDONALD'S; RUBY, MUSEUM OF CRYSTAL BRIDGES; RUBY, LUNCH ADMIN, AHST COMMUNITY SCHOOL DISTRICT. Mixed in were Happy Meal toys, nail polish, an old purple double dong grayed and dirtied at its tips, two lotto scratchers, and a lavender button that said SHE'S GETTING MARRIED, I'M JUST GETTING DRUNK in curly font. Not long before she left, I'd gone to the county court office to get my license renewed when I saw her walk out through the glass double doors with an older man on her arm who was dressed in a denim pearl-snap shirt and a tan cowboy hat. The man had taken off his hat, rubbed his peppered beard, and nodded at me as they walked past. I'm sure they were on some beach in Texas sipping Coors while the new tenants scrubbed the stains out of her carpet. I'd rifled through the remaining items, hungry to hoard what I might not get otherwise—the double dong and a crocheted wedding gown from the 1970s, a good get—and kept the apartment key in a jewelry box on my dresser. Sometimes I pulled the shoebox out from under my side of the bed to stare at the dong, wondering if I'll ever use it. Daddy doesn't know I have it, at least I don't think he does, and it's always good to have a little secret now and then.

I finish pissing, click the plastic cap over the cotton wick of the test, and wipe a drop away with my thumb.

"Do you ever wonder what our future child will be like?"

I pose the question while Daddy and I are lying in bed. What Daddy is thinking, I can never tell by the look on his face. I ask him questions hoping it will bring us closer.

"No," he says. "I don't think about the future like that."

He rubs the keloid on his jaw, then the bags beneath his eyes. The way he carries himself, his chest and shoulders are always tense—a taut exhaustion that lets go only when he is drunk enough to sleep.

"When I think about the future," he says, "I think about winning the lottery." His eyes light up when he says it.

"Is that how you'd pay for our wedding?" I hear Momma in my words, but I can't help myself. I know it comes from desperation. It's present in her devotion to the church and the ever-present push for the afterlife. That is what we are saving ourselves for, she says. Not life on this earth, but eternal life. *Be saved,* Momma whispers. *Don't let me end up in Heaven alone.* But my devotion is to childbirth. I wish she knew that. I fear living life without ever experiencing it.

"Things were going real good between us," Daddy says. Elevens carve through his brow. "Why are you bringing this up right now?"

"I—I just felt like asking." A tiny fear etches its way through my chest, attached to one of Momma's pronouncements. Fear is bad for the baby, so I push the feeling aside. I can't wait anymore, though. "I took another pregnancy test today," I say.

Daddy breathes in deep through his nose. I put a hand on his chest, dark and leathered by landscaping work, and curl my fingers around his hair.

"It was positive," I say. "The little blue cross? I did the test twice."

"You have a rough enough time with the bugs," he says.

"I'm not getting any younger, Daddy." My voice turns down in frustration, as the words of Momma and all those doctors saw like a serrated knife through my mind. He's always trying to teach me about them damn bugs, to get me to feed them for him, care for them. I don't mind touching them, but the cages make the room smell musty, and sometimes we have to do things with the bugs I don't like.

"A baby's not like taking care of a pet or a plant," he says. "Be prepared if this is the step you're going to take—"

"I can take it," I say.

"You still have the mentality of a child," he says.

A dull spot cavitates my chest. I had spent all spring purchasing parenting books from Goodwill for just a couple dollars: *What to Expect When You're Expecting*, *The Attachment Parenting Book*, *Mindful Blessings*, *The Baby Sleep Book*, *The Ferber Method: Solve Your Child's Sleep Problems*, *How to Break the Cycle and Not Become Your Own Parents*, and *When You're Expecting Twins, Triplets, or Quads* (in the off chance). I piled them at my bedside and flipped through them whenever the urge hit me, poring over illustrations of serene mothers holding angelic children.

"You're *scared*," I say.

"I'm only trying to help you," Daddy says.

"I know it's about money. You could apply at Mike's."

"Oh god," he says. "Your meat factory? No thanks. Blake offered me a job the other day, but I didn't commit. Picking up insects from Florida and bringing them up to Virginia to sell."

"Aren't there already bugs in Virginia?"

"These are exotics—orchid mantises, scorpions you can't get elsewhere. Usually you have to go through a whole bunch of red tape to get them through customs, but if we pick them up for this guy, we'll get a few thousand dollars. I might even be able to get some of the specimens for free."

"Can't you get in trouble for that? Sounds complicated. Like tax fraud."

"Only stupid criminals get caught," he says.

Daddy used to be a dealer but claims he quit it years ago. Momma will berate me even more if she finds out Daddy's gone back to anything that smells like criminal work, even though I've been good all my life, follow the rules as best I can. It's Sloane who was the destructive influence, not that Momma'd ever seen it. But that's what draws me to Daddy—and what drew me to Sloane. His defiance made him seem exotic to me; I admired it.

"I could make the trip easy," he says. "It's twenty hours there, but just a drive up the coast."

I pout. "Twenty hours," I say. I'm thinking about the ring now and if it means he won't get it.

"I don't know what the hell else I'm supposed to do if I can't find work," he says. His gravelly voice squeezes into a whine, and he slams his fist on the bed. My shoulders tense and I apologize.

"It's fine," he says. His lips press together, and I can tell he's grinding his molars, his cheeks taut with muscle. "It's fine."

I decide it'll be good for him to see Miami. He can scout it for our honeymoon.

"It feels different this time," I tell him, rubbing my belly.

Daddy leans his head back against the wall. He doesn't touch me to comfort me, but that's all I want.

"It *does*," I say. "This one will stick."

"Okay," he says. "Just please, don't tell anyone—anyone, including your fucking mom—until you're far enough along."

A minuscule muscle at the edge of my eye twitches, and I try to blink it away.

It's too late, I think. *I've already told her.*

XXXX

I keep hoping one day Momma will tell me she loves me, that she'll say it aloud. I think she loves me, but I can't be sure until I hear it. Maybe once the baby's here. When Sloane got pregnant, it drew out a tenderness in Momma, something I never thought she possessed. Everything I had known about her was harsh, as though the very nature of her mood had aged her: marionette lines at her chin, permanently frowning, even when she wasn't upset; lips forever drawn into a tireless scowl. Her eyes, so light that when the sun hit her just right, sometimes she seemed ghastly. Hair, dull brown and grayed at the temples, and her hands, long, slender fingers with knobby knuckles, the backs of her hands covered in fine, spidery wrinkles. I was six the first time she slapped me for disobedience. It was in the Fourth Commandment. The damning word squeezed, bulbous and full, from her mouth: *obligation*. What a lesson of my life. Duty. At the time I tried to infer its meaning but was too afraid to admit my ignorance.

The fear of God—how His authority extended, unpredictable, from my parents' fingertips—made little sense at the time. The rules were never consistent, or at least they felt that way. One minute I'd be playing happily with my toys, my little stuffed animals and dolls, singing songs to myself, then there'd be a sudden flash of red, and Momma storming in, telling me to shut up. I'd cry, which was the opposite of what she wanted, so then she'd yell at my father to pull out the leather belt, dark brown and carved with intricate flowers.

"Make her quiet," she'd say.

Right across the backs of my thighs. I'd cry and fight while Momma pulled my pants off, the belt slap harder, and I'd turn around, face red, wet as autumn. His face wrenched at me, like he was helpless and sorry, and Momma would get mad again and tell me to turn right back around, like she despised seeing the pain in my face. The punishment came no matter what crime I had committed, and it was never explained. It was automatic. I learned to lie, not about my faults but about everything.

But no one could be angry or disappointed when holding a baby. I'd seen how Momma was when Sloane got pregnant. I can just imagine that baby's sputtering mouth, its bright baby eyes compelling Momma to love it.

In bed, I push myself up against Daddy and ask if he wants to look at the test.

"It's got piss on it," he says. He rolls away and flips open his laptop on the nightstand to watch a show about sexual assault victims. I place my hands on the cool skin of his exposed back, so pale and wide and fat, and tenderly scratch at his skin. I press my lips against the nape of his neck, pulling him back. If I could compel him the way I feel compelled, he'd understand. Daddy doesn't move against me, though the hair on his neck rises against my mouth. He adjusts his hips, and the creaking mattress interrupts the show.

"I'll keep looking for work," he says into his pillow. "I don't know what I'll find that's got health insurance, that'll pay enough to raise a kid. S'what you want, isn't it?"

I massage his shoulders as fantasies of motherhood invade. Pastor Anderson taught us the best religious work was staying out of the job market to be a wife, to raise a child. It was the only good thing about his sermons—I hated work, would trade everything to be a traditional wife. Birth the baby, make dinner from scratch, play therapist to Daddy, fulfill every one of his sexual needs. I'd be happy to play that role as long as I needed if I never had to slice another chicken breast into fingers ever again.

"Remember when you got Meredith?" I ask. "She was just a nymph. Smaller than your thumb. Now she's as wide as my palm. Once you have our baby in your arms, you're gonna feel so good. It'll work out, it always works out."

I kiss his back again, and he turns around. He puts a hand on my cheek, and I roll my hips against him gently. He hovers, the breadth of him pushing the air out of me. I trace the shape of his face in the laptop's light. He kisses me, an all-encompassing kind of kiss, his lips wet and full and suffocating my own, then he pulls away when I start to kiss back. The sweat transferred from his skin to mine leaves me cold as he moves to lay on his back next to me. This part I always dread, but I want baby cribs and scrambled-egg mornings and singing nursery rhymes to my pastel-clothed child.

"Get the boys," Daddy's gruff voice says in a whisper painted with beer.

"All of them?" I ask.

"Just a couple."

Daddy leans on his elbows as I walk up to the glass terraria on the shelf. There are many: the cockroaches, the beetle, the mantis, and cages of feeder moths, crickets, fruit flies. I open the lid of the Madagascar hissing cockroaches and stare inside.

"Mist them first," he says. "They like that."

"I *know*," I say. I spray the enclosure, peering at a piece of driftwood covered in moss. The cockroach rattles like a maraca when I pick him up. On my palm he quiets, his antennae whisking air. I stroke his back, a smooth firmness to it like polished wood. I place my hand, palm up, on Daddy's chest, and he closes his eyes, readying himself for the roach to crawl. The first time he told me he liked this, I seized with disgust. But I noticed how tender he was with them, especially the mantis. Daddy blamed it on his childhood. Once, his father found him experimenting with a friend and beat him senseless.

"I'm not gay," he'd said. "It's nothing like that."

I got sad thinking about it. "Do you still want to sleep with men?" I asked.

"I'd rather not talk about it," he'd said.

But I wanted to talk about it. I wanted to say, *You do not understand how profoundly I relate.*

He wasn't allowed to visit the boy anymore, so Daddy says he began collecting insects instead. He liked when they crawled over his fingers and toes, the exquisite touch of their spindly legs. The tickling made him feel light, he said, like when you get that run of euphoria on hearing good news. His desire grew, I imagine, the way my wish to have a baby grew: a kernel-sized thought that popcorned through my mind until it was all I could think about.

The armored bug steps from my hand into the curlicued hair on Daddy's chest. Daddy sucks in his bottom lip. Sometimes I think he likes his bugs more than he likes me. He probably does; a bug can die and be replaced, but no other woman would do this for him. I pluck another cockroach from the cage and place it next to the one on his chest. Droplets stick to my hands and I wipe them on the comforter. Their indented heads move about, led by their roving antennae.

I slide on top of Daddy's lap and excite him with my hands. Pure bliss spreads across his face as one roach crawls slowly toward the thick gold chain resting on his clavicle. It nears his neck, and Daddy burps a delicate *oh* sound. He grows hard and girthy in my hands and bucks his hips. My thighs, thick and doughy, sweat onto his, chafing against his hairy skin. When he first started with the insects, it was like a pain thing, he said. He had told me he was a bit of a sadist—my ears perked, wondering exactly what he could mean. What he wanted was for the insects to crawl on me, which scared me. He wanted to see me that way, scared, and something about that drew me to him.

When he enters me he places his massive fingers around my neck, his thumb and forefinger beneath the sharp bone of my chin, and I let my weight lean into his hand. This moment excites me most about him. I suspect he's killed people before—he always talks about the mechanics of death when we watch his murder shows, repeating the same facts, the same way he tries to teach me about the bugs. Strangulation, he likes to say, takes at least four minutes of pressure to the throat to cause brain damage or death. And even then, he says, many people do it wrong; the person passes out but doesn't die.

Shows always made murder look fast and clean. Although, he'd add, a garrote can cut strangulation time in half if you know how to use one.

He applies pressure to my throat, and my pulse bulbs behind my eyes. I touch his wrists, too afraid to touch the insects. It thrills me, the possibility he's strangled people, that he could do it with precision. I want to collapse toward his chest but am careful of the roaches. The second one explores his nipple. With Daddy's hand on my neck, he's so in control I know he'd never hurt me. I want to say, *You can slap me. You can tear me open. You can kill me, if you'd like.*

XXXX

I lean against the living room wall and close my eyes. An image of me beating myself in the head with a hammer whips through my mind, then burns away like the flash of a camera bulb.

"Pain has its purpose," Momma says. It's midnight. She's woken from what she says is a prophetic nightmare and wants to make sure I'm okay. The deeper the pain, she says, "the louder God is trying to tell you something. Don't you remember anything from Sunday school?" she asks.

I haven't been to a church service in years. Sometimes when Daddy's asleep I'll watch the TV preachers shout and shake on-screen, their little mouths wailing. Daddy hates the TV preachers, so I watch with the volume turned to one, the bedroom door closed, and listen as their tinny voices beg for tithe.

"We're constantly under attack from Satan," Momma says. "Satan tries so hard. The more persecution you experience . . . the more you know you're on the right path."

"God protects you," the TV preacher says. "That's what pain is. Tells you something's wrong, it changes you, God changes you." He flaps his hands like they're wet and sings the words, repeating them against the organ music. I ask Momma about the nightmare.

"Your baptism, sweetie. Do you remember it?"

"Of course I don't," I say.

Her tongue shucks across her teeth. "When you were born, the nurses took you from me. You weighed so little, couldn't breathe on your own. They came in the room to put ash on my forehead and wouldn't let me hold you. I was worried you'd die. The hospital, they tried to baptize you right away. But I wouldn't let them.

"Anyway, Dee-Dee, that's the pain of separation. My steadfastness to the old-time religion kept you alive. You're not holding out that this new baby will survive, are you?"

The blank spot in my head opens up again, the ball-peen end of the hammer making extra depressions inside the cavity. *Don't name the baby,* I tell myself. I so want to. Eliza. Janice. Or Miracle. I will dip the baby in baptismal water and she'll emerge new, with a name, a legacy. Miracle, the blood and bone of me.

"What miracle?" Momma says.

XXXX

On Sunday Daddy and I wake up to the sound of mewling beneath the bedroom window. I split the blinds open with my fingers to look at the car. Same make and model as mine, different colors. I peek at my own car and notice tiny handprints on the paint. A toddler with the most shock-white hair hanging about her chin crouches on the asphalt, looking beneath the vehicle. No one else is out there.

"There's a kid," I say.

Daddy climbs out of bed, puts on a pair of basketball shorts and a black tee. He walks into the bathroom to brush his teeth.

"Did you hear me?"

"Just a new neighbor," Daddy says with a mouthful of foam.

I step outside and check the mailbox, which hangs in a rusted metal box affixed to the siding near our door. It's a good day; it's clear of clouds, there's a gentle breeze. The green trees and sweet sky couldn't be more emblematic of summer, and the humidity hasn't yet settled in. Daddy follows me outside and lights a Pall Mall. Next to our stoop, barely hidden by the gnarled and scraggly hedges, two tabbies nibble at a pile of cat chow in the dirt. A few others mewl from deeper inside the shrubbery.

In front of our fourplex there are a handful of stairs, so few that one could jump down or stretch one's legs long enough to skip all of them, that lead to parking spaces for everyone in the building. I scan for the toddler near the cars.

"I don't see the kid anymore."

"So?" Daddy blows smoke, then taps the cigarette with his thumb. "Mind your own."

I pick up a gray kitten that has stumbled out of hiding. One of its eyes is a thick blue gob with white filaments like webby stars. A crown of pus seeps where it meets the lower eyelid. The other eye darts around, the pupil a thin slit.

"Shit," he says. "That cat's all fucked up."

"You think they belong to the neighbor?" I ask. "Maybe I should take him up to them." The kitten squirms in my hands.

"Leave it," he says.

"I'm going up there."

My feet clunk up the wrought-iron stairs to the second floor and I knock on the door. I cradle the cat inside my jacket against my chest. It claws feebly at my breasts and gives a meager cry, and I want to protect it. A gust of wind blows dead leaves against the building. There's no answer. My curiosity hangs over me like an awning and I knock again. As soon as I turn away, the bolt unlocks, the door swinging partway open.

The woman inside scratches the top of her messy ponytail, her small mouth in a frown.

"The fuck?" she says. She has that slept-in look, in a way that looks glamorous only because she looks so good without effort. She spends a moment taking me in, and suddenly, recognition hits both of us. "Daisy?"

It's Sloane. Her voice is raspy, and she takes me in a quick, distant hug. Her slight frame fills me with lust and angst. All these years apart, I thought she hated me, and now she's moved back. Our town is small, and this is the only apartment complex. Everything else is double-wides and houses built in the seventies. Behind her, the fair-haired toddler rolls around on a blow-up mattress. The apartment is nothing like it'd been, the carpets replaced, and the air from inside smells nice, like clean laundry.

"Sloane." I can't stop smiling. I want to caress her arms, touch her skin. I go in for another hug, and she raises her arms instinctively to stop me, then opens up and puts her arms around me loosely. I tighten, pat her back with my free arm, then pull away. I'd forgotten how much she made me afraid of my own movements.

"What are you doing here?" I almost stutter.

"Dad has dementia," she says. "Mom needs some help."

That's just how it went around here. It seemed you were always losing somebody to sickness of some sort. People slipped into drug use or mental failure, or they simply expired.

"I'm sorry to hear that," I say. "You know, when I lost my dad—"

"It's fine, really," she says. Half a smirk turns into a sneer. "He's a bastard. I'm in town just for Mom." She points at the one-eyed cat, and I hold him out to her.

"One of yours?" I ask.

"Not that one, no," she says. She puts her hands behind her back and looks past me. "You live around here?"

"Beneath you," I say.

"Wow. Fuck," she says. "Absolutely not surprised, with how small this town is. It's been a long time—long, long time . . ."

A thousand curdled memories ease into me: Patchy fields of grass. A metallic-pink plastic hairbrush. Her arms rocking me. Candied bread. Her fingers searching through my worn clothes. My father and the wide welts left by his leather strap. I feel woozy. Then I remember the pastor.

"Did things ever work out in Kentucky?" I ask.

She waves her hand. "Oh god, no," she says.

"Oh."

She points back into the apartment. She says, "Okay, well."

The moment decays, but I can't let go just yet. After high school there were so many things I gave up because I was afraid; Sloane was the last time I had put aside my fears until I met Daddy.

"Should we catch up sometime?" I ask. I don't know what I'm asking for. I'm afraid of meeting with her, but still I offer.

Sloane nods. "Why not?" she says. Her movements are stilted, and she walks back into the apartment. She turns and speaks from the crack in the door. "Okay, bye, wow, good to see you."

At the bottom of the stairs, the landlord, a ruddy man with a face like a slapped ass, taps his foot. He walks about the property as though he's the captain of a cruise ship.

"Rent check," he says, with an extra-hard *k* at the end. He presses his thin lips together and smiles, a twitch in his upper lip. I forgot the first was on Friday.

"I'll go get mine," I say. The kitten makes a small chirp from my jacket, and the landlord's eyes go to my chest. In my stupor I'd forgotten it was there. I know what he's going to say: New pet, new deposit.

"It's not mine. A stray."

"Lots of strays here," says the landlord. He presses his foot into the pile of kibble and it makes a distinctive crunch. "Ya know, that new girl"—he glances up at Sloane's apartment—"just got out of an abusive relationship, nowhere else to go. I'm a good guy, I had to rent to her, even though she has no credit or nothing. She's pretty at least."

"I'll go get you that check," I say.

Daddy scoffs when he sees the kitten struggling in my hands.

"Landlord." I put the cat down and grab the checkbook. I'm so stunned I don't say anything more. I get like that sometimes. When I'm afraid, I'm just internal. My mind gets buzzy with thoughts, but I don't say a damn thing. I guess that's because of the church, or Momma. Some undone puzzle I just don't want to deal with. Daddy doesn't notice anyway, so it's fine.

Outside, Blake is leaving his apartment. He stops at his car, parked on the other side of the lot, and stands there scratching his beard. The landlord nods at Blake as I hand him the check and ambles off toward another unit.

"You know why I'm waiting, don't you?" Blake says with a blunt affect. He adjusts the ball cap on his head.

"Sorry." I let my tongue hang on the last half of the word. "I mean, look." I point at the red Volvo as I walk toward him. He shakes his keys.

"Told your man I got a job for him if you let him work it." He runs his fingers through his beard again.

"I want him to stay out of business like that," I say. Blake makes to get into his car. "It's not personal. You can't be a good parent and do those things, too."

"The kids stay with Sarah," Blake says. "They don't live with me."

"Not you," I say.

Blake stops for a sec, and I proudly let him acclimate to my announcement. In the normal world, I'm nothing. A chubby girl with an upturned nose and cracked red skin. Hands like water-filled plastic gloves. But with pregnancy, my corpulent body suddenly acquires purpose.

"Shit." He opens the car door and throws his jacket inside. "Let me know if you need anything, right?"

He gets in, shuts the door, and starts the car as I make my way back to the apartment. He pulls out, crunching the transmission with his gearshift. Behind me I hear the whir of a car window.

"If you need to park closer, use my spot. It's fine."

Back in the apartment, Daddy sips coffee and watches a reality show about naked people surviving in the Australian outback. A man and a woman have trekked into the wilderness with two cloth bags, each containing a single survival tool. On the show, women's bodies are displayed as bodies are: from thick and matronly to shrunken and saggy, their imperfections for the world to see. I sit on the couch watching the bodies shamble awkwardly through desert and brush. I think about Sloane's body, now with babies pushed through it. I think of the smooth concave curve she used to have between her hip bones as a teen. Her first baby would be grown by now—or had she given it up for adoption? I envision her changing from maiden to matron, the saggy sack of belly she might have. It feels good, vindictive even, to see her single and alone. For the first time I have something she doesn't have.

"Where's the kitten?"

Daddy shrugs. I crouch on hands and knees to look beneath the couch, an asteroid belt of crumbs. We'll have to buy a new vacuum, I think, as well as plastic doorknob covers, soft gummy corners for the sharp points of furniture, to protect the baby.

"Guess we'll give it some kinda name."

"Don't name a thing you aren't going to keep," Daddy says. He pours a shot of rum into his coffee from a bottle on the table.

"You brought him in," I say.

"I didn't bring in the cat," he says.

"You did."

"No," Daddy says. "I didn't bring that cat in. You did."

I squint at him, can only remember going up the steps with the cat in my jacket. Everything else was smeared with Sloane.

"We can't keep that thing. The bugs," he says. "Meredith."

A slight scratching sound comes from inside the pantry, and an object falls. I walk over and open the door to see the kitten on the lowest shelf, bobbing his head back and forth. I brush my fingertips along his greasy fur.

"It's fine," I say. "We'll keep the bedroom door closed."

"What did the neighbor say?"

My heart pounds as the two most distant points of my life connect. I imagine Daddy meeting Sloane, being taken with her. The same way I was, the way everyone is. I don't know what I'm more jealous of: Daddy leaving me, or me not having Sloane.

"I want the cat," I say.

"You don't even take care of your houseplants." He points to the crisp brown branches of the fern by the window.

In the bathroom, I open the drawer with the pregnancy test, just to be sure I hadn't dreamed it. The stick is white as bone, in a mess of old face creams, pink razors, pads. The blue cross is there, but faint. My survival tool. Daddy won't leave me if I'm pregnant. My stomach lurches—morning sickness, a shiver. I treasure the test in my hand and wrap my arms around myself, stroking the delicate skin on the backs of my arms, bumpy with ingrown hairs. I caress myself, fantasizing about people holding the door for my massive belly, giving up their seat at the DMV. An image of Daddy and me, standing in the middle of the room with light around us as he coils his arms around my belly in a protective clasp; my own arms holding the sum of all my yearning.

No one is taking this away from me.

1996

It didn't snow that winter, but ice storms hit. Sleet paved the roads and sidewalks with patches of black ice, and rain-soaked trees burst in the night. Sloane and I walked home together after Sunday school, passing trees split into thousands of pieces, our noses pink and sniffling, my pits sweating but my hands ice cold. Little icicle-fingers deep in my pockets. We passed the river that flowed through the east side of town. Middle schoolers snuck to the shore to smoke and throw stones at the packs of stray dogs that lived off the garbage, middle schoolers who seemed cooler than me, whose only retort to us or anyone older was always "Fuck you."

Sloane and I trudged along the river, following the current halfway home before turning left into our subdivision, and the pit in my chest grew. We didn't need to see the river to know when we were getting close, but the temperature dropped, haunting prickles into my skin. It reached us with its smell, too, humid and with an unidentifiable form of decay.

I don't know why Sloane let me hold her hand. One moment we were talking about school and the next she was gripping my hand tightly. We walked past Victorian houses that faced the river, the curving, ornate designs carved into the facades like looming faces, their doors yawning. Everything about her was delicate, down to her fingernails, which were glossy and pink, the whites grown out a slice.

Clean, like when you leave a hot shower. At the end of the street we had to go to our own homes, but she stopped. She didn't say a word, just looked up toward her street, staring into mid-space. She didn't want to go home. I turned to her. Her fingers gripped hard. Wind blew stray hairs that stuck to the polish on her lips.

"Why did you lie at church?" I asked. I'd been wanting to ask since I'd touched her at her deliverance. She loosened her grip. "Why did you let them believe you were possessed?"

God was ethereal. We understood perhaps there was something greater than us, but Sloane was smart enough to question it. She had figured out early how the church was using God and Jesus and Satan to control us. She wasn't afraid to ask questions like the rest of us were, prodding teachers into frustration: "Why does God allow suffering?" "How do we know our church is the right path, that we aren't being led astray?" "If God has free will, doesn't that mean He can do evil?"

When I asked her about herself, Sloane looked at me like no one had ever questioned her motives before. She was used to getting away with things; as usual, a luminescent quality clung to her face. Natural pinkness to her cheeks and freckles. She looked like a painted doll whose creator had taken great care to get every stroke of color correct. I imagined a fine horsehair brush making lean lines of her eyelashes. Nobody wanted to turn away from a face like hers and risk missing out on her charm. Sloane flexed her fingers in my grasp.

"I don't know," she said. "I don't like being at home, and when I'm lying, I get to pretend I'm in another place. It's fun to trick everyone into thinking something that isn't true."

I was glad she included me in her game. I wanted to kiss her. The desire slowly filled me like water in a basin. I hadn't considered why she might not want to go home; all I could think about was the petal-like graze of lips against teeth, a touch I'd only ever imagined by pressing my mouth against pillows and the crease between my thumb and first finger. I thought of my home. It was simple there, but treacherous, though lying in bed with my stuffed animals, I could read or listen to whatever I wanted as long as no one barged in. I could listen to pop music and dream about what it might be like to be held. Did Sloane have a sanctuary like that? We stood there for a long time, looking at a wooded thatch that obscured the river, letting the dark encroach on our vision. My palms grew wet.

Life in the church felt tied to our small rural town, as though escaping Cassville might give us freedom from Faithful Floods. We'd heard that people out in cities went missing all the time, but maybe they just wanted to start new lives. It's easier to lie to strangers, to become someone you really want to be, when you aren't bound by a past.

"Would you run away?" I asked. I wondered what she would run away to—something better than here.

"Yeah," she said. She gave my hand one last tight squeeze before letting go, wiping the sweat on her jacket. "I most definitely would."

XXXX

I call Momma and tell her the heartburn is starting. My doctor's appointment is tomorrow, and I'm nauseated every day, and "my skin is getting softer, Momma. I've never been this smooth! I'm fluttering inside. Daddy won't come with me to the appointment; Momma, I'm so tired. This is it," I say, "this is really it. Momma—I'm scared."

Momma could've said any number of things. *I'll come with you to the appointment. Trust your instincts. David should support you more in this. You're worth it. Would you like me to come visit for a few days?* If she loved me enough, she would say these things. Wretched, when even grandchildren won't make Momma love me. Instead, she aims for the one thing she knows will hurt me.

"I heard the news about Sloane," she says.

The phone trembles on my ear and my tongue goes dry. "What news?" I ask.

"Oh, don't be like that," Momma says.

"No, tell me."

"She said you're neighbors now."

"You knew? That's just like you," I say. "As much as you talk, you're a terrible communicator."

I wake up at three A.M. the morning of my first appointment with pain in my side. The sheets are damp, pulling raw against my skin. I turn over and grip Daddy by his upper arm, squeezing breath through my throat, but he doesn't stir; he has half a bottle of whiskey to sleep off. It's typical of him. He claims he's stone-cold sober now, but when he says that he means hard drugs. Alcohol doesn't count. I walk doubled over to the bathroom, the door squeaking closed as I flip on the ugly yellow light. I search through the medicine cabinet and knock a bottle of aspirin to the floor. But I'm too afraid of miscarrying to take medicine, even something OTC. I slide down against the wall, planting my palms on the cool linoleum. A slow drip has formed a red-orange puddle beneath the rusty pipe connecting the toilet to the wall.

The window to the right of the toilet is dark except for the streetlights by the bar at the end of the street and the county museum. Beyond that, an illuminated sign flickers in the distance. I can't make out the words, but I know them well: FAITHFUL FLOODS. I haven't been to that hellhole of a church since Momma left town. It's nestled on a sparse plot of land between the VFW and an RV dealership. The building, two double-wides stuck together with a giant community room in the center, is hidden from the road, so all you see is the sign until you're right up on it. But if you walk past it on a Sunday morning, you can hear the organ pounding away in reverence, the people singing so loud you can practically see them in your mind: hands raised, holy fire burning, tongues flicking away in utterance.

My side throbs again, and I'm taken back to one of the pastor's sermons. "The flesh has no strength against sin or against the world," he'd said. "Sin is stronger than us." He removed the microphone from its stand and walked to the edge of the stage, singing the words of his sermon as an organ played. He did this dramatically, standing on the tips of his toes, to signify being raised to Heaven. That's what the pastor liked to do: act like he was channeling the very powers of God Himself. These moments made me uneasy. The adults were eager to please, approaching the altar in groups. There is something about the force of group ritual that encompasses you, even if you are skeptical. You don't want to believe it, but the belief of everyone around you is so powerful, your mind commits to the bit. This was why I was so fascinated by Sloane. At her deliverance, she somehow resisted this. She was outside of its power. I hung back, looking for any sisters I might recognize, but everyone moved too fast when the music upped its tempo, the bass pulsing through my teeth.

"We cannot overcome the flesh alone," he said. "Prayer isn't powerful. The presence of *Jee-zus* is what's powerful!" He pulled a monogrammed handkerchief from his back pocket and patted his forehead and jumped toward a group of people to his left who'd begun that staccato sound of tongues.

Momma says speaking in tongues is the purest form of prayer. That was our baptism—in our faith, it's not through water, but through being dipped in holy fire. That's what the Church calls it when God speaks through you, that's how you know, Momma says. It's electric when you're near someone who's been chosen, she says, the fire sparks from one person to the next. Your insides fill with the brightest, sharpest light. At church I'd close my eyes, Momma and my father on either side of me gripping my hands tight. They'd raise my hands up high, and I'd try to find that hidden part of my brain where my secret language waited to be freed. But there I found Sloane instead. She was always inside me, licking her teeth, smirking and writhing and sweating out on that flat church carpet.

My stomach cramps, and I fill a glass at the tap. The water is sour with the taste of metal, and I drink until my stomach hurts. The fullness evens out my cramping, and I reassure myself that the baby's just thirsty. Taking care of myself means taking care of the baby and I'm a good mother. I drink another glass and observe my stomach. When it distends this way, I breathe out tranquility. This is how I'm meant to be. Growing life.

At work, I corner my floor manager to get time off for my doctor's appointment. He takes me back to his closet of an office. With the desk and filing cabinets, there's barely enough room for us to stand. He puts his hand on top of stacks of schedules and customer orders and leans on his arm.

"I don't think I can let you go early today," he says. "A broiler in barn four tested positive for H5N8 and we might have to quarantine the whole lot."

I lick the sweat away from my lips, astringent from the constant misting of sanitizer. "It's urgent," I say. "I'm having a baby."

The fluorescent light casts shadows over his face, smooth except for the occasional pockmark and pocket of wrinkles.

"We need the hands," he says. He moves a stray paper into another pile. He blinks at me, his eyes nestled into his pudgy, soft sockets. It's not that he doesn't care; he looks exhausted. There'd been injuries at the plant, and the ownership had told management we weren't killing fast enough. They'd applied for waivers to the line speed, increasing it to 175 per minute. That's what made little sense to me. You'd think they'd want us to go slower. The ring of the buzzer transported you into the frenzy for hours as you moved the same parts of your body over and over and over and over until your muscles tightened or sometimes seized. You'd have to fight against the pain and keep going. The floor manager used to work the line; he knew what Mike's was putting us through.

"How old are your kids?" I ask.

"Teenagers," he says.

"Please," I beg. "You understand how important this is. It's my first appointment. *Please*." I busy my fingers with a stray thread on my scrubs. "Tomorrow you can put me on barn duty. I'll help. Whatever you need."

He sighs. "I'll let you leave early, but you can't do this to me again."

I nod. It's practically unheard of to get time off with a same-day request. I acknowledge the privilege, hold it in my stomach like a tiny treasure.

Number Three on the deboning line walks up to me as I shove my duffel bag into my locker.

"Thanks a lot," she says in a tone that shanks guilt right through me. The team will have to work faster to make up for my absence. "Next time, don't fucking come in."

She shoulder-checks me as she passes, and another brilliant pain gut-punches me. The buzzer reverberates through the warehouse, and we head to the floor where the death counter's massive red numbers read: 000,000,000.

I pick up the pneumatic scissors as the first of the carcasses roll into the room. Number One pulls the skin from each carcass with a set of pliers, then Number Two uses a paring knife to slash the thighs and wings off and cut long slits into the breasts. The girl who shoulder-checked me earlier, Number Three, grasps the two pieces of flesh at the breast slit and pulls them straight off the chicken with her hands. Number Three tosses the breasts onto the conveyor belt and I cut them into strips. Once the line gets going, I can't watch the other crew anymore, too focused on the task at hand. At the shift's halfway point, I've cut thousands of breasts. Their bodies have been reduced to their simplest forms—no head, no feet, no feathers, no blood. Just fat, flesh, cold and shiny beige objects, which makes me feel less complicit in their deaths. I get lost in the repetition, pleasant and soothing, like a blank spot inside my brain. Chickens find no redemption at Mike's.

The death counter clocks fifty-five thousand birds when it's time for me to go. In the bathroom, I peel off my disposables, stained with specks of fat and meat, grit from skin and bones. My clothes are damp under the armpits, in between my thighs, the areas where my waist and hips fold in. I'm looking forward to the aseptic dry of the doctor's office. I take my pants off and set them in my pile of scrubs, grab a purple tee from my bag and pull it over my head. The cloth clings, its cool fabric a brief respite. I turn on the faucet and splash water on my face to rub off the grime. My skin flakes white, my cheeks splotch red. Only when I compare myself with Sloane do I see my ugliness. Without her, I'm almost pretty, and I'm unconvinced there's anything other than beauty that makes a woman valuable. Or a child. When I told Daddy about the first pregnancy, he seemed distant, sure, but beneath the fear there was a hunger in his face, like he recognized at last who I was inside, and wanted it. The way I remember people looking at Sloane, a glossy wobble of unmet need coating their eyes. I'd go through a hundred pregnancies for Daddy to look at me like that again.

I pull my underwear down to pee. When I push, something more than piss leaves me, the weight separates my lips. A bright red shock of blood no bigger than a half-dollar is on the crotch of my panties. I grab a wad of toilet paper and wipe myself, which exposes more blood and a scant trace of mucus. My hands shake and panic breaks. I stare at the glob in the toilet and question its formless possibility. I want to grab it, wrap it in tissue, and take it with me to the doctor. The rim of the toilet is crusted in black mold, with little hairs stuck to the crust. I think better of it, wipe again, and flush. Red thins out, then disappears.

"We all have a thorn in our flesh," Pastor Anderson said at that sermon. I try to recall everyone's faces: Momma's, my father's, Sloane's. I try to re-create Sloane as I once perceived her, before she left. But now all I can see is the older mid-thirties version of her. She probably tells Momma all about the wicked things we did as teenagers to gain her favor, and Momma probably tells her all the things she wishes I would do that I don't do. Momma can't cope that I'm unwed and don't have a child yet. Momma didn't tell me Sloane was moving home because she sees Sloane as a model daughter of Jesus, reborn into the arms of Christ, and she thought I might expose her to my sins. And Sloane didn't want to hug me when she saw me, I knew that—but I had hoped that any weirdness between us had fizzled out with time. Momma has infected her with these ideas that I am bad, and they're both hypnotized by the church. The only savior I have is Daddy; he's smart enough to see through it, but he's not smart enough to see through beauty like I am. I see Sloane standing next to Daddy, and they're both holding the hands of the blond toddler I'd seen by my car. Light radiates from behind them like they are angelic. I push the warped images out, but they emerge from every corner. "Everybody has a weakness," the pastor said. "The body is weak. We have to break it, because if we don't, that weakness will destroy us."

XXXX

I walk through smudged glass doors, plastered with a poster of a smiling family holding hands, into the clinic, which sits between a shuttered King Pizza and a tire shop. A heavyset woman at the counter with medicated eyes and manicured eyebrows hands me paperwork. The forms ask for my income, medical history, an insurance card with a group number. The factory doesn't offer health insurance. Daddy always says if there's an emergency we'll just go to the ER and never pay the bill.

"Do you have two recent pay stubs?" the receptionist asks.

"No one told me I had to bring them in," I say. I've never gotten pay stubs anyway—I think they're electronic.

"We charge on a sliding scale only if you can provide proof of income," says the receptionist. Her voice is flat and uncaring. When I don't respond, she goes back to tapping on her keyboard. "I'll just make a note in your file."

I sit down in one of the waiting room's maroon vinyl chairs. A small TV high in a corner plays a cartoon. On the way to the clinic, I passed a billboard ad for a local hospital. On it a digital counter ticked above a giant baby, recording each birth since the hospital opened ten years ago. When the billboard was put up a few years ago, the number was around forty thousand. Today it was 56,867. We kill at least that many chickens in a single day.

A girl walks into the clinic wearing bike shorts and a big sweater. She's large, as large as me or bigger. I stare at the shape of her ass through the neon fabric of her shorts, every little ripple that gives way; it's almost sheer, and I can see the outline of her underwear. I can't stop staring as she waits for the receptionist, and I wonder if she can feel my eyes on her the way you can sense a cloud covering the sun. My stomach grumbles, and I realize I haven't eaten—stupid of me. I get up to look for a snack machine, but there's only an old water fountain.

Once when I was six, Momma sat me at the kitchen table and fixed special pastries from scratch. She removed her wedding rings and placed them in a tiny glass bowl by the sink, then kneaded her fingers through stringy eggs and flour, folding cherries into dough, wiping wisps of dark hair from her forehead with her forearm. She placed the baked scones under a bell jar. I could eat one scone a day, dry, with a cup of tea. She monitored everything I ate and wouldn't let me have my daily scone if she had seen me eat something unhealthy. "Gluttony is a tool of temptation," she said, returning the scones to the top of the fridge. "We must manage our temptations on the path to righteousness." She meant to hammer in that a good Christian was always under attack from everything from outright persecution to our own bodily functions, but all I did was fantasize about the thick, sweet cherries in that dough and how badly I wanted to feel them spread flat and wet against my tongue. I snuck back into the kitchen after dinner, hoping to get one, but stopped when I heard Momma on the phone with Aunt Mae. Momma never let a week pass without calling her— that was an important part of keeping the faith, too: maintaining good relations.

"She's growing out of junior sizes. I can't stand looking at her this way. She'll never get married. Don't understand how she's gaining."

Later that week, Momma bought me a training bra. It was white and too tight around my ribs, leaving deep red welts. She made me wear it to school all day, then every night Momma stood in my room, watching me take it off.

"This is what you do to yourself when you eat," she'd say, slapping the welts until my eyes watered.

I follow the nurse to the back of the clinic after she calls my name. She leads me to a scale, and I step out of my shoes, her nameless, blank face moving the sliding weights across the beam of the old mechanical scale. I'd gained weight with the past pregnancies, ten or fifteen pounds, and stepping on the scale comforted me. It meant something was growing in me and I was growing with it. I don't enjoy being smaller; it's suffocating. This is the only rebellion against Momma I'm brave enough to have. The nurse seats me next to the scale and wraps my arm with the blood pressure cuff. She looks like she could be a mother, too. I eye the roundness of the flesh on her back, the jiggle of her upper arms. Her hair is pulled into a taut, simple ponytail, and I construct a schedule of her morning: waking up, getting ready for work, tying her hair back, going into the baby's room to pick him up. The child clings to her like an animal, and she gets him ready for the day and places him in a car seat and drops him off with a nanny. It must be painful to be separated from her child all day. She probably gets photo updates from the nanny when he's eating breakfast, lunch, and when they go to the park together. I bet that makes her day better, but it's a struggle to survive this way, to work full-time and be away from your baby.

"Do you have children?" I ask. She pulls off the cuff and directs me to the toilet next to the lab and gives me a slip of paper.

"No," she says, and leaves.

The slip of paper has a sticker with my name on it. I shut the door and pee in a cup and slap on the sticker. The toilet and the cup are free of blood. What happened earlier must have been a false alarm, a mistake. I wait in the lobby until a new nurse takes me to the examination room. The room is chilly, and I change into a cloth gown and sit awkwardly on the bed with its paper sheet crinkling against my ass.

A few minutes later there's a soft knock on the door. The doctor looks young but well put together, like she's never hit the snooze button to sleep in. In front of her she holds a clipboard and asks for the date of my last period. Then she asks for the dates of the recent positive tests and the rough test dates for my earlier pregnancies. I list all of them, all five. When I answer, her eyes widen a little. I mention bleeding this morning and describe the red toilet glob in detail, even the trail of blood it left in the bowl. The doctor's eyes move from the clipboard to me as she writes, and I avert my eyes to her mouth. She purses her baby-pink lips, the skin wrinkling like crepe.

"All right," she says in a grating way, like she's preparing for something bad. "The urine sample came back negative."

"I had two positive tests," I say. I lean forward on my hands, as if to correct her. I tell her I must have been pregnant as early as last week.

"I'm sorry." Her voice is flat, nothing there for me. "It's likely what happened was just your period, maybe a few days late. Are your periods normally irregular?"

"I could feel it. The glob—"

"It's possible it was just clotting from the period. That happens, sometimes women pass large clots. If you had been pregnant, you'd still have pregnancy hormones in your urine."

"The HCG? I know—I know all of this—"

"Home tests aren't always correct."

"I took two of them," I say.

"It's possible you didn't take the tests correctly."

My eyes avoid hers. I don't understand what's so hard about pissing on a stick. I can anticipate her next canned response. I bet lots of young, hopeful mothers come through these doors hoping for good news only to be treated so matter-of-factly. She should be a butcher.

"Let's have your blood drawn to determine if anything else could be going on," she says.

"You mean like a tumor?" I ask.

The doctor shakes her head. "If the pregnancy is very early, the hormones are just too light to detect," she says. "About the bleeding, if you'd miscarried, you'd still have those hormones in your blood. We can test those levels."

I can't hear this again. There's no other way for me, no other future. This is it. I can't afford in vitro or adoption. When the nurse places the tourniquet on my arm, a part of me hardens, as if a great passageway is swelling shut.

I squeeze my palm to make the vein pop. The needle goes in without a warning, and the nurse attaches a small vial to catch the blood. He removes the vial and clicks in another. I wince, wondering which bits of me make up the human growth hormone, which bits will be separated into the baby's blood, eyeball, tongue. Then he does another. Little spurts of blood drip, each one perfectly round, becoming one with the fluid at the bottom of the vial. A baby will always need me—that perfect round yearning within.

"Give a man what he needs and he will stay," Momma says. "How does that contrast with what he desires?"

I'm silent on the other end.

"A man needs a woman secure in herself, Dee-Dee. Someone who is useful and doesn't give too much away."

"I am useful," I say, my voice cracking.

"You have to withhold a little," she says. "That's how courting works."

I try to imagine Momma giving my father what he needed. The more the years pass, the less I remember about him and my childhood. Momma was a waitress when they met. I picture her wearing a pastel dress uniform, an apron, writing his desires onto a sheet of paper with the carbon copy underneath. My father sits in a vinyl booth with a scraggly beard and dirt-colored hair, wearing a cotton polo and bell-bottoms, when loving Jesus was a New Age thing. He graduated the same spring the Vietnam War ended, missing the draft by a few months. How had he proposed? Momma never talked about it. Romance wasn't of any importance anymore to her. All I remember is as a young girl she told me she wanted to travel as a flight attendant but instead became a homemaker.

I've never asked her which she wanted—or needed. Is she satisfied with her choices? Will I be one day? If I ask, she'll deflect, no doubt with Scripture.

"Do you understand how what a man needs differs from what a man wants?" Momma says.

"I don't know," I reply.

"No," Momma says. "You really don't."

1997

Second semester of sophomore year, acne broke out on my face for the first time, but my breasts remained undeveloped. The acne was horrific: cystic, like little volcanic ridges across my cheeks. Sloane had curved out that summer, and she was always showing me her bras. Lifting her black T-shirt, she'd say, "Look at this one," happy to match her tits to the rest of her wardrobe. My tits were just baby fat, squashed flat by the training bras Momma made me wear. I'd wondered if anyone else was seeing Sloane's bras or if it was only me on account of her wanting to show off. I didn't know how to characterize the intensity of my feelings for her, but I knew others might think them wrong. I'd never tell her or anyone about myself.

Even if Sloane didn't like me that way, our bathroom breaks fed rumors we were making out in the stalls, which was way more exciting than what usually happened. She would hand me a cigarette while wearing neon-lime fishnet gloves and tell me about the cute boys in her classes. I'd take a drag, never able to finish a whole one, positioning my legs into a crouch with my thighs open the way a boy might sit, resting my elbow on my knee, as Sloane took a seat on the toilet, kicking the stall door with a steel-toed leather boot. We'd trade the cig back and forth, her black lipstick smearing up the filter. I'd hold in a cough, then blow the smoke out slow. Before the school day ended, I'd watch her grab a brown paper towel from the dispenser, wet it, and scrub the black from her lips until the skin crusted and peeled.

The week after spring break, we skipped class, bicycling through the crisp March air to the open prairie on the edge of town. We sat eating pastries in the tall, itchy grass, smoking musty cigarettes, drinking sweet iced coffee, pretending we were French losers, outcasts from the art world. We'd speak in accents with each other: *"Mah-dam-mwa-zel, have ze tried le crehm doh-nutz?"* Spring onions were sprigging green in the dead wild grass. Sloane told me about the perverted things she found online at the school library: drugs that made sex ten times better, animated comics of animals with human genitals, which the school's porn filters couldn't catch. I dropped the fake accent, my armpits hot again, too focused on the made-up images of nudity flitting through my head. Wind pierced my skin, riding the shock wave down to the center of my hips.

"You hung out with Allen last week," I said.

"And?"

"Did you guys . . . ?"

"Poor Mizz Deh-zee," she said, keeping her fake accent, *"ave yhoo ev-air keesed someone?"*

My cheeks burned pink. "You know I haven't," I said.

"Have you even jacked off before?" she asked, dropping the French act.

I laughed a little, in that nervous way when you're caught being lame. "I wouldn't even know how," I said. But it wasn't the truth. By that time of my life, I had been trying to get off in any way I could. Hands, brushes, candles, markers—anything long enough to stick inside me I would try. I was too ashamed to tell her this, with no barometer to measure against. Then there was the rubbing, the insane, ecstatic rubbing, like when people felt touched by the Lord. At least three times a night I lay belly-down on my bed with my palms pressed up against my pubic bone, rubbing against my hands until something began to spark there, until my legs shook. But jacking off—it seemed to imply some kind of finish, an end. That never happened.

"Allen gave me a little of this . . ." She picked up a cream donut and licked out the center. Sloane held the licked donut out to me, cream still left in the center. "Go on, be a cunt-licker." She shoved it into my face, getting the cream on my nose, and I recoiled, even as I licked my lips.

"You've never been curious?" She pulled her sunglasses down her nose, judging me.

Of course I was curious. Most of the time my fantasies were of her, of what she tasted like, if she felt inside the way I felt inside. I said nothing, wiping the cream from my nose.

"I don't get it," she said. She rolled off into the grass, pinching a few dandelions at the stems, then weaving the ends to make a flower crown. It felt like an opportunity to steer the conversation further into sex, but all I could think about was Sloane in her bed, white socks poking out beneath a mess of sheets, rubbing away with her hands. There was more I wanted to say. The anticipation leading up to saying what I wanted, or the fantasy of it, felt so good, and I kept wanting to push on, but I didn't. Speaking it aloud would ruin the anticipation, and to me that was the best part. She let the silence grow, imperceptible to my discomfort, and placed one of the dandelion crowns on my head.

"Queen Daisy, patron saint of virgins," she said. "It's incredible. There's an entire world out there they're not teaching us about. Here, sit up and close your eyes."

I did, and my pulse pounded dull in my throat, like a little hammer right beneath my jaw. Her fingers curled back from my palm. She traced a delicate circle and what felt like a cross, and I went dizzy, thinking about those socks of hers, thinking about how I might like her wily hands pressed against me. Then she did it again, but with something warm and wet across my palm. Another shock. With my eyes closed, I almost lost balance. I heard her whisper.

"Don't worry," she said. "I'm not cursing you."

"Ha-ha," I said.

Then she spit into my hand. I ripped my hand away from hers and opened my eyes to Sloane sucking on her index finger.

"Wait!" she said. "You need to make a fist or the spell won't come true."

"What spell?" I asked, regret washing over me. Now all I wanted was for her to place that perfect spit of hers into my palm. *Make my world different*, I thought. *Change my life for good.*

She placed a dandelion in my palm and closed her hands around mine. Her plastic nails, a jewel-tone purple, moved like a spider wrapping prey.

"Just make a fist," she said. I opened my hand a crack and saw small bits of blood mixed with her spit and the dandelion.

"Keep it closed. It's a spell for good luck. Sexy luck."

So I did. I held my fist closed, until the flower got shriveled and pulpy, the bitter-smelling petals staining my palm deep marigold.

1997

In the summer we hung out in front of the gas station hoping someone would buy us cigarettes, our foreheads sweaty and shoulders red from the heat. One day Todd showed up with a pack on him. Todd had been staying with Sloane for a few months, and I'd assumed he was her cousin. I didn't ask, and Sloane never said. We walked toward the river embankment and under a shroud of trees that opened onto a clearing, where we smoked behind some shrubbery while Todd talked about nu metal and his profound love of Nietzsche. He was mildly handsome, with scraggly teeth and long brown hair pulled into a high ponytail, the sides of his head shaved. When he wore it down, his hair fell across his face, complementing his light mustache and hiding his glowing olive eyes. It seemed a little wrong to admire him when my crush on Sloane was so deep. It was okay, I told myself, because they were related and had features in common.

Sloane and Todd talked a lot about God. They questioned and supposed a lot of things about the universe that I never could've thought up on my own.

"It's like a kind of energy," Sloane said. "God isn't like a patriarchal thing, or whatever. When the congregation is speaking in tongues they don't even know what they're tapping into. It's an energy beyond their comprehension."

"That just *sounds* like what they call God," Todd said.

Sloane sat up, defensive, flicking ash on the ground beneath us. "I've felt it," she said. "And I'm a huge skeptic."

"I thought you faked it," I said. "Like at your deliverance."

It was hard not to feel bored by it. I didn't understand. This frustrated me about her—she was supposed to lead me away from God, to my freedom.

"No, that *was* fake. But that's not what I'm talking about. There's an energy in me. I've spoken in tongues before. And I've felt other things." She looked at Todd in a pleading way that sought his approval, or permission—a look I'd come to recognize in myself with Daddy years later.

"Rituals," he said, coolly blowing out smoke.

"We've accessed things," she said. Her eyes got wide, searching for the words. Her blood and spit in my hand—nothing had happened yet. Did she think something would actually work? I wanted it to work.

"I don't understand," I said.

"The energy comes from outside," she said. "Tongues—that's just a different kind of ritual. They aren't accessing what they think. But the way it works is . . ."

She looked frustrated for a second, as though she didn't know how to explain. Todd put his hands up. It sounded like she was suggesting that these Good, God-Fearing Christians were channeling something darker than they imagined. Something that was holy not because it was like Jesus but because it was something completely different, an absence of light.

"Okay," Todd said. He licked his red lips, raw from the summer heat and soda. "The energy a person puts out into the world gets echoed elsewhere. When the church is scrambling themselves into a trance, they're expelling something. A belief. And that belief can affect other people. The energy builds. It animates what's around it. And there are things—things you can manifest."

"The energy feels big," I said. "You know that, I've been there. It gets tight in your chest when you're around them, even if you don't"—I put bunny ears up—"'feel the call.' But I don't get how it affects things."

"You're not getting it," Sloane said. "You know the story of John the Baptist?"

"Um, no," I said.

"How he was beheaded? What about Judith and Holofernes?"

"Yeah," I said. "She was trying to fight against King Nebuchadnezzar or something. I only ever remember the name because it's so catchy. Didn't she trick Holofernes into bed and then decapitate him with his own sword?"

"Right," Todd said.

"Sick."

"There's beheadings all over the Bible," he said. "Why do you think they did that?"

He put his hand on Sloane's knee in an intimate way, like he was claiming some kind of ground. The cigarette in his free hand was pinched between his first and middle fingers, which made him seem older, more sophisticated. Why did I want him? And why didn't Sloane move his hand from her knee? Her expression changed a bit, like her mind had gone off somewhere. Where was Sloane going?

"Why do Christians bury their dead?" Todd asked. "You ever thought of that?"

"Our bodies need to be intact for the Rapture," I said. "For when Jesus returns."

"Right. Cremating the body is a crime, it keeps our souls from being freed. It's the same principle with decapitation, really. If you really want to curse someone, you'd need to trap that energy."

I could tell he was loving this, the attention from both of us. He loved flexing his intellect like it was beefcake.

"You'd have to remove the head from the body," he continued. "It's disrespectful and more than a symbolic act. More like ritualized soul torture. You'd prevent them from ever being free or saved. That's *our* culture. That energy in us—tongues, what have you—takes the shape of the room we allow it to have in our lives. That's why some people see Jesus in toast. But that's why other people see ghosts or aliens. Their culture is the fear of guilt, or of technology, rather than God. But they have the same space in their heads and hearts for Jesus, even if they deny him. They look for aliens because they think the aliens will save them. They all have 'original sin' syndrome, thinking humans are innately flawed and that something greater than themselves will take them away from this hell on earth."

"I guess I get it," I said. Jesus was killed, too, and that was more than symbolic. That was literal. But its purpose was more like to free us, I guess. "You're saying Jesus is a big hallucination."

"No," Todd said. He patted Sloane's knee, rubbed it with his palm. Something in my pussy tickled, followed by jealousy—not of Sloane, but of him. I imagined licking the stray hairs on her kneecap. Todd was boyish in a way I'd never be. Slender, tall. The knobs of his elbows were wider than the rest of his arms. He was smart, if a bit too impassioned. I don't know why I remember so much of Todd, except that maybe some small part of me wanted to emulate him into my adulthood— the gauntness that made him ultimately ethereal so any philosophical knowledge he gave seemed more sage-like; yet there was still a masculinity about his waifishness that gave him superiority and power. No matter how hard I tried, I'd never possess the slim, aerodynamic body he held; even if he didn't work for it, it communicated to the outer world a sense of discipline, as though his thinness were a result of religious fasting.

"Jesus was an entity that visited earth in the form people needed," Todd said. "You get it? Back then, no one knew anything else other than humans and animals and light and dark. That's why when they said they saw God, they had to say he took the image of a man. They didn't know any better. But now you have ghosts and aliens and Bigfoot and the Loch Ness Monster and all kinds of shit."

The conversation went on, with Todd's arm draped over Sloane. The entire time Sloane said nothing, chain-smoking Kools, lightly touching the glitter beneath her eyes that made her look like she'd been crying, but in a fashionable way. Eventually, she said she had to piss and told us both to leave. She got up and walked into the heavy thicket. I followed Todd out of the clearing, the animal scent of his body trailing behind him. Twigs crunched as Sloane pulled down her pants. Todd and I had our backs to her, stealing glances at each other; his smirk was as wide as mine. I turned around, weaving my head; branches and leaves formed a mosaic of her flesh.

"I see you peeking, Daisy, you weirdo!" Sloane yelled.

"Just trying to see if you're done!" I yelled back. My head rushed with blood as I realized I'd been holding my breath. Todd looked at me and laughed. Maybe he recognized the pervert in us both.

"Okay!" Sloane said.

I turned, watching as her ass cheeks squeezed and popped into her jeans.

"You fuckers," she said. "Can't give me any privacy. Happy now?"

"Queen of pissing in the woods," I said.

"Virgin," Sloane said.

On the walk home, Sloane wouldn't hold my hand with Todd there. I hung back, feeling left out, sulking. What Todd said had stuck with me, though. There was something to this idea of energy, of it all being the same type of entity, and how to access it. I held my fist closed, wishing I could open it and see the flower there again from Sloane's spit spell. If I could direct my energy enough, believe enough, I could get what I wanted.

XXXX

This time the red Volvo is parked in the spot right next to mine. Two full laundry baskets fill the back seat; the passenger-side footwell is full of trash, the windows filmy. My phone vibrates, and I let the call go to voicemail. In the mirror, I push at tiny blackheads on the tip of my nose, wiping the grease on a tissue from the glove box. I pick up my phone to listen to the message, a nurse reading test results like a eulogy. My HCG test was negative. No evidence of a pregnancy. I listen to it, zombielike, a refusal to accept this fate. I simply don't believe it. An empty itch at the edges of my eyes hints at tears.

The front door to the apartment opens, and Daddy walks out in basketball shorts and a white tee, cigarette in hand. From a distance I'm reminded of how good he looks, like a scarred war veteran or a man who'd die or kill to protect me, insects be damned. He lights the cigarette and steps back toward the apartment when he sees me sitting in the car. I turn it off and climb out.

"I didn't know you were home," he says.

"They let me out early," I say. It's a lie. I'd faked a stomachache to go home, rushing out of the warehouse before Number Three could shoulder-check me again. I deserve a day off to marinate in my grief, like a dying mammal. I move to the other side of him, upwind from the smoke, unable to speak.

"Did you hear from the doctor?" he asks. "It's been three days."

Something claws up my throat. I think about why I'm afraid to tell him. If I say I've lost the baby, he'll tell me he was right about everything. He won't take me in his arms, or caress my hair, or make me feel like it's not my fault. He'd just stand there smoking, put the blame on me, absolve himself of the contract people make when they're supposed to be in love. I can't rely on him to fix this. But I'm still loyal to him and I don't understand yet what the pull is. Maybe I'm afraid. When I look at his deep scar, the sharp lines of his profile, I recognize he is the best I will ever have. I think about how I felt so influenced by Todd and Sloane. Daddy represents pure intellect for me. He is a brain I do not have. And by being with him, I can possess this—the safety of a smarter mind. I'm too dumb to survive in the world alone. And I don't really want to be alone, I realize. To be alone means supporting myself, which I can't afford. Filling up the space without him. A free afternoon after work would terrify me. The structure his presence creates allows me a semblance of motherhood, a pretend life I'm happy to act out. I cook his dinner; I listen to him speak about his murder facts, insects, and his former drug deals, but I absorb none of it. I listen to him tell me about how the world isn't built for men like him anymore. In that way, I'm useful.

"They said they'd call me," I say. "I don't know what's taking so long."

Daddy takes another drag and I lean into him. He wraps an arm around me. My muscles relax and a soft ache hits my lower back. My feet throb. I want to lie down in bed and cocoon myself.

"If we have this baby, will I have to work?" I'm pouting now.

"Depends," he says, "if I win the lottery." He blows out smoke and glances over at Blake's apartment.

A silver pickup with tinted windows pulls into the parking lot, the exhaust rattling a trail of black smoke. Hanging over the end is a white leather couch held down with bungee cords. The truck pulls right up behind my car and the red Volvo, a blue tarp flapping in the draft. The door clunks open and Sloane jumps from the cab in a pair of denim cutoffs, her hair in a messy bun.

"Daisy!" she says, her voice cutting through me. She waves and goes around to the back, joined by a gaunt older man with close-cropped hair and a scraggly beard.

"Could you help us move the couch?" she asks. "There's beer in it for you."

Daddy nods. "You know her?" he asks.

"Kind of," I say. I hang back, trying to perform as someone who would act casually about their first crush meeting their current long-term boyfriend, as he puts out his cigarette and walks over to them. Daddy and the older man work the couch up the rusted iron stairs while Sloane shouts directions. They get the couch up to the patio and she opens the door. I doubt the landlord has changed the locks since Ruby moved out. When Daddy gets back downstairs, he tells me they invited both of us up for dinner in a few hours.

"You didn't tell me your super-hot friend moved in upstairs," he says. My heart is knives. I twist my hands around in my hoodie pockets.

"I didn't think you would care. She's an old acquaintance from high school. It's a small community."

Sloane's apartment looks put together when we go over for dinner. Besides the couch, she has a new love seat and a flat-screen TV on a black trunk in the living room. An older woman who looks vaguely similar to Sloane sits on the couch. The blow-up mattress is gone.

"Daisy, you remember my mom, Barb," she says.

"Hello, hi, dear." She reaches out her hand for me to shake. Her fingers are plump and chill like dried Italian sausage. "I don't much remember you," she says, retracting her hand, "but you look familiar."

The guy from earlier sits next to me on a foldout chair.

"This is my old man," Sloane says. She squeezes his shoulder. It prompts a smirk to spread across his face, crinkling all the skin on his forehead and around his sunken eyes, which are puffy around the edges. Then he breathes in a thick rail of air through his nostrils like he's had a sinus infection for weeks.

"I'm Kevin," he says, offering a hand to Daddy.

"David," Daddy says. They shake unceremoniously, sizing each other up.

Sloane hands me a bowl of chicken pasta. I eat, avoiding the crinkle carrots. The whole meal tastes of pepper. I focus on getting full and let the small talk burn out into the background. My stomach spills over my tight jeans; I'd put on a crop top and knee-high fringe moccasins before going up, hoping it would accentuate the roundness of my stomach and lift my spirits, but I just feel fat, even fatter than normal. Kevin leans over and touches my bare arm.

"That's some nice ink you got there," he says. Sloane arches her neck to see. The tattoo is ten years old and splotchy; I forget it's there.

"It's the Ugly Duckling," I say.

Sloane stifles a laugh. "Oh, Daisy," she says. "You haven't changed." She walks over and lifts her shirt, exposing the ragged outline of a naked woman with angel wings and, on her back, a man with a scythe on a horse, a dagger, a rose.

"These are all stick and poke," she says. "I got them in prison."

I almost choke.

"Oh, damn," Daddy says. "You did time?" Interest lifts his face and he leans forward to look. The naked woman ripples along her ribs. She has the most enormous tits and looks a little like Sloane.

"I did do time," she says, "but it's not what you think."

We all wait for her to explain. Barb lights a cigarette and, exhaling, turns to look out the window. Kevin watches Sloane, never looking away, not even when a car backfires outside. Sloane pulls out a cigarette and holds it between her fingers.

"I got caught with heroin, but now I'm off the shit. It's why I moved back here, actually. Dad is sick, but I needed to get away, too. I've been clean for twenty months."

I count the months in my head backward. She must have been tying off right after her baby was born.

"Your kid?" I say. I want to ask about the other one, from before, but I think better of it. It still feels like we're strangers even though we're not.

"She's napping in the bedroom," she says. "But yeah." She cups the cigarette out of habit and lights it. Her nose flares when she thumbs the switch of the lighter, and I notice her nose ring for the first time. Her cheeks are so flush I want to bite them.

"Mom took the baby in," she says, blowing out. "But now I have custody. Everything's going to be better now." She glances at Kevin, who's looking down at his hands in his lap, rubbing them together. His denim jeans are spotted in dark stains, maybe oil or car grease, so dirty they look gray.

"Yeah, sweetie pie," he says. "You got me now."

"It's taken me so long to just find someone who believes in me and checks all my boxes. We're still trying to take things slow, but it's a relief at this point to think there is potential for a life with this guy."

"Gonna be my little homestead wife." He says it in an easy way, too easy, like it could just be a sentiment, but the promise of a wedding could be waiting on the edge if she hung around enough. He chuckles a little bit.

He has so much energy in the way he speaks to her. God, I get so jealous of people at the beginnings of things, instead of mired in the middle of them, like me and Daddy—where the butterflies have all gone, but something still keeps me there: duty, belonging. "How long have you been together?" I ask.

"Three weeks," Sloane says. "We got to know each other so fast because we were spending every day together in his van, driving cross-country back to home. But now I'm here, and I got my daughter back."

"It's a shame what the judicial system does to people," Daddy says. His voice is soft, like a low-lit lamp. "You needed rehab, not prison time."

"I did stupid things," she says. I wonder if she's going to mention the first baby, if Kevin knows about it, if they spoke about it on their road trip—but the story she tells about them starts later than that, much later, as though Kevin had miraculously spawned himself into being at precisely the right moment she needed a ride to Missouri. And so the history between me and her doesn't exist. She goes into the kitchen and pops open a beer with the lighter, then hands it to Daddy. My hands go cold as a smile moves across his mouth.

"When I was on Adderall, I didn't hurt nobody. I did steal my mom's microwave, though."

Kevin laughs, raspy and wet. He sounds worse than Momma.

"Another time in Kentucky," she says, "I broke into my friend's house and stole a Crock-Pot and a box of yarn, no fucking clue why."

She laughs really hard at that, encouraged by Kevin's laughter, and leans back, exposing her throat. As she comes back forward, she places her hand over Daddy's to stabilize herself, leans into him like she's fallen. Their bodies don't touch, but her fingers are right on his for the smallest moment, then they lift off. A shudder hits me, and I rub my hands together, trying to stop the cold shrieking into my wrists.

"I don't even know why I stole that stuff," she says. "I haven't done anything like that in a long time."

No one seems to notice what's happened, that Daddy and Sloane have touched. Their fingers, the most sensitive parts of the body, intertwining for that one shocking second. Pressure rises in my skull. Barb looks as docile as a cow, and Kevin laughs his raspy, coughing laugh. Maybe there's something wrong with me.

"You don't have to worry about what we think," Daddy says. "I went through detox myself, a long time ago." He takes a sip of beer.

He never told me about detox. The praying mantis, his beetles, that's simple. He told me once the scar on his face was from a bad drug deal. The tension in my body makes everything ache like the flu, and my nausea creeps up again. She's had two kids and yet is thinner and blonder than me, her skin still smooth whereas mine has leathered. Even her fuckups make her more like Daddy. I'm jolted from my thoughts when Kevin offers me a beer.

"Oh, I can't," I say. I stroke the roll of chub protruding from my poor posture, ready for this opportunity. I try to stifle a smile as everyone's face turns toward me and prepare my lips to say as naturally as I can. "I'm pregnant."

Daddy shifts at the counter, and I look to the floor, stunned by my own words. I cradle my arms in my lap, imagining my future baby. I look up and Sloane is staring at me, her sharp blue eyes so light they look beady. I'm hit with the memory of her face in mine, the sweetness of her breath, and feel embarrassed by my longing.

"Fuck," Sloane says. She smirks at Daddy. "I'm excited for y'all." She pauses dramatically, then looks me right in the eye. "Y'all will be excellent parents."

Her voice carries a practiced positivity, like a church lady, so different from the way she was confessing her sins just a moment earlier. Barb leans across the coffee table and pats my hand. "Congratulations, dear," she says. Kevin nods, too.

Sloane raises a beer. "Be prepared for all your friends to abandon you," she slurs louder, taking a sip. "Your child-free past is in a grave. *Dead*."

Barb tuts, and embarrassment stings me once again. I think about what I could say to ease the situation but come up empty. I'm too thrilled to say what I want out loud: that I want more congratulations. But their stares prod me to express something else for the sake of social grace. Why didn't anyone say something special?

"I'm sorry," I say.

Daddy taps his tongue against his teeth. He always does this when he's nervous. He gets quiet, working a crackle of spit with his tongue.

"I shouldn't have said anything," I say. "I think I'm going to head down."

Everyone trades goodbyes at the door, deciding this is the right thing to do, and Daddy follows me back to the apartment.

Daddy grabs a few beers from the fridge and holds them in his hands while I pull on my pajama shorts. I sit on the edge of the bed rubbing lotion into my prickly knees, waiting to see what he says. I know what is coming: my eclipsing, the ultimate extinguishing of my importance, but I'm not ready to go down like that just yet. His footsteps move from the linoleum and go silent as he steps onto the carpet. Then he appears at the door.

"Are you going to sleep?" he asks.

"Yeah," I say. "I'm nauseous. Think it might be morning sickness."

It's a lie. I feel sick from the anemic pasta Sloane fed me and her willful embrace of Daddy's hand. I scratch an itch on my nose. He just stands there with his beers. He's a few in; I can see the gears clunking slower than normal.

"I'm tired. And I have to work in the morning."

"I'm heading back up there," he says. "You mind?"

I have nothing left but to give him the permission he wants. "Not at all," I say.

He stands in the doorway for a moment, then turns around and comes back to the bed.

"You shouldn't tell folks," he says. The beers clink in his hands. "It's too soon. And you never know with these people."

"I know Sloane," I say, more defensive than I should. He leans over me, scratching his jawline against my face.

"She could be a serial killer or something!" he whispers.

"Okay," I say, taking in his joke. His lips part softly and wet my own. I want him to stay here with me, with our bugs and our baby and our one-eyed cat.

When he leaves, I hear the conversation upstairs through the ceiling. His deep voice, then Sloane's and Kevin's, all ending in laughter. I pull out my phone and look at myself in the camera. What a man needs is different from what a man wants. All I've ever done is give people what they want. I angle the camera toward my body and flex my muscles to imitate a little pregnant belly, taking photo after photo, and think about what I want. I never understood the idea that pregnancy ruins a woman's body. A woman has never looked more sexual. On my phone, I search online for pregnant bodies: pornographic videos of lithe European women being massaged with oil. Their legs protrude froglike from their glowing abdomens. I save a video playlist of third-trimester pregnancies, the ones where the babies are so big you can see them move beneath the skin. They're shot from the mother's point of view, angled downward, and if I place my phone just right on my belly, I can almost make myself believe it's me. I do Kegels and pulse my pelvic floor every time the baby's movement sweeps through the belly on my phone.

My mind wanders to how I'd lay out a nursery: a small crib in the corner painted bright cherry, Winnie-the-Pooh decorations on the walls, a felted mobile of bears and honey pots dripping delicate chimes over my sweet sleeping infant. I remember the call from earlier and eject its truth immediately. I'll get pregnant again, I tell myself. It doesn't matter that I've lied; it won't be a lie once it happens. The doctor didn't know what she was talking about. My tests were positive, and—fuck her—I'm pregnant. I place my hand on my stomach. The Baby Site says that by now the baby should be the size of an olive. When I press into my belly, something sore and round is there, I feel it. The baby is so much larger this week.

I hear the front door open, and Daddy calls my name before stumbling into the room. "You're going to love hanging out with these people," he says. "They're fucking great!"

I place my head in my hands, wiping my eyes. "I gotta get to sleep," I say into my palms.

"That's fine," he says, not noticing my despair. "We should all hang out with them again soon. Kevin is great. We have a lot in common. I just came down to grab something."

He's slurring. I watch him cross the room and pick up one of the small plastic cages we use to transport the bugs. He lifts the lid off the stag beetle enclosure and places his hand in. My heart turns up; a rash of heat spreads across my chest. I reassure myself he's not going to do anything weird. Of course he would show her his bugs. He's like a twelve-year-old. When he pulls his hand out again, the stag beetle on his thumb flutters its wide U-shaped jaws. He shakes it off into the travel cage.

"You're taking Jeff?"

He walks over to me in bed. Daddy is always more affectionate after a few drinks. He leans over and kisses me, the warmth of his flannel on my naked skin. He puts his hand on my stomach and leaves it there. Everything, for a moment, feels okay. The plastic cage presses into my side and pinches my skin. I don't want anything to change. I look at him pleadingly, but it doesn't register.

I hear the front door close. He's left the bedroom door open, and the one-eyed cat comes in to lie with me. I pet his head, careful not to touch his bulging eye. If Daddy cared, he'd go get maggots to eat the dead flesh around his lid, then spend five hours explaining to me how maggots are the cleanest of bugs, that they eat the bad disease-causing bacteria. The dark mass inside the cat's eye has grown and it looks painful, but I don't know how to fix him. We lie together for some time, and I feel comfort in welcoming this nonjudgmental, helpless creature into my embrace. I close my eyes and picture my future baby—first faceless in diapers, then in a dress I'd once seen in a shop window—midnight-blue velvet with embroidered stars. I see her without eyes but with a pale smile full of sharp teeth. I dream of birthday parties at the park, each one marked by lighting a candle on top of a placenta-shaped cake. I blow out the candle. I bite through the umbilical cord with my teeth. Then I eat the cake, filled with offal, meaty and dripping. The kitten next to me mewls for a taste. The kitten's eye grows and grows until it bursts.

The open bedroom door frames Daddy's silhouette. I rub the sleepy ache from my eyes and let my vision adjust. The silhouette doesn't move, and I think I might be dreaming.

"The cat," he says. He closes the gap between us and puts his face right in mine, hands on either side of me. He leans over, and I consider the weight of his body on mine: he's taller, but I'm wider than he is, and I think we weigh about the same. If there were a moment he would kill me, this could be it. His pupils are tight pinpricks, the surrounding irises pale blue, like sea-colored hard candies.

"What's going on?" I ask.

"You let the cat in the room," he says. Sweat drips from his forehead onto my cheek and I move to wipe it away, but he grabs my wrist.

"I didn't mean to," I say. I twist around, patting the blankets, but the cat is nowhere to be found. When I look over to the cages, the lid to the cockroach enclosure is ajar, and on the desk, a casualty: one roach has been half chewed, its white guts bulging from the split seam of its torso. Daddy follows my eyeline to the desk.

"Fuck," he says. "Fuck. Fuck." He puts his hands on me, one over my stomach and the other on my cheek. The in-out whistle of air through his nose is labored. His scar pushes into my cheek, and it feels like putty. He pushes harder, our skin pinching between our conjoined jawbones.

"I fucking told you not to keep it," he says to my cheek.

He gets up and whips the blankets off me. The cat, wrapped in the sheet, hits the wall near the bed with a thud, and its yowl seizes my chest.

"Get dressed and take the cat outside," he says. "Goddamn it!"

He throws sweatpants at my face. I do the breathing exercises I picked up from *The Baby Book* to calm my panic—*hehe-hoo, hehe-hoo*—struggling to push my feet through the legs of my pants and slipping my bare feet into my sneakers, the tongues folding in on themselves in my haste. My inner voice tells me to defend myself, but I don't.

The cat runs into the pantry, and Daddy grabs him by the tail and jams him into my chest. He leads me out the front door, slamming it behind him. A gentle rain freckles the cement patio, slowly picking up in fervor.

"Get rid of him," he says, and points. I follow the trail of his finger to the dark brush and bramble and the gurgling canal behind the apartment complex. The channel had been dug out last summer when the rains fell so hard the parking lots had flash flooded several feet, almost causing me to lose my car. At the far end, the water is sucked through a metal tunnel as wide as a man, with concrete poured over, and I consider if Daddy might push me in. Thick globes of rain hit my cheeks as the cat scratches against my shirt. Daddy puts his palm on the small of my back, rushing me outside. His foot catches the pile of cat food, crunching the kibble into powder. I picture the grave Sloane mentioned at dinner, a deep well, each moment a handful of dirt being thrown inside.

Second Trimester

XXXX

The streetlights thin as we pass through the outer boroughs of Cassville farther into the country. Daddy points, and I take a right hairpin turn down into a valley where wide fields sit for sale between river cane and forest. A porch light shines through a grove of trees, and we stop at the end of a driveway marked by a rusted gate held together by bits of scrap wire. Daddy's phone lights up the cab as he makes a call. "Here," he says into the receiver, and hangs up. A few minutes later, an older guy in a Carhartt jacket and Levi's sodden with mud taps on the passenger-side window with a finger. Daddy rolls it down halfway and crisp fall air pours in. The man adjusts his glasses and slides his hand in, clutching folded bills. Daddy takes the money, puts four plastic cylinders containing the egg sacs of orchid mantises into the man's hand without a word, and the man nods and waddles away like an overgrown baby back into the darkness. I pull back onto the road, imagining what the man is going to do with those bugs, alone, in his dilapidated house. I don't want to think about her, but my mind drifts to Sloane. We've texted on and off, but I've been too tired to make plans between driving Daddy around at night and working early in the morning. Out the window, the hospital billboard with its bright red number flies by. *This is what he's saving up for,* I tell myself.

A black sedan is parked in front of the apartment. Behind it, a uniformed man is talking to someone I can't make out.

"That's an unmarked car," Daddy says. "A fuckin' cop. Shit, shit." Daddy shoves the money into the glove box, then runs his hands through his hair. "Do you have any gum?"

"Center console."

He rummages through receipts, throws a pen out onto the floor, some change, but comes up with nothing.

We roll to a stop, and I put the car in park. Daddy tells me to stay in the car, but I get out and follow him. Everything about the cop is shiny—black boots, utility belt, taser, gun, nose. When I get to the officer I lean in close and he backs up a step. OFFICER BARCLAY, his badge says. He's been talking to our neighbor Blake.

A ragged Yorkie chirps at us from Blake's window, and Blake turns and whispers forcefully, "Georgia, shut up." The officer clicks on his penlight and shines it in Daddy's face. A perfect circle lights him up, and the black in his eyes turn to pinpricks. All that beautiful light blue, framing the dark of the night. Daddy shields his eyes—the one time he doesn't want to be the center of attention.

"Officer," he says. Daddy has on his work boots. His jeans are covered in sod stains, his hands in black grit. He'd been landscaping with Blake earlier, stomping into the foyer in the afternoon, wafting his sharp, salty stench mixed with sweet fertilizer. It was the first gig he'd landed in weeks, and his skin was flushed from exertion. I could have licked the potash from his skin. Then Blake said he had another job for him. I hadn't wanted to drive around all night, but Daddy insisted.

"ID," the officer says. Deep ravines from his nose to his chin accentuate his sneer.

Daddy pulls his ID out of his wallet and flips it over with two fingers. The cop clips it to his clipboard and eyes Daddy's scar.

"Not a driver's license?" he asks.

"No, sir," Daddy says. The cop writes something down. The gun on his belt is right there. Daddy puts his wallet back, and when his hands fall to his sides they're shaking. He presses his knuckles into his thighs.

"We got reports of an animal being mistreated some weeks ago," Officer Barclay says. "A woman told us a cat was thrown into a ditch."

"I don't know anything about a cat," Daddy says. When Barclay looks at me, I shrug and wrap my hands around my belly.

"Officer, I can't be around cats," I say. "I'm allergic, and besides, we have a baby on the way. You know how cats can be around infants. We wouldn't have a cat even if we wanted one."

"That's what I told the officer," Blake says, too helpful. He pushes a shoulder-length strand of hair behind his ear and crosses his arms. "We got a cult of strays around here, but I never seen anyone do harm to them."

The officer says he'll be right back and climbs into the passenger side of his car. My neck feels frigid and exposed, like a river stone. I shiver in my coat, glance in the officer's direction. I wonder if he's running Daddy's ID for warrants. I wonder if Daddy has outstanding warrants, maybe in Arkansas, or somewhere else, from before we met. He had been through rehab, he had done a lot of things, before me—things he never thought to speak about until Sloane was around. I wonder now what Sloane is doing, if she's watching from the apartment above, feeling embarrassed for me or pleased at the pitifulness of my life. Still, this is the most exciting thing to happen to me since her moving back. I'm scared, but something in it makes me feel alive. Blake takes a long, dramatic drag on his cigarette, sucking it to the butt, then goes in on Daddy.

"I can't be having the cops around like this," he whispers. He rips what's left of the cigarette from the filter, tossing the cherry to the ground, and pockets the filter. Daddy shakes his head.

We maintain to the cop we haven't seen any cats. We've never seen cats. We don't even know what a cat is. Meanwhile I'm working over the memory of the night with One-Eye, wondering who could've called, who might have seen. In our apartment, you can hear everything that goes on upstairs. I surmise the reverse is also true. Daddy cursing, flinging the cat into the wall, followed by its screeching yelp. Had Sloane seen us walking out of the apartment and leaving the cat by the ditch? I walk toward the tributary and look at the side of the building where our bedroom window is. Hers is right above ours. Maybe she saw us. Maybe this was her sabotaging my life.

The cop walks back, his shoes crunching broken asphalt, and I notice he's left the clipboard in his car.

"Your scar," the officer says. "Your ID must be ancient, you don't have one in this pic."

"It was a car accident, sir." Daddy takes the ID. "My sister died."

"Sorry to hear that," Barclay says. "I'm an uncle myself, sister's got three fine children." He rests a hand on his shiny gun. "Couldn't imagine them livin' in the world without their mother."

"Thank you, sir." Daddy moves his hands from his sides to the front of his waist, clasping them together. The officer mushes his lips together.

"One more thing," he says, shifting his weight. "This ID is out of state. It's Missouri law to get an in-state ID within thirty days of moving here."

"Shit," Daddy says. He puts his hand to his forehead, mimicking surprise. "I'll get that done right away, sir."

"Okay then. I think we're done here."

As the cop turns away, Blake mouths to Daddy, *What the fuck.* Daddy mouths back, *I don't fucking know.* Daddy and Blake smoke outside while I stare into the gloom behind our apartment building, remembering that night and imagining it from the perspective of Sloane's window.

Inside Blake's, the boys talk about how close that was, about doing a run again from Mexico to Colorado, while drinking beer from green cans at the kitchen table. This time, they would transport a batch of emperor scorpions, thousands of dollars' worth. Daddy is meticulously laying out the Madagascar cockroach corpse onto pieces of foam. He'd rescued the body, dried it out, and then re-wet it in some kind of humidifier box to make it moveable again. I look at it with guilt. He tenderly splays the legs out with little pins, crisscrossing them to keep the shape of the appendages. I sit on the couch and drift off. Did someone find the cat's body? I remember Daddy's fingers in the shape of a gun, shoved in my spine. He'd pushed me through the hole in the chain-link fence, right up to the cement edge of the ditch. It wasn't very wide—the length of a car—and I just thought, *If I can throw the kitten far enough, he'll land on the other side.* When I didn't throw him, Daddy ripped the cat from my hands. The current was rushing, full from rain. The only sound was the sloshing water.

At the factory, death comes from precision. Stunning, bleeding out, and beheading the chickens take seconds. They go from animal to product pretty quick. Daddy said another thing TV got wrong was how long drowning takes. "It looks peaceful, the body just giving up and floating away, but your entire body is on fire," he said. "And your lungs feel like they're bursting." I asked how he knew. "The brain can survive almost ten minutes without oxygen," he said. "That's a long time when you're holding your breath." I asked what's the longest he'd held his breath for. After three minutes, he responded: "The lack of blood to the brain causes damage." I wish I'd seen what happened to the kitten after Daddy threw it.

Blake laughs and I jolt awake from a dream of the exchange between Daddy and the cop. Daddy slurs an apology for being so loud, and I tell him it's okay. I gnaw a fingernail, afraid to upset him.

"I never knew you had a sister," I say. That's what he'd said to Officer Barclay, that the scar was from a car accident, that she'd died.

"I never had a sister," he says.

"Stupid pig," Blake says, and they both cackle.

I can never tell what is real and what isn't with him unless I ask. Though I hardly ever pry, I know he has family somewhere, long abandoned, at least a mother he hates and a father he's never met. He can't hold out forever. Eventually, he'll get used to the demands of a baby and child, and I want to experience his personal evolution alongside him.

I grab my cell phone from my purse. On Blake's patio, crickets make their familiar noise, and the occasional car passes by on the highway. The lights are out in Sloane's apartment. A part of me wonders if she's still standing at the window, watching. I call Momma, who, of course, answers.

"Dee-Dee," she mumbles into the phone. "What time is it?"

"I need to tell you something."

"You need a friend," she says. "Sloane says you haven't talked to her."

Momma waits for a response, but my silence burns on. I can't tell Sloane this. She's waiting for an excuse to get in between Daddy and me.

"Dee-Dee? Sloane needs a friend, too, you know. That's part of building a good relationship, reciprocity. Lord knows you don't have it with me, either. But you've got to learn, especially with a little one on the way. And *especially* if you think David is going to hang around after that child is born. If he don't have a reason, nothing can stop him. That's why marriage is so important, child."

"Momma?"

A pang of loneliness careens through me, like *real* loneliness, a solitude that feels like death, and suddenly I'm aware I'm all alone and it's my fault. That all of this, indeed, is something that *can* be helped, if I just put in a little more effort, if I just try a little harder to be vulnerable. But it was bullshit. I'd been vulnerable all my life, and all Sloane or anyone ever did was take advantage.

"It's nothing," I say. I hang up and go back inside to lie next to Daddy's warm body on the couch. The felted quilt gathers between his legs, and I burrow against his damp skin and fall asleep.

In the morning, my body feels too light, like I haven't eaten in days. Like the baby's gone. The baby has gone, I remember, but the baby is still here in my heart, I mean. The baby's here, she's just waiting. I'll get pregnant again, all I need is to show up for the right opportunity, to open the doorway for her again. The only thing that can put me at ease is filling the space inside. I drink two glasses of whole milk from Blake's fridge until my belly distends, thinking, *Baby, baby, baby.* I picture her in my arms in the delivery room, a delicate patch of peach fuzz on her squished forehead, vernix in her eyebrows. Then I'm full, full, full. Only then do I feel right inhabiting this walking cage; otherwise my body is merely a grotesque, useless thing. I want to chop myself to bits and be fed to the fish in the canal.

I arrive at Mike's late and keep to the sides of the hallways to avoid my floor manager. When I get to the line, Numbers One, Two, Three, and Five twist their eyebrows in anger. I imagine them sneering underneath their masks. They've started to quarantine more of the hens, and I've noticed the ones we're cutting now are a little bit smaller in size, as though they're too young. I butt in and sulk as I cut.

Work goes by quickly, and at home, Daddy drinks at Blake's all Friday night and I join them, sober. Trick or treaters come and I hand out candy until no more kids ring the bell, thinking how Momma would scold me for engaging in the depravity of Halloween. I eat what's left and fall asleep from a sugar crash. We wake up on Saturday and barbecue in the yard space our fourplex shares, and they drink again all day. On Sunday morning when I wake up on the couch, they are both gone. I make a pot of coffee on the camp stove on Blake's kitchen counter. Blake's stovetop stopped working months ago, and the landlord never came by to fix it. We all live this way: things fall apart and their corpses rot in front of us as we adapt to a lesser way of living.

I grab a brick of orange food-pantry cheese and a dozen eggs from the fridge, and I crack open five eggs into a frying pan and add the sour-smelling cheese. On the counter, I find a note from Daddy. He's gone with Blake to work a job tree trimming. I want to trust that he's actually out there climbing trees with Blake and not smuggling insects. I slide my omelet onto a paper plate already smeared with mayonnaise and hot sauce and eat. I stop by the apartment to feed the other insects, careful to latch their lids tightly, then I throw on a stretchy tank top and pat my belly, marveling at its plumpness. I fill a water bottle with more whole milk, put on my rain jacket, and walk the gravel road past the apartment complex. The pathway follows the canal for a bit and is lined with forest shrub, occasionally trimmed to reveal decrepit prefab houses, RVs, or single-wides with tin siding. I walk for a while until I discover that I'm outside of town. A game hunter's shot cracks through the woods. A flock of chickens grazes behind a fence, their feathers full and thick, their bodies proportional, not at all like the creepy meats at Mike's. Pleasant clucking follows me down the road as I turn back around.

1997

Momma made me wear my pink peacoat, which was too bright for my taste, and my black patent-leather Mary Janes with white tights. I was sixteen, but she dressed me like I was five. She insisted on me being immaculate for Sunday school. Even in winter, a proper girl couldn't wear trousers to church. The wind cut through my tights as I walked the few blocks to Faithful Floods. There was no sidewalk, so I dragged my feet across sections of frozen yellowed grass and gravel driveways. American flags flapped against the dull sky. Some houses already had their Christmas lights up. On one lawn was a plastic Nativity scene, Mary in her ocean-blue robes and Joseph prostrate before a light-up baby Jesus in his wooden crib. I wanted to take that baby Jesus with me all the way home.

I reached the church and swung open the heavy glass door against the wind to a whoosh of hot cinnamon-scented air. The choir was practicing before the kids' Sunday school lessons, and I made my way to the classroom in the back. Drawers and cabinets held illustrated Bibles, colored pencils and crayons, construction paper, preprinted coloring sheets of Jesus feeding the faithful with fish or Old Testament figures like Job and Zechariah. I was too old for such things, but the teacher believed younger kids benefited from having us older kids around. Coloring sheets from the week prior, with varying levels of skill, were pinned to the bulletin board. They were of the same image: Samson.

I pulled a coloring sheet from a cabinet. Samson's long hair caressed his shoulders like a cape as he slept on a bed. Behind him, Delilah held a pair of scissors with one hand and a lock of hair with the other.

A question had come to me before my father died. Pastor Anderson had referred to a line in Hebrews, in which both the words *transgression* and *disobedience* appear. I learned transgression concerns crossing a threshold, to go beyond.

Momma asked if I understood the first sin of Adam. "Knowing or not knowing is the difference," she had said. "Some disobedience is subconscious."

"I thought we were already redeemed," I said. "Why do we have to seek redemption?"

"Scripture is more perfect than our failed degenerate language," she said. "Jesus already bought us with his sacrifice, and soon he will return to us again. That's why we must continue to lift our heads for salvation, to prepare for the seven-year tribulation."

I didn't understand how to hold simultaneously the competing desire to sin and desire not to. I figured I had time before Jesus was here. Desire was ingrained in my DNA. And Samson had *perceived* God just fine; he had looked to God for salvation. God Himself, all-knowing, had placed him in the position to be tempted by Delilah.

God wanted Samson to decide, but God knew Samson would tell Delilah all his secrets. God saw what Samson didn't: Delilah was working with the assassins who aimed to kill him. Samson's disobedience rested in what he couldn't have known. God *knew* Samson would have to die among the Israelites when the columns of the temple came crashing down on all of them. That was Samson's deliverance.

How could that be just?

I try to remember if Pastor Anderson had said anything about the Samson coloring page to the class. If Momma had accompanied me to church that day, I wouldn't have shown up alone. If my father hadn't been sick, if Momma hadn't sat by his bedside, they both could have gone. But Momma wouldn't let me come to the hospital.

The choir hollered and sang in the other room. An energy stirred within me, tightening my chest. I considered what Sloane and Todd had said about how energy presented itself to you. At times I was relieved to be away from its pull. In that place full of screams and swelling organ music, it was tough to breathe. Even if you resisted, the feeling curled up inside you, got in your head. I picked up a pencil and colored Samson's hair dark brown. His face had the serene look of an untouched lake. Delilah, with the scissors behind him, looked content, too. As if she was meant to betray, fulfilling her destiny.

Samson's struggle was familiar. The instant when Todd touched Sloane's knee had stayed with me. His hand, large and knobby at the knuckles, caressing her knee like a crystal ball, rubbing until her skin looked oily. Yearning flushed in me to a place with no direction. If Samson was so mesmerized by this woman's beauty, it made sense that he'd betray himself.

The organ beat a thumping hard rhythm in four-four time, shaking the walls. I heard a muffled cry from inside the utility closet. I knew what the sound was, didn't need to be told. A grunting and the soft release of breath joined in rhythm and intensity with the choir music. Slaps like small hands clapping. I sat rigid, holding my pencil to the paper. I crept over to listen. The door was open slightly, and I peered through the crack between the door and the jamb. The outline of a man's plump ass, which deflated with each thrust of his pelvis. His white-collared shirt was pulled halfway up his back, the pits stained like piss. He had a hand on the girl's skull, pinning her face to the wall. Air flowing through the split in the door smelled of corned beef and cheap cologne. Then a hand reached around and clenched his ass, making divots beneath each purple nail. The hand belonged to Sloane. A gasp caught my breath, and the pastor turned his head, eyes wide. My Mary Janes tapped out of the classroom, into the lobby, and through the doors. I ran down the street, past my house—I couldn't go home—to the river, where the water flowed beneath sheets of ice. Cold mud sucked at my shoes until I found a boulder to sit on and catch my breath. The rock pulled the heat from my thighs. The pastor's thrusting ass had seared into my mind. I breathed into my hands, the air hot and sticky against my face. I warmed my leaking nose, then stuck my fingers into my tights and cupped myself, rubbing to fight off the cold. I squeezed myself, tenderly at first, pinching then expanding—remembering now makes it so hard to face her in person. The way his hand pressed against her skull like he was smashing a piece of fruit, and if I had known then what it would lead to, I would have swung open the door. Sometimes I cradle my own head at night, thinking of the way he gripped her, what it would be like to pull her hair through my fingers. When I was too cold to sit any longer, I went home with my muddy shoes and a rip in the knee of my tights, keeping my secret.

XXXX

It's gonna happen at any moment. A new pregnancy. A new doorway for *her*. She should be coming back to me by now. Something must be done about it. The more I visualize myself with her—cradling her close, feeling her little hand wrap around my finger, watching the way she moves spit around in her little baby mouth—the closer I know I'll get. If I spend enough time working toward all the things pregnancy entails—weight gain, breast changes, mood swings—her presence will be attracted to me by my will. God will reward me. I've done good. I deserve this.

In the mornings before work, I plan out my route: there are three twenty-four-hour drive-throughs on my side of the highway, and if I take one of the frontage roads there's a taco place. I can hit all three drive-throughs before my shift starts, I can fill myself full, I can manifest my new life. Full body, full of baby.

I pass two burger joints when I see the sign for the Chicken Palace and I take the exit. The Chicken Palace has combo meals that all come with this so-called special sauce, which is just horseradish, mayo, and ketchup, and crinkle-cut fries that have the crunchiest, batter-like skins and fluffy insides. I order the chicken finger sandwich combo meal, which comes with a limp leaf of green lettuce on top of the fingers in a toasted kaiser roll. All the chicken comes from Mike's. I most likely cut the tenders myself. I order extra sauce and a Coke. I don't want to order more because I worry the drive-through clerk will judge me. I drive two blocks to another chicken place with different combos.

"May I take your order, ma'am?" the attendant fizzles over the speaker.

"I'll take a bucket of mashed potatoes," I say.

"What?"

"Mashed potatoes with gravy," I say, leaning my head out the window. The sky is turning gray, still lit by streetlights.

"We haven't made the gravy yet," says the attendant.

"Biscuits? Macaroni?"

"Biscuits have just started, the wait'll be fifteen," she says. The clock on my dash blinks 4:45.

"I'll wait," I say.

As the car idles I take giant, shameless bites of my sandwich. The tenders scald my tongue, and between each bite I suck down a mouthful of soda, the tangy special sauce smeared around my lips. I hear a knock on my window, and the attendant is holding a plastic bag, full of biscuits, butter packets, and macaroni. My stomach groans as I lower the window. Before I've even pulled the car out onto the main road, I squeeze fake butter onto chunks of steaming biscuit. I spoon macaroni in my mouth only to spit it back out. I'm too full, and the grainy consistency makes me queasy. The soft grit coats my mouth, but I try again, then force in a bite of flaky biscuit, a sip of soda. With each bite, something grows in me. I drift into the other lane as I grope for more butter packets. A tight turn comes up, so I put my crumbling biscuit down on the passenger seat and place both hands on the wheel.

Before my father died, he said the biggest mistake people make when they navigate a hairpin is that they brake before the turn. "What you have to do is hit the gas," he said. Press down on the accelerator and the car will hug the road like a twin. "In a sharp turn, never brake.

You swing into it with everything you've got." That was one of our last moments together before he got too sick: my father in the driver's seat, his bottom lip fat with tobacco. His normal grimace had loosened, the taut fibers in his neck relaxed. My eyes followed the white line that ran imperfectly against the shoulder of the road as I replayed a fight I'd had with Momma the night before about my weight. My anger was a hard ball inside.

My father rolled down the window and hocked a wad of tar-colored spit. "You can't keep fighting with your momma like this," he said.

"You fight all the time," I said.

He laughed. "That's different. She hates me. She'll always need you. She hasn't needed me for a long time."

"Maybe not."

"You know what I did before we moved to Cassville?"

He rolled the window back up and turned on the air conditioner. We came to a bridge over a small river, its shadow ominous as we passed beneath. It disappeared in the rearview mirror, a rusted hunk held together by fist-sized bolts.

"You were in the army," I said. "It wasn't for long. I remember your uniforms. But you left me alone for months—"

"Damn it, Daisy," he said. "Don't be self-absorbed."

I shifted my seat back and stared at the car's roof and the unlit dome light in the center. "I don't understand what this has to do with Momma," I said. "Or with you." I held back angry tears.

"Sit up, please," he said. "You need to pay attention to the road. The double line in the center means you can't pass. And why?"

"I don't know," I said, still looking at the dome light.

"Once, during Desert Storm, I was in the middle of a busy market," he said. "The crowd began heading in one direction. I had no idea where they were going, but I followed them till I got close enough to see. Some guy had restrained another man and had put a tourniquet on his arm, right below the elbow. The crowd was captivated. Then the guy placed the man's wrist on a stump and hacked his way through it with a massive butcher knife."

I saw the scene in my mind as he recounted the story: a yellow rubber tube for the tourniquet, all the bearded men, the blood mixing with desert sand. It sounded biblical. I wondered what it was like to be that close to the rule of God, the way He used to rule in the Old Testament.

"Another man," my father said, "they decapitated. They cut his head clean off with a sword. I'd never seen anything like it. As the only American in the crowd, I almost pissed myself, thinking I was next."

I said nothing as scenes of blood and gore flowed through my mind. He was being judgmental, but I admired it. What did my father know about religion, anyway? *In the army, you get so used to the structure they provide, you must become mentally weak as a result,* I thought. *The only god in our military is death.* At least the men he had seen had something greater than themselves to contend with. I imagined him with cropped hair, muscles straining beneath his BDUs. I'd always wondered if my father had joined the military because he felt guilty for missing Vietnam. His brother had been drafted and died, and he never once talked about it. Now my father was sick. The heavy makeup he wore to camouflage his pallor had caked beneath his eyes and collected in his wrinkles, making him look even sicker. It was so pathetic, the way he was trying to pretend he wasn't dying. He leaned over, one hand on the wheel, to open the glove box and riffle through papers. He pulled out a ratty paperback with a red cover and placed it in my lap. I turned the book over in my palms.

"*Pigs in the Parlor?*" I read, flipping to the back cover:

A practical handbook, offering valuable guidance as to determining . . .

- How demons enter
- If deliverance is needed
- How deliverance is accomplished for others and self . . .

The book claimed it could "revolutionize" the way schizophrenia "has been traditionally viewed by the medical profession!"

"The pastor gives one to all young men in the congregation considering ministry," he said. "But I wanted to pass on my copy to you. I haven't done a good job at ministering to you and your mother, I admit that. We have to fight against the evil in this world, Daisy, against the corruption of this nation. Globalism, capitalism, modernity—they're our enemy. The new world order." He spit again out the window and coughed. "I know it seems like the day-to-day doesn't make sense right now, but I worry about you. I worry about your relationship with Sloane. Satan tries so hard. Your relationship should be with the Living Word. It's spiritual warfare, child."

I turned to face my window, nausea twisting my stomach, and I threw the book to the floorboard. "This isn't going to help me," I said, my throat growing tight. "Other girls at school don't like me. No one at church likes me, either."

"You shouldn't worry about what kids at school say," he said. "Your teachers, your friends, they can't be trusted, they aren't who you think they are. I'm at the Father's feet with this, Dee-Dee, asking Him to teach you the truth in all things. There's not much time left for us, for me."

On the last day of junior year, Sloane slipped me a note in the hall. I peeled it open in fourth period, my sweaty thighs spilling over the metal seat.

The cemetery. Tonight.

As the sky yellowed into evening, I worried Momma might call Sloane's or that Sloane's mother would call my house and we'd be found out, but Momma had no real reason to suspect I wasn't where I said I would be. I walked alone until small crunching footsteps alarmed me, and I turned around, shining my flashlight toward the sound.

"Relax," said Sloane. She blocked her eyes from the beam of light spreading across the trees behind her, revealing a deep green. She bent to pull down her long maxi skirt, revealing ripped and dirty jeans beneath, and grabbed a flannel shirt from her backpack.

"My mom bitches when I wear pants," she said. "I told her we were doing Bible study."

She slipped the tie from her French braid and tugged the strands loose. Her hair was like silk unraveling, and the sweet smell of her shampoo carried with each swing of her head. Sloane was my only exposure to the feminine grooming habits I assumed most women had. Momma never allowed such vanity. She was very plain, with clean but ruddy skin, and an eternal red rim around each of her watery eyes. No name-brand products, no perfumes, no lotions. Just a bar of medicinal orange soap and a bottle of sickly green two-in-one shampoo and conditioner in our bathroom. "Why would you want to tarnish the natural beauty God gave you?" Momma said.

I slung my backpack over my shoulder, and Sloane led me to a clearing. She laid out a blanket and dumped her bag into the center, glass clinking as she set five jars in a circle between us. She took a lighter to each, and flickering candle flames cast shadows against the brush. She patted the space next to her and I sat cross-legged. A small bowl sat in the center of the candle circle. She pulled four sweating bottles out of the pile she'd made.

"Wine coolers," I said. "Where did you get these?"

"Todd." She smirked and popped one open with the lighter.

"You're such a show-off," I said.

"Don't be a bitch," Sloane said, handing me the bottle.

Sloane's aura that night seemed elegant, as if a new, smoother version of her had been chiseled from her younger, formless self. I imagined the pastor's dimpled, clenched ass, pressing into her. It'd been a few months since I discovered them. I wanted to ask her how long the affair had been going on, if all those times we walked home together after Sunday school she'd seen him, if he dripped from between her legs, if she was aware of the dampness with every step. If she couldn't wait to get home and shower him off right away, or if she lay alone in her room, reliving each and every moment. Part of me was afraid for her. We were warned not to walk home alone at night, not to tempt men with immodesty. Even if I thought the rules were stupid, I couldn't break my conditioning. I wished I knew what it was like to take that violence inside you. I took a long drink of the wine cooler, sweet and vinegary. We stared at the glowing candles for a while.

"I'm getting kicked out," Sloane said suddenly.

I put my hand on her exposed knee, which was cold from the rip in her jeans. Tears edged from her eyes.

"I'm pregnant," she said. "I'm really fucked."

My chest tightened. The perfume of her, the burning smell of the candles, the black branches of the trees—everything closed in on me. Sloane's hair whipped in the breeze, covering her glasses and sticking to her glossy lips.

"What happened?" I asked. I curled up to her, my hand still on her knee the way I saw Todd do, my thumb caressing all the little hairs she missed when shaving.

"It was fun at first," she sniffed.

I pushed my fingers through her sweaty fist and her hand bloomed open. She sat looking at my hand in hers for some time, tears peppering below. I closed my eyes and moved my mouth toward the heat of her sweet breath and pressed my lips into Sloane's. The feeling of my skin against hers made me hungrier than I'd ever felt in my life. She jerked her head back.

"Jesus, Daisy, knock it off. How am I going to get out of this?"

"I'm sorry."

All I could think about was the color of the hair between her thighs. I pulled my hand out of hers and turned away. A million anxieties stretched out before me, each one taking her away from Cassville, away from me. All the birthday gifts we'd never exchange, the long nights never drinking beer, the older boys we'd never mess with, the road trips we'd never take through the desert to California, where Sloane's hair would bleach to boiled lemon and our skin would bake to a tender sheen. The baby would not be with us, wearing adorable little sunglasses and chewing on cucumbers. I cleared my throat.

"Let's run away," I said.

"There's nowhere for us to go," she said flatly. "My parents are sending me to my uncle's place in Kentucky." She wiped her red-tipped nose.

"Kentucky?"

"Ken-fucking-tucky. They'll make me go."

"I don't get why your parents are such assholes," I said.

"My uncle is worse," she said. "He used to work at a conversion camp or something. I'm pretty sure he tortures people. My dad says his brother has a *gift* for saving the unsaved."

My tongue was dry like hay. I turned back to her, fighting the urge to touch her stomach.

"Ken*sucky*," I said. Sloane laughed.

"Ken*fucky*," Sloane said. She laughed again, flashing her crooked eyetooth. I sat still, wishing she would take my hand again, but she didn't. She rested her arms on her lap, her hands wringing away, and stared at the shadows dancing on the blanket. My thoughts crept back to the closet.

"How far along are you?" I asked.

"Three months," she said. "I haven't even been to the doctor yet. That's how long since my last period."

I was thinking about Missouri. I was thinking about the one clinic in five hundred miles that might take her in, like a refugee. It wasn't out of the question, not yet. But at the same time, the idea of family, of harming an unborn child, made me feel a kind of sick I couldn't describe. It had been whipped into us, the value of human life, born or unborn; to abort would be taking away a chance at rapture. I thought of the words of my father then, of God's unborn army, holding up their mothers' bellies like shields in Roman formation.

"I'm not giving the baby up for adoption," she said. "My dad thinks it's a sin to keep a baby conceived out of wedlock," she added, her voice deepening in mockery.

I finished the wine cooler and grabbed another. When Sloane saw me struggle to pop the cap off with the lighter, she snatched the bottle and opened it.

"Who is the father?" I asked. "Is he going to take responsibility? You never told me you were seeing someone."

"It's no one at school," she said. She pulled the ends of her sleeves down to her thumbs.

I wished she'd just tell me, confide in me.

"I'm afraid to say anything. If anyone finds out, he might run away." She lay down, placing her head in my lap. "I don't want to be alone right now, and I can't be at home. I need to be here."

I brushed my fingers along strands of her hair. It was a welcome compromise.

Leaving the cemetery, I turned around and walked toward the river. The road that sat on the bank of the river went up into another subdivision, and I turned toward the pastor's house. I felt driven there. Every window in every house on the street was dark. The pastor's house had a wraparound porch that I followed to the patio, my sneakers crunching the dry grass in his backyard. The light in the dining room illuminated a portion of his living room, which was furnished with a brown sofa set and a small TV; I hadn't seen the light from the front of the house. The curtains were open, and the sliding glass door revealed Pastor Anderson in a recliner. On the TV I could make out nude figures, a bloated mouth. He flung his head back, which bounced against the headrest as his body shook. I tiptoed closer for a better look, and when I did, a small white mutt trotted up to the glass door. He sniffed, then pawed at the glass and whimpered. The pastor's head turned, and I hit the dirt, crawling on all fours to the front yard. I ran all the way home.

The pastor's sermons grew in intensity. Either my paranoia had poisoned the atmosphere or the pastor knew about Sloane's pregnancy. How could you live another life—one your wife didn't know about? His wife liked to greet everyone on the way in, her blond hair rolled into a stoic bun. They didn't have children; they'd only just gotten married the year prior, otherwise the town had never seen him with any woman, young or old. He had a certain charm to him, the kind that springs from power. He loved to make us afraid. At the pulpit he told us stories of children being stolen from compounds in Texas and Christian families being shot in the woods in Idaho, all because of their faith. It wasn't just that straying from the right path had caused these terrible things to befall God's flock, he said. It was because the Christian mind and heart was always under attack. He said that the FBI would come out to these places in the middle of the night, kidnapping the children to reprogram them as part of the new world order.

"The ax is already at the root of the trees," he yelled, quoting John the Baptist, "and every tree that does not produce good fruit will be cut down and thrown into the fire!" He waved his hands, spittle forming at the corners of his mouth. "I baptize you with water for repentance, but after me will come One who is more powerful than I, whose sandals I am not worthy to carry. He will baptize you with the Holy Spirit and with fire!"

He slammed his hands onto the podium and surveyed the crowd.

"Cults come and go," he said, "but the Pentecostal Church is forever."

I ran home to my room to cry. My bedroom was the only space not tainted by my father's sickness. I stole my father's Mossberg from the hall closet and hid it under my bed, tracing the slender metal of the barrel with my fingers until I fell asleep. I even got so angry I stabbed the drywall in the back of my closet with a kitchen knife, wanting to see how far my anger could take me—what it would be like to stab something without holding myself back—and hiding the triangular slits in the wall with my clothes. I was afraid of the secrets I was keeping for Sloane, especially the ones she didn't know I had. A little voice pleaded in my head: *Save her, save her.*

I stopped eating breakfast, which was when Momma noticed the change in me. In my weakness, I longed for Momma to accept me. I thought if I told her, she would comfort me. Maybe she'd help. All I needed was to ask one question of her.

We were sitting at the table, and she was sipping her coffee, and I, milk. The morning sun shone golden through the curtains. My father was showering, getting ready for work, and the water banged through the old pipes. Sloane's name writhed out of me like live bait from a bucket. I told her everything—that she might be kidnapped like the kids in that church from Texas or sent to a reeducation camp. I cried heaving sobs, snot collecting on my lips. "Please let her stay with us," I begged. "Think about what might happen to her baby."

"Her baby?" Her rigid posture loosened. She took me in her bony arms—even her hugs were awkward and uncomfortable—and I sobbed into her fleshy chest. "A baby?"

"Yes," I sniffled. "They're sending her away. Momma, please." I rolled my face into the crease between her freckled breasts. "I need Sloane with me, with us, because she's my friend."

My inner monologue reassured me: *Because you care about her and she's your only friend. Sometimes you get confused about things, but just because she makes you feel something, a greed that runs from your tongue to the base of your spine, doesn't mean you're interested in her like that.*

"Where are they sending her?" Momma asked.

"We could all raise the baby together," I said. "It would be like I had a sister, or even like I was an aunt."

Her body rocked with mine, and she ran her fingers over the bumps in my spine, pressing into each one gently. I looked at her. Momma's eyes welled up and the whites turned pink, the green of her pupils a bright teal in contrast. I loved her for holding me and wanted to stay in her arms. I wanted to kiss the smooth skin beneath her jaw, run my thumb along her chin. But I hated her for crying. When she'd found out my father had pancreatic cancer, the year prior, she held out on me for months, sitting silent on the couch with her eyes tendriled red.

She'd pull back her lips as if to smile, but she only ever managed a grimace. That year my father drank more than normal, or maybe I noticed his drinking for the first time. I'd hid in the bathroom with the thrill and terror of their impending divorce, not understanding he was dying. Finally, I remember thinking, *Something interesting is going to happen in my stupid life.*

My father continued dying, of course, when Sloane came to live with us. He slunk around the house in baggy clothes, wearing foundation to conceal his jaundice and the clay-colored bags beneath his eyes. That could have explained why Momma was being so lenient with me. The love of her life, her ballast, her man, was leaving her behind for Paradise. We would soon bury his body in the earth and await the return of Christ to see him again, when his body would then rise and fight for the army of God. With death hovering, Momma was desperate for something to remind her of life on earth.

1998

We lit candles on my dresser the moment we heard Momma go to bed. Sloane put on a Bratmobile CD, and I ran to turn down the volume. I loved the lyrics; they featured girls' scratchy voices singing about being ugly and fighting back and being mad. She pulled up a leg of her pajama pants and scratched at her shin. There were little freckles on her shoulder where the spaghetti strap of her top had slipped down.

The newness of our lives filled me with a certain kind of giddiness. It started in the pit of my stomach, then wiggled its way out to all my limbs. We stood in the tiny bathroom across the hall staring at ourselves in the mirror, toothbrushes moving in our mouths. Foam fell from the side of her mouth onto the face of the Paul Frank monkey on her tank top, and she pushed me out of the way to spit. When she bent over I could see some pudge protrude from her stomach. The extra flesh made her torso look heavy, like a bag of flour. I hadn't admitted then how desperate I was to be a part of Sloane's pregnancy. Having Sloane with us had revived Momma—more than my good grades, my perfectly recited Bible verses, my eventual graduation. She welcomed the distraction from my father's chemo, the slew of pills he took on precise schedules. He trusted only her to give them out. Like if she didn't remind him to take the CoQ10 at eleven o'clock and the ten thousand milligrams of vitamin C at 11:30 and the N-acetyl cysteine an hour later on an empty stomach, he might just drop dead right then and there.

"You'll probably end up becoming one of those boring Kmart moms if you ever get pregnant," Sloane said. She had stretched out on the bed, taking over the space. I craned my neck up from the floor in front her, fiddling with stray carpet threads.

"I'm not boring," I said. I picked up a lit candle from the nightstand and let the wax drip down my fingers. The quick heat disappeared, leaving a hardened shell around my fingertips.

"You're afraid to do anything!" she said. "You're so controlled. You don't even listen to music that isn't country. You listen to country because your mom does."

"That's all she lets me listen to," I said.

"She's nice to me."

"Just wait," I said.

"Does she hit you?" Sloane said.

Sloane was such an independent, charismatic person; I never asked why she was the way she was. Her parents seemed to ignore her unless she did something terrible, and maybe attention was fine even when it was abuse. I wondered if the way Todd had touched her had anything to do with it, if she was looking for something in him. Or if she got love and sex confused. I couldn't tell when she was being friendly and when she was being sexual, and that worked for her. Her target could interpret her behavior as sexual, even if Sloane had no intentions of following through, because, Sloane had said once, sex was what motivated people the most.

"Momma doesn't hit me," I said. "I've never been hit. She sometimes hits my dad, though."

"Then she doesn't seem so bad," Sloane said, contorting her face.

She picked up her Caboodles case from her side of the bed and tossed out nail polish, lipstick, and an eyeshadow compact. I was fascinated by the little pots and bottles. Sloane continued her rummaging. She pulled out a safety pin, rolling it between her thumb and forefinger. She held the pin out to me: "Prove you're not boring."

The CD player switched to a new album, and the room filled with surf-guitar riffs backed by keyboards. I winced. Should I pick my belly button, the only place I could hide a piercing from Momma? Shadows had cut Sloane's face into sharp angles, and as usual, I sat there, doing nothing. The pain scared me more than the blood. After a minute, she got up and grabbed the candle from the dresser.

"Fine," she whispered. "I refuse to become a boring mom with a sensible haircut and no tattoos and Kmart khakis, bitching at my kids for dirty laundry or loud music, even though I'll remember how fucking hard it is to be this age. I swear, mothers fear their daughters only because they're afraid of their own fucking deaths."

She scraped something—dirt? mascara?—off the pin with her nail and passed it through the flame until it gained a coat of black carbon. She handed the pin to me.

"Sloane," I said. I pinched the safety pin delicately between my pointer finger and thumb. She pulled off her pajama pants and tossed them to the floor. Then her panties. I'd never been naked around another girl before. I turned my head. I was terrified of my eyes resting too long between her legs and Sloane calling me out.

"Fuck, you're such a prude," she said. Sloane spread her legs wide. "Once, at the library, I found a history of body art. There was a whole chapter on body piercing. I want an eyebrow piercing so bad. But it's probably better to have one people can't see. I saw this amazing drawing of a vagina with piercings on it."

All I could see was that basic image from sex ed, which looked nothing like the real thing, even with a mirror. Mons pubis. Labia majora. Urethral opening. Anus. So clinical. To name it was to give it shape, give it purpose, and I didn't like that.

"Come on," she said. She pinched one side to demonstrate. "Pierce it."

My mouth went dry. She lifted her legs up onto the bed, the bottoms of her feet arched toward me. I got lost in the wrinkles of her soles and the crinkle under her nubby toes. I wanted to lick them, to put each wriggling toe inside my mouth.

"Go on. I'd rather die than let either of us become dull, dumpy bitches."

The carpet was rough beneath my knees. Her cloud of peach body wash revealed a tangy musk, which suffocated me, as if something sweet had been buried to ferment then dug up. My hands shook.

"Where do you want me to pierce?" I said.

She placed her hands on either side of her pussy and spread herself open, pinching her labium and stretching it out. "Here. It doesn't hurt, see, you can even pinch it," she said, clawing with her nails. "I just can't do this myself."

She was in an awkward position, which shifted her belly rolls so they jutted out. Her breasts lay flat in her tank top like fried eggs. The hollow of her armpits invited me to pet them with their small patches of hair. With my free hand, I pinched her labium between my fingers, then let go. I wanted to take my time to make the experience last. I touched her again, rolled the thin skin of her lip between my fingers, and got dizzy.

"You're taking too long," Sloane said, looking up at the ceiling.

My breath let out slowly, and I picked a spot to push the pin through. Near the top would look cute with a little ring.

"This is insane," I said.

"Just do it!" Sloane said.

I pressed—I had to push harder than I expected—and my blood pressure bottomed out as the needle passed through the skin and

pushed out the other side. My knees buckled. Sloane shrieked. There
was a little blood, and I squeezed the safety pin closed. My breathing
was rough, like when I'd seen her with the pastor and when I had been
sitting on the rock at the river; it was so hard my lungs felt like carved-
out gourds. Euphoric relief worked its way to my pelvis and suddenly
my mind was sharp. Hurting her felt simple and good. I could've
pierced her again if she asked me—I could have pierced her in more
challenging places, I could have done anything, even deliver the baby
if she had begged.

A door slammed across the hall, and we heard the muffled sounds
of fighting. Sloane stiffened her body, eyes big, and put a finger to her
lips to shush me. She looked down at her newborn piercing, and I
grabbed tissues, handing them to her in a big wad.

"There's blood!" I said, as she dabbed at her labium.

"Of course there's blood."

"We need disinfectant," I said.

I tiptoed to the door and pressed my ear to it. In the hallway, Momma
spoke through her teeth. The harsh whispers crawled up under my
nails. "No," my father was saying. "No, no, no. We cannot allow that.
She can't stay here." Momma's pleas were followed by another door
slam. Feet rushing down the stairs. Then Momma yelped, "Prick!"

"Oh my god," Sloane said. "Did he push her down the stairs?"
Sloane stood up, her ankle bones popping as she slipped on a pair of
panties. The fabric was tight around the safety pin. I wanted to stroke
the little outline through the cotton fabric.

"I don't know." I'd never heard Momma cuss before. The screen
door screeched open, and the front door slammed hard enough to
knock a blown-glass dolphin from my desk hutch, the fin breaking off.
We both gasped, and Sloane put her hand to her mouth. I went to the
window and saw my skeletal father stomping to his car. He swung the

car door open so hard he lost balance, coughing, hacking, spitting onto the pavement. I pressed my nose against the screen, smelling dirt and the breeze. The car roared to life. The fan belt in the engine squealed, and the Continental lurched into reverse, limestone gravel popping beneath the dusty wheels. I knew I was supposed to feel pain or fear, but my adrenaline soothed me, like sucking on a lollipop. The car turned down the road, bronze paint glinting in the lavender evening. *Finally,* I thought. *Something interesting* is *happening to me.*

XXXX

Taped to the glass window at the Dollar General is a pink flyer for upcoming pregnancy classes at the big hospital, Mercy, a town over. The closer you get to the Wal-Mart headquarters, the closer you are to God. The Walton Family Foundation funds much of Mercy's programs and even builds many of the hospitals. I know people think flyover country is ten years behind the rest of America, and it used to be true for the most part until you get to Wal-Mart country. Cleanest libraries you've ever seen and not a Costco in sight. The Waltons have invested considerable funds in building out services in the public interest, and the Mercy hospital system is no exception.

"Think of the classes as part of the foundation of your house," the patient advocate says over the phone. "The house is your life. The childbirth classes are the joists and studs holding your house together, and Jesus is the cement."

"So what you're telling me is that my foundation is empty," I say.

"Oh no," she says, drawling out the last *o*. "Please don't think of it like that. I'm saying your foundation will move with the earth. Without something solid, the house will crack."

The childbirth classes would be full of upper-middle-class women just like how I imagine the woman over the phone looks. Brunette hair highlighted into that strange blond color. Women whose work schedules consisted of selling plastic body wraps, tacky leggings, and eyelash-lengthening fiber mascara to all their gullible churchgoing mom-friends. They'd all be pore-free like in Olay commercials, some with a little bit of pudge, but none like me. They'd be on the fourth floor next to the nursery. The thought of being near all those newborns makes me woozy, like I'm in a deep, warm bath and I just want to relax further into it. I decide the classes will help me visualize my own pregnancy better. Once I *believe* in my pregnancy, I will *receive* it. And I need to receive it. There's no other way to guard Daddy from Sloane.

"Count me in."

"Great," the patient advocate says. "Will you be paying by credit or debit over the phone today, Mrs. Adams?"

I pace in the sterile waiting room until the woman from the front desk looks up.

"Are you all right?" she asks.

"I'm here for the pregnancy class?" I say, my voice weak, the intonation rising at the end like a question.

"That doesn't start for another hour," she says. She asks for my name, my information, and types something on the keyboard. "Looks like you've already paid up, so just have a seat." She goes back to work at her computer as I sit down at the other end of the waiting room.

A blonde with a square jaw dotted with dark moles walks up to me, smiling. The name tag on her light blue scrubs says EMILY. "You're Daisy?"

I nod.

"Would you like a tour while you wait?"

I nod again. She smells like melon-cucumber lotion and holds a clipboard close to her chest as she leads me through an open door, several inches thick, like a heavy bank vault. The birthing room is immaculate with a full-sized medical bed in the center, white sheets tucked tight beneath a blue fleece blanket. I imagine myself there, legs in stirrups, Emily smiling between my thighs as she tells me, *Don't push with your abs! Push like you're pooping! That's it! It's crowning!*

"The birthing tub is inside the bathroom," she says, sliding the door open. It looks a bit like a torture chamber, the IV poles next to a table of medical equipment. On the way out I spot a closet with white robes and a lonely set of pale scrubs.

As we walk through the ward, Emily explains what it would be like to give birth at the hospital. She talks to me about the OR, and I ask to see it, but a patient is currently in there. The ward is mostly empty, though. I wish the floor was filled with women about to give birth; I want to hear a baby's first cry echo down the hall. Emily takes me toward the elevator. At the other end is a hallway with the same vault-like double doors and large signs that say ALARM WILL SOUND WITHOUT BRACELET. On either side of the doors are two white boxes with little lights in them, like a fire alarm.

"Where are we going?" I ask.

"I'm going to show you the emergency room now," she says. "When you come in for your birth, you'll enter through there and tell them you're in labor. They'll have you sign in and direct you up here. Even if your doctor has you scheduled for an induction, you must come in through the ER."

"I'd hoped to see the nursery," I say, looking toward the closed doors.

A customer-service smile spreads across her face. I want to punch it.

"Unfortunately, we can't show you that," she says. "Security risk."

"Surely you don't think I'm a risk," I say.

"It's not personal. Just standard practice, hon." She shakes her wrist, jostling a peach-colored hospital bracelet with a black sensor on it.

In the emergency room, she introduces me to the receptionist and hands the clipboard over to her. Emily tells me what documents I need to bring with me for the birth. She tells me to remember a hospital bag and thanks me for considering Mercy hospital for my stay.

"When are you due?"

"In spring," I say. I swallow hard. "Ah, April nineteenth? I mean twenty-third." I put my hands in hers then, gripping them tight, and I thank her overdramatically for the tour.

"Are you here for the pregnancy class?" she asks.

"Yeah."

She goes to pull a hand away, but I keep it clasped in mine.

"Thank you," I say. "Really. This has been a pleasure."

"No problem, darlin'," she says, looking toward the hallway leading to the classroom. Her drawl is more drawn out than usual for the area, and I tag her from east of the Ozarks, maybe Tennessee. Her sugared smile twitches, and we part ways.

Along the long stretch of hallway to class, I keep my hands closed at my chest, clutching the bracelet with the sensor in my fist. A line of pregnant women amble toward the classroom, like shiny buoys in a lake. I slip the bracelet into my bag. A brunette with a billowing tie-dye maxi and salt-sprayed hair turns to me, and I panic. I'm certain she can tell I am faking, and a greed lurches inside me. I want that, I want to look like her. My body is a terrible mistake. I feel empty, hollowed and ripped apart by the assembly line. My breath grates against my palate. I want this so bad. I walk faster, past the brunette, into the class, and sit, gripping the bottom of the chair with my hands, the cool air-conditioning crusting the sweat above my upper lip into salt. I'm not going to let anyone, not even myself, take this opportunity away from me.

Another summer night at the cemetery, Sloane dumped half-burned candlesticks, some bits of wood incense, and a small metal bowl onto a blanket. She had been looking distraught lately. Sloane put the candles in a circle and lit them, then rocked trancelike as she lit the wood incense. Her sweaty palms squeezed my hands.

"Don't break the circle," she said. The canopy of the magnolia tree filtered the dusk, and the moon looked like little particles broken up. It was full, a bright night. I knew it would be, because my period had started syncing with the full moon after Sloane told me about her pregnancy. Before that it was synced with hers. Sloane adjusted herself, sitting cross-legged, and tucked her chin while keeping her eyes pointed up at the sky, the whites beneath the irises like porcelain bowls. I had no clue what we were about to do, but at least she was touching me.

"How's the piercing?" I asked, to lighten the mood.

"I got a ring for it, *dahling*," she said, raising a penciled eyebrow. She let go of my hands and pulled a glass jar from her bag. "Maybe I'll let you see it later."

Inside the jar was a rolled-up piece of paper tied with blond hair.

"Is that . . . a cigarette butt?" I asked.

"I've got bad news for you," she said.

I put my hands on my knees and looked at her. It'd been only two weeks since she'd moved in. Momma said my father was staying in a Super 8 motel one town over. Momma said she was praying to God every night that he would change his mind. He was dying; she didn't want him to die alone. Never once did Momma talk about God's love, or about fate or free will.

"My parents still want to send me to Kensucky," said Sloane.

"But you're with us now," I said.

"They said I have until the baby comes to decide what to do. If I give the baby up, I can stay. But if I don't, Dad said they're going to report me as a runaway and make my uncle adopt me."

"We *should* run away," I said.

"And go where, Daisy? With what money?"

She unscrewed the lid and poured honey all over the cigarette-butt-with-hair. When the jar was full, the butt looked like an insect trapped in amber. Then she covered the top in sugar and screwed the lid back on. She took out a safety pin, pricked her finger, and smeared a red candle with blood.

"Here," she said, and pricked my finger. The tip throbbed as she milked the blood on to the candle and mumbled something beneath her breath.

"What are we doing this for?" I asked.

"I'm trying to stop them from sending me away," she said. She put my finger in her mouth and sucked. It felt like something I knew I wasn't supposed to touch. I swirled the tip against the wet rough of her tongue, wanting badly to explore further. She pulled it out and held my hand in hers again.

"Remember, freako," she said, squeezing. "Don't break the circle."

Sloane began to chant. I closed my eyes and felt a heat move into my hands. Woody smoke curled into my nose. Her chanting was less frenzied than speaking in tongues: it had purpose, control. Clarity. I moved my lips to Sloane's meditation until I memorized the words.

Lovers eyes shine the best.
Lust lives in my mouth.
Fire in the east and west.

Blood to north and south.
Easy as breath, you will be mine.
On your heart, I will dine.
Predatory as the owl,
Be my subject, be mine now.

I opened one eye, then the other. This was not the spell she implied. Sloane's head was down, lost in her chanting. Our sweat mingled together in the tight grip of our hands. Her glasses magnified the freckles on her cheeks like a child from a storybook, and I nursed my yearning for her near the edge, imagined my fingers teasing her open. A stray hair stuck to her upper lip, but she kept her eyes closed, a breeze billowing it away. My palm itched, and without thinking I let go of her hand and scratched it against my jeans, then took her hand again.

Sloane stopped chanting and glared at me. She appeared entranced. She dipped her finger into the open jar of honey and scooped a dollop into her mouth. She leaned forward. My pulse thumped against the crotch of my jeans. She placed her hand on the button of my pants and began to undo them just slightly, reaching her hand deep inside my panties. I closed my eyes, self-conscious of the tampon stuck inside me. Behind my eyelids it was dark. I pretended I was Todd, with the fortitude to touch her, but stayed very still. Her fingers pet against me, feeling around the softness of my definitely-not-Todd parts, then found the string. She placed her lips on mine, her lip gloss sticking to the edges of my mouth, and pressed through with her tongue, her spit thinning out the honey. The thrum between my legs released a drip as her tongue traced my teeth—everything for a moment was heady and perfect—and then she ripped the tampon out like a rip cord, pulling it right out of the top of my pants. It left a trail of red on my stomach. She pulled away and my early terror rebounded.

She was looking at me, but she was far away, her eyes unfocused. She held the tampon like a pendulum, the bloody thing swinging back and forth. There was red clot-like slime at the very tip of it, where other parts had absorbed it. She wrapped the string around her finger, closed her eyes, and put the whole thing in her mouth and sucked. She sucked it clean dry, then took a finger to her lips and wiped away the blood. That was her, consuming me. It felt cruel and perfect.

"If I told you, I knew you would freak out. You need a virgin's blood." Sloane cackled. I retreated inward. She tossed the tampon into the grass. She had drawn me out of myself, only to tease me back into hiding. I said nothing as we packed up our stuff and headed back to the house.

Later I slid into bed with Sloane, hoping she would let me stay. She coughed and pushed a sharp elbow into my ribs. I was wearing a thin night-robe that didn't cushion the pain at all.

"Floor please?" she asked, her eyebrows pleading. I got the feeling she felt guilty about the silence between us earlier. I didn't want to move—I was mad about the tampon—but felt I had to. On some unspoken level I thought if I didn't do it she might abandon me. I sulked and took my blankets to the floor, twisting them around myself, hugging my knees as close to my chest as possible. Then I thrashed my legs open dramatically, flopping onto my back. The streetlight outside the window graded from light to dark on the ceiling. I couldn't stop thinking about the kiss and how badly I wanted another. I deserved it. I'd been there for her, made myself available for her any time she wanted. Something inside pushed me to ask her to kiss me or to force myself upon her. I swallowed hard and thought about the dandelion I'd palmed into pulp. It predicted all of this—she'd said the ritual was for luck, and all I'd wanted was her presence, and now she was here, right in front of me. I sat up quickly, pinching my face together, ready to confront her for bewitching me. Sloane lay there with the blankets pulled up to her chin.

"It's not you," she said, her voice a whimper. "My belly is getting too big."

She shifted in bed and sat up to face me, her wet hair dangling around her face like little ribbons.

"The baby's kicking now," she said.

My eyes went to her stomach, covered by layers of blankets.

"But it's small. Like a mermaid or fish living inside of me. I'm a fish tank."

"Maybe it's a demon," I said.

"Shut up." Sloane leaned back in bed, rubbing the bump.

"Can I touch it?" I asked.

She pulled the blankets down and lifted her sleep shirt, a black tee with SLAYER scribbled on the front. Sloane hadn't seemed like she gained much weight at all. The bump was smooth but angular at the bottom where the baby sat. The bed creaked as I climbed in on my knees, hunching over her like an animal. I wrapped my hands around her belly, ensorcelled by her skin. She was perfect. I slipped my fingers beneath the top of her panties and pushed my mouth into hers, hard, teeth mashing against lips, and dipped a finger inside her. The rest of my hand traced along the edges of her lips, and the cool metal of her piercing pressed against my palm. The tip of my finger curled into her, and she squeezed tight around me. I pulled my finger from her heat and rubbed the slickness along the firm knot of her clit with my middle finger, moaning. This moment, which my entire life spun upon like the blade of a helicopter, had spread out slowly like a pat of butter over hot, steaming bread, but it was over in seconds.

Her hands pressed against my clavicles. "No," she said. "No, no. I don't want this."

I clenched my teeth, almost biting her as she pushed me away.

XXXX

Number Three smokes a cigarette out front before our shift. She is giving me this look, with her eyes tight and her eyebrows pushed together, like she is angry at me, but she is also looking in the direction of the sun just rising over the horizon. I pass by without making eye contact, as though she might strike like a snake if I look too hard. In the locker room, I try to slip on my sexless scrubs. They are impossible to pull up above my hips until I untie the knot at the waist. I slip on my plastic protectors, which are like condoms for my arms, and then my hairnet. The machines drone and the sanitizer slops. The chickens that roll through are too thin today. They're not sick. They're just young. Maybe thirty, forty days at best. They're more beige than they were before, off-white instead of their usual peach. The death counter hits fifteen thousand, and my line manager walks into our section, light blue medical mask covering his mouth, with a clipboard beneath his armpit. He tugs on the shoulder of my scrubs and we lock eyes. I look in them, into his tight pupils and the rings of dark around the amber-brown irises. The sclera is marked by tired little veins. If he is saying something, I can't hear him over the machines. He walks me into the hallway, and the deboners keep working without me, filling in the space I've left like a spoon removed from jelly.

He pulls the mask down, taking a deep breath. "Hut three," he says. "I need you."

I follow him through the hallway. It is eraser-bright, the angle of the sun through the windows so perfect that you walk directly into it, unable to see. I'm thankful to be out of the disinfectant humidity of the assembly line, but I'm scared for where the line manager is taking me. The flu must have spread.

Heat emanates from the hut's door. The smell is like the inside of an old coffin, like something rotting inside had pressed itself into the wood, inseparable. The sharpness of it, like old blood plus earthy mushrooms, but stronger. The chickens by now have been quarantined for weeks.

"Two other huts have already been quarantined," he says. His mask is still pulled beneath his chin. "We have almost twenty-seven thousand birds to cull."

I blink slowly, working to comprehend the number.

"One by one?" I ask. My chest gets tight and I breathe in deep, into my diaphragm, to loosen it up. My hand searches under my scrubs for the warmth of my stomach to comfort me, and I squeeze the flesh there, knead it around even though it hurts. The baby is the focal point at the end of my road. I need to follow every line toward her, one minute at a time. The idea of being around so much sickness makes me feel scared, and I wish I didn't have to be here anymore. The line manager pushes me into the barn, and that's when I take my hand out from beneath my scrubs and put it to my mouth, to shield me from the smell. All the birds—the thousands of them—they're already dead. It's just a massive field of pink and white on the barn floor, the deafening sound of flies, and that sharp, punching stench. I turn back quickly to run, but he keeps me there, blocking the entrance. I bend over and puke immediately into my face mask, pulling it off my face, vomit weaving through stray strands of hair, all across my mouth. The line manager walks over to a sanitizing station and pulls out a puff of thin blue paper towels for me to wipe my face.

"Have they all died from the flu?" I ask. The remnants of vomit are viscous on my mouth, and I fold and fold the paper towels, pressing down hard to get it off my lips.

"We shut off the ventilators," he says, watching me wipe my face clean. "It was the only way to kill them off. Hut four is locked down right now."

"Ugh." I put the wadded-up towels into my pocket because I don't know where else to put them. I grip them nervously, wadding them tighter and tighter. They're damp inside my hand. "What am I doing here?"

He hands me a tub of Vicks VapoRub.

"Put this on," he says, "beneath your nose. It will help with the smell. We need people to collect the bodies and take them out back."

My head hurts from the smell of it, my sinuses burn. The line manager leaves me there to clear the hut out. I look at the tub of Vicks and open it up. There's a finger dip in it. It's already been used. I think of the baby, of the sacrifices I have to make to be with her and provide her with a better future, and dip my finger in, too. *Whoever was here before, I'm here with you.* I wipe the menthol jelly across my upper lip to block the smell and begin to breathe only through my mouth, which exhausts me more. I pick up the first body, already stiff from rigor mortis, and look at its pathetic, yellow-stained feathers and the exposed pink beneath. Its skin is so thin you can see dark blue bruises. Daddy has a lot to say about death, but he has never said anything about death like this. Ventilator cutoff. That's how they killed so many at once. Like keeping a dog or a child in a hot car. The chickens all suffered from heatstroke, hearts failing, organs pooling blood like water balloons. It must have taken hours for them to die. The most disturbing part of touching the birds: they are cold. When they were in pieces, I never minded the frigid temperature of their flesh, but whole, like this, my body expects a response—warmth; some instinctual sense that blood is moving beneath the skin. Instead, it feels as though the heat is being sucked from my hands into them. My upper back is tight and clenched, like my shoulders are up to my ears. I solemnly pick up more bodies, throwing them into the first crate, each with its own different bruises, strange pale blue shapes, like some kind of oil painting. They are mesmerizing to look at, and soon I become lost in the motion of it, picking them up, looking at them one by one as though I am honoring each one with my touch, tossing them in the crates, until a stack of them five high is full. Where was God in all of this? Was He as moved by His dead as I felt at this moment by mine? Terrible light at the entrance of the hut overwhelms my eyes, which are tired from looking at the floor for so long. I don't smell death anymore, so the Vicks worked. Or I've just become accustomed to it. I feel fluttering in my stomach: the baby, not hunger, even though I feel like I should have had my break by now. I walk out of the hut, take off my mask and my gloves, tossing them in the trash can by the door. The sun is high yet rain begins to patter down. The devil is beating his wife—that's what Momma calls it when it rains and shines at the same time. Dark clouds linger on the plains, and the air is sharp and chilly.

The field between the hut and the factory glistens. Wild grass sways in the breeze like the ripe thighs of a beautiful woman opening before me. An empty lot Mike's hasn't mowed because of fuel costs. The cold air makes the grass smell like the freshest, sweetest grass I have ever smelled. I suddenly feel lifted, then I begin to sweat. My mouth is so dry, and my nose is so dry I can't breathe through it at all. I need water, and badly. I walk around to the back of the factory, where it receives deliveries, to see if I can sneak into the cafeteria for a quick break. I go to the locker room, take off my scrubs, shower, and put on new scrubs, but I still smell like death. When I had lost the first few pregnancies,

I didn't fear what left my body in its bleeding heap. But something about the chickens puts me at unease, like a brutal truth tugging me below the surface of my preimagined normalcy. *No,* I say to it. *The baby hasn't died. She's with me, in me. I can feel it.* I wash my hands but feel as though there's something on them, a residue.

I go to the cafeteria and sit on a lone bench. I don't know what time it is, not without the death counter. I look out the windows, leaning forward on the table, trying to ease the aching of my back. The sound of machinery overtakes me, it gets so loud. I am walking in a dream after being in the huts; my eyes are still adjusting to the brightness. The Vicks must be wearing off because the smell comes back. I think I'll smell like death for days. It won't come off. I get a bag of chips from a vending machine, and the bag smells the same. When I eat, there's the feeling that filth is still on my hands, making it to my mouth. A giant yellow excavator comes into view around the corner of the building, dropping hundreds of chicken corpses into a giant dumpster. Hundreds or thousands. A waterfall of bodies. In it, there is an inescapable pull of power mixed with my fear: the act of human consumption, the cog of need. How many thousands of millions of mouths fed each year, how many millions of pounds of chicken breasts cut, pumped full of saline like little sluts, wrapped in Saran wrap, shipped all over Missouri, Arkansas, Oklahoma; frozen and shipped even farther than that. The factory churns, its mouth eats the bodies and spits them into the trash in an endless cycle, it eats our energy, and here I am, my energy makes it. The dumpster has a special mouth with many rotating metal teeth to catch the bodies. Each load that's dropped, they're crushed into a ground-up liquid of bones, fat, feathers, and flesh.

Back at the apartment, the drizzle has become gray and regular. Daddy sits on the couch, like he's been waiting for me. The TV is off. A mason jar is cradled in his lap, and he pets it softly. At first I think it's june bugs, but I go over to him and crouch. My face close to the glass, I see them zoomed in: bloated drops of insect with creamy yellow-and-black fur, the hairs slightly dandered with pollen, gossamer wings tucked politely at their backs like the tails of a tuxedo jacket. The end of their abdomens come together in a sleek, small stinger. Bumblebees. One tries to fly, its veiny little wings pinioned, and the sound inside the jar rings, like the jet engine version of the buzz of a fly.

"Smuggling exotic honey?" I say.

He rolls his eyes at me and swills a mouthful of booze. He looks down into his glass as though it might swallow him. He never gets sensitive like this until he's about six drinks in.

"There's things I won't discuss with you," he says. "I hope you trust me when I say I'm trying my best."

He looks at me, the whites of his eyes pink and glossy. Broken capillaries like fine hairs color his cheeks. I sink into the couch, reflecting on what to say that would sound convincing. Daddy takes the jar and throws it in my lap, irritating the bees.

"Bedroom," he says. "Now."

I sense that, if I don't do what he says, I might lose him, or lose my life. I cower as one might prostrate before a god. When he stands up, I can see he's already hard for me. I never questioned him, and I didn't, not until this moment. He picks the jar up and the bees buzz again at the movement. It sounds powerful. The light through the blinds turns low and cool, wind hisses through the trees outside, bringing the storm with it, and behind the trees, I know there is a little fenced-off tributary burbling away the water. I'm overwhelmed, remembering the mass of chickens in the burning huts. It must have taken hours. It's true I have no remorse, but I'm angry to be made to feel guilt this way, that I feel I can't speak out. I'm angry I let myself be controlled, by him, by Sloane, by Momma. My boss.

Daddy bends me over the bed and slaps my ass pink, one hard smack at a time. I close my eyes to go deeper into the feeling. He likes it when I whimper and so I do, phlegm at the back of my throat catching a little bit. There's the metal scrape of long, thin tongs against the utility shelves, the hollow ring of the jar's lid unscrewing. The bees' wings lose their deep echo for a moment, and I hear the lid screw on again. Bent over, I can't see it, but I can hear one bee's attempt to flee, I envision it pinched between the tongs, threatened, frightened, confused. Daddy's hand spreads out the fold of skin on the back of my thigh where my ass meets my leg, then there's the strange, delicate feeling of the bug's fairy legs against me, then its massive sting. He does this maybe a half dozen or a dozen times, each like a cigarette cherry burning off a hole of skin at the spot. My closed eyes run the imagined burn in high definition: the skin released from its tautness against the singe, shrinking back from the heat. There are, of course, no holes; just an ever-present stabbing that shoots to my knees. Waves of nausea soothe their way into my pain, distracting me and dulling it out. I wrap my arms tight around me, facedown in the covers. I fight the nausea. Adrenaline grinds my willpower to a fine dust. Then I begin to cry. Daddy slaps the burning spots, hard, then puts his hands over mine. A vein pops out on the back of his hand. He fucks me from behind until he comes. This—the snot and tears and vomit leaving my body—feels cleansing. This makes me better than an ordinary person.

XXXX

A quick knock on my door wakes me. It's Sloane, disheveled in buffalo plaid pajama pants and a wrinkled white tee.

"Do you want to come up for coffee?" she asks. She sucks her bottom lip into her mouth, biting it with her teeth. I say yes. Even now, almost twenty years later, I'm greedy for her consideration. I've been able to avoid her for so long because she hasn't sought me out. It's not like I didn't think of her all that time, wondered what she was doing.

I make Sloane wait out front while I get dressed in a pair of jeans and a peplum top. The peplum top is too tight, but it makes my belly look larger than it is.

I check on the bugs. I adjust the light to the stag beetle cage and notice the top has been edged off just a hair. My heart jumps and I lift the lid to look inside, parting the neon-green foliage. I lift the tiny rotting log in his cage, but he's not beneath it. I turn on the bedroom lights and check under the bed, in the covers. I check the windowsills and the closet, find nothing. My heart drops, as either it's with Daddy, or it's missing and it's my fault. I drop a feeder maggot into the praying mantis enclosure and a lettuce leaf into the roach cage. The roaches don't eat, but Meredith rocks back and forth on her delicate legs between some leaves. Her cage is lined with a mix of real and fake foliage. She's the length of my palm, with a lime-green sausagey thorax. Every time the maggot dances a bit, she takes one step toward it. Her meat hooks unfurl, her pinprick irises move about. Meredith is studying her prey. Daddy once told me the praying mantis has five eyes. Three sit in the middle of her head. She's fast—she snaps up the maggot and begins eating it from the middle first. It tears in two, and she drops one piece, still wriggling, and eats the remaining half.

I walk up the stairs with Sloane and check the parking lot for Blake's car. I don't see it, and Daddy hasn't left a note.

Sloane's apartment is stuffy, cemented with the smell of raw flour. In the corner of the living room, Steg throws around rainbow Duplo bricks in her playpen. Sloane brings me a black cup of coffee, and I sit at the table. It's acrid and weak, burned from sitting in the pot. Steg screams and runs back and forth, picking up toys and throwing them over the railing.

"She's so beautiful," I say. I imagine her as an infant, palming her sweet skull, caressing her fontanelle with my thumb, scraping the cradle cap from her scalp with my fingernails. Steg squeals and bares her solid, tiny teeth between bulging cheeks.

"Thank you," Sloane says. She sits across from me and sips her coffee, not making direct eye contact. Like there's air she wants to clear. I want to clear the air, too. I want to know what happened to the first pregnancy. I want to know if she lived the life I had imagined she had. I want her to be the one to bring it up, but I can't wait.

"Why didn't you ever call me after you left town?" I ask.

She swallows her coffee and holds the mug to her lips, hiding the lower half of her face. She has crow's feet, just slightly, and her forehead looks like it's been beat by the sun.

"After I moved to Kentucky," she says, "I had complications."

She says the word *complications* like it implies more than that.

I say the only thing a person can say when someone masks their trauma so vaguely. "Oh my god, I'm so sorry."

"It's fine," she says.

I imagine the worst. I wonder if late-term abortion was legal in Kentucky then. I imagine the speculum inside her, the doctor snipping the baby into pieces, like chicken fingers. "It's okay if it isn't," I say.

"The boy, Aaron—something was wrong with him. He lives in a home. He's sixteen now."

"Do you go visit?"

"No," she says. "I felt fucked up by it for a long time. Still, I spent a lot of time rigging when I shouldn't have. Then I got locked up, but things are different now. I'm on the program. I'm sober. I met someone. And after Steg, I kinda felt better. I'm moving on now. I've been moving forward for a long time."

"You moved on from *us* pretty easy." My neck tightens as the words form, my ears burning, and I get embarrassed again as soon as I say it.

"You were a good friend to me," she says. She sets the mug on a coaster and looks away. "I haven't forgotten that, Daisy."

She'd say that even if it wasn't true. There's no way of knowing if she's being truthful or just cordial, or if she's trying to trick me.

"You never told me whose it was."

"I didn't need to," Sloane says. There's a twitch at the side of her mouth, and for a moment, fear makes its familiar path through my core.

"All that talk about how bad the church was, but you still went to him?"

Sloane puts a hand on the table and leans toward me. "I'm not a hypocrite for exposing someone else's hypocrisy," she says sternly.

"But it did give you a kind of power," I say. "You loved being able to control people."

"That's not fair," she says. "I was trying to prove to myself—to you, to everyone—that all their charismatic crap was a lie. Prosperity worship, give me a break. Oneness doctrine is the worst thing to happen to Christianity since . . . ever."

Sloane's gaze softens. "I always worried about you," she says. Her admission fills me with the slightest buzz, but then it's killed immediately when I think of the way she touched Daddy's hand, how she'd said nothing of it.

"You never showed it."

"I mean after I left," she says, "I thought about you, often."

"And now?"

"You seem . . . happy," she says. "Well-adjusted. How is your baby?"

I dig through my purse, pawing between old drive-through receipts and sticky candy wrappers, and pull out a sonogram, but I can't remember where I got it. I don't even know how I knew I had it. It just felt right, like the way you reach your hand to your nose to touch it and know where it is. I can place myself at the hospital last week, remember the maternity ward and the nurse with blond hair. The name tag EMILY. There was a dark room, a doctor's office, a granite countertop with pale tongue depressors and Q-tips and a pink poster about the fetal growth cycle. Then the doctor. She was short with me, but I remember thinking her white teeth and salon-quality hair were signs of her superior morality. She wrote things down on a piece of paper. Everything else is a blur. I show the sonogram to Sloane.

She takes the ultrasound, rubs her thumb across the paper. "Look at that," she says.

The ultrasound is crinkled. Small text in the upper right-hand corner says "fourteen weeks." Other text is cut off.

"This is the nose," I say. I lean over the table and put my finger on a point attached to a rough-edged semicircle.

"Precious," Sloane says. Her demeanor shifts into something saccharine.

She hands the ultrasound back, and I fold it up and slip it in my purse.

"You know," she says, "I've gotta run soon. It's a doctor's appointment. Do you think you could watch Steg for an hour or so?"

There's a pleading look to her face that I didn't realize I'd missed until she made it.

"For me?"

"Yeah," I say. "Sure."

Sloane sets out a paper plate with salty buttered crackers and a few slices of cheese on the dining room table, puts our coffee cups in the sink, and kisses Steg on the head an inordinate number of times before leaving the house.

I sit on the dining chair and scroll on my phone through dazzling filtered images of pregnant families and nurseries, letting Steg run around, as she pulls books off shelves and tissues out of Kleenex boxes. She starts ripping the tissues into the tiniest of pieces, then comes up behind me and pulls at my knee, then runs away, chasing a cat into Sloane's bedroom, and a stench settles behind her. It's strong and musky; it turns my nose. She's shit her diaper. I'm drugged in my scrolling and don't want to get up. Each image feels too good to look at. I'll change it later. But then I get up, thinking about the missing stag beetle. The last I'd seen the thing was the night Daddy and I had come up for dinner, the night Sloane touched his hand. The wooden drawers in her brand-new dresser slide out like a fork from a newly baked cake. I slither my hands beneath the folded laundry, then move on to her nightstand. I don't know what I'm looking for, really, because an insect cage would be obvious. I find a greasy pink condom wrapper behind a photo frame, alongside face lotion, a bottle of massage oil, and a few books. Nothing incriminating. Steg tugs at my jeans.

"Hungry," she says.

In the fridge, nothing looks appetizing. The milk smells as though it's turned. There's a little tub of cooked spaghetti, complete with red sauce. There's no bread, only rice and boxes of Hamburger Helper. When I inspect the rice further, I find little weevils. I get the spaghetti and pop it in the microwave, but it needs something more, so I put Steg in her playpen and give her a light-up toy, hoping it will occupy her while I go downstairs to grab something from the fridge.

At home, Daddy's cell phone is on the kitchen counter. I don't know how I'd missed it earlier. A corner hangs off the counter's edge, the silver case like a mirror. It looks like a trap. Daddy did that sometimes, Scotch-taping the door or placing a hair on a doorknob to test if anyone had broken into the apartment. I quiz myself to see if I can remember his passcode and end up using his birthday: 0409. The phone unlocks and a sweaty thrill swells my chest. Maybe Sloane was wherever Daddy was—I still hadn't heard from him. The hand touch, maybe it developed into something more. A doctor's appointment on a Saturday? Seemed fake. Even if the free clinic was open weekends.

I tap on the little envelope in the corner and scroll to a person tagged only as "S." There is only one message in the thread, from Daddy.

She makes me want to stab myself

The way it's written, it's clear that some conversation had been going on, but the messages were deleted. Bile hits my throat as I put the phone back down. Sloane's hand against Daddy's plays through my mind on repeat, my vision zoomed in so closely I can see the pores on Sloane's hands and the delicate white hairs springing from them. The slide of his knuckles against her smooth, unswollen palm; the space between each of her fingers like a porn star's thigh gap.

Something in me bursts. What day is it? The popping of chicken necks between my hands, the rusty smell of blood. My breath goes ragged. Am I supposed to be at work? I yearn for the meditative slicing of my scissors against chicken breasts and the numbing drone of the warehouse. My skin grows cold with sweat. I think of the ultrasound. I'm not barren. This whole time I must have been carrying her, my Miracle, while telling myself I'd lost her so I didn't have to face my fears. I put my hand on my stomach and a heart pounds against my palm. She is here. I hear the wail of a baby from upstairs and my legs wobble. Sloane's baby? Worms crawl into my vision. I lean over the kitchen sink, my palms against the porcelain, as bitter coffee ejects from my mouth.

1998

Rumors spread about Sloane. People thought she had been sent to a faith camp, or was turning tricks, or had been doing hard drugs and got knocked up by a junkie. One person in the congregation would offer up a theory, and the rumor would deform and spread out into the wider community. There was never any way to fight the rumors, if you managed to hear them at all. Whenever I walked into the restroom at school, if anyone saw me, they'd wait until I was in the stall.

"Dykey Daisy! Dykey Daisy!" they'd shout through the crack in the door, their teeth flashing as they cackled. Each harsh syllable made my self-esteem spiral, but another part of me would spark alive with rage. I'd fantasize about crushing their mouths into the sink faucets, of smashing their faces into the mirror, holding them there, cheekbones churning into the glass, their pretty white teeth splintering.

Sloane had started to show so much it was impossible to hide. She dropped out of school and stopped going to church with us, and Momma stayed home with her. She insisted I was the one to go to services. I walked alone, knees and knuckles numb from the cold, then came home and reported back to her the details of the sermons. On the walk back, I imagined Sloane and Momma in the kitchen, warm in front of the stove, patting their flour-crusted hands into thick dough to make drop biscuits.

Parents at church would not make eye contact with me, Sloane's mother included. Barb claims she doesn't remember me, but I think somewhere deep down she does. She swayed with the rest of the congregation, eyes forward, as though she knew I was watching her. Their ecstatic prayers grew in intensity and circles of people formed beside me, though none would let me join. Some desperation rose inside me. I wanted to be known, to be truly vulnerable with somebody—maybe with God, a god, Sloane, Momma, somebody. But it terrified me. I wanted to receive the spirit gift if for no other reason than to be special, so I could go home and tell Momma I was like her.

On this particular Sunday the pastor whipped his microphone cord around him as he walked across the stage. I wished it were a noose wrapped around his neck.

"The devil knows money is a weapon against you," he said.

"Hallelujah," the crowd said. The way they sang it, people lifted their hands up and repeated the praise until the words ran together: *Hallelujah. Hallelujah-halle-lu-lah-hall-ley-loo-la-ley-loo-la-ley-loo.*

"The wicked shall see it and be grieved and melt away." His soft whisper then rising voice brought the congregation to choir. He blotted a handkerchief against a pulsing forehead vein. With circles of sweat in his pits, he raised a hand high, the mic in the other hand, and skipped across the stage to where Sloane's mother stood. She and I locked eyes, finally, while everyone around us shouted the lost syllables of *hallelujah*. The pastor chanted and the organ rose and the crowd went *la-ley-loo*. She glanced at her feet. Her lips moved, the same *la-ley-loo*. I needed the presence, the energy was too much, I became afraid of the power. I wanted to give myself up to it. I began to move my mouth, too.

The people shouted. Some convulsed—large, theatrical jerks. It was overwhelming to fight the feeling rising in my chest while seeing the crowd act out with such seriousness. The music warbled with arpeggios.

"If you want to torment the devil," the pastor sang, "let prosperity come into your house. Wealth is a virtue against Satan! It is! Let it come!"

The corners of his mouth crusted over in a white film as the words went sticky. I wet my lips in response.

"Satan knows money can be used as a weapon against him. This is how the Davidians became trapped, they were *foolish* in their renunciation of prosperity. And look what happened to *them*— murdered, *slaughtered* like cattle."

The amber tilt in his voice, rich.

"Don't you get it?" His voice deepened with conviction. "The Gospel is *free*, but the means to deliver it is *expensive*."

The tongue speakers got louder. I continued to mouth the words. I wanted to find the open space inside me where God might be hiding, but when I searched, all I could picture was the moment I spent inside Sloane, my finger soaking in her, then the pastor's head shaking against the recliner, his manic hands, then them in the closet. Cells blooming into embryo. My lips against her teeth. The needle through her skin.

"We gotta get ready to finance the *Gospel*," the pastor shouted, feedback crackling through the speakers.

In one of the prayer circles, a man began to foam at the mouth. His hands grasped at his throat as though he were choking, but when he looked over at me, he sucked in a long, hard stretch of air and spouted gibberish. Another woman shrieked orgasmically, each vocalization building on the next. She yelped and pulled her hair out of its pinned rolls. A man's knees gave out and he hit the floor. "O Lord," he said, followed by incoherence. He hugged his cane, bared his dentures, and bit the resin handle so hard a fake tooth cracked. Others near the stage threw money at the tithe bowl.

The pastor leaned in my direction, and my eyes searched for Sloane's mother. She reached her hands toward the stage and dropped folded bills at his feet. She saw me looking and stepped in my direction. My throat tightened as she pushed through the crowd, tiptoed over a young woman in a bright blue skirt and blazer. The woman had ripped her blazer open, tears streaming down her face, hissing, "*Spiritspiritspirit.*" When Sloane's mother got to me, a sneer popped onto her face, then she pulled me over by the wrist. Her nails scratched my skin as I pulled my hand out of hers. My shoulders rose in fear, my whole body tense.

She turned away. The next thing I remember, her back slammed my hands into my wrists, like I had pushed her. She toppled over into a prayer circle, grabbing on to a woman's emerald dress as she fell to the floor. The dress ripped. A few people turned in my direction. I stumbled back then turned to the exit, hoping I could get lost among those who weren't yet gifted.

XXXX

I count the cars in Mike's parking lot as I walk, today only a few minutes late, sucking in air with each number I mouth. Once inside, I scrub up and hit the floor. The alarm sounds just as I open the door to my section, and Number Three shoots me a dirty look, waving her hand frantically for me to assume my position on the line. I'm so thankful not to be in the huts today. The fall weather is mild but in the factory it's hot. It's always hot. She pulls her mask to her chin; it's left indentations on her cheeks.

"Shit," she says. "You are *fucking up* lately."

Sanitizer sprays between us and the line buzzes to life. I pull up my mask, ignoring her, and begin to cut.

Sloane thinks I should be going to church, but she doesn't understand how painful that is for me. She says I should be going to Catholic Mass, swears it's different. She thinks I should be talking to Momma more; she's always talking to Momma, I swear it. Momma's been calling me less. Why does Sloane think she's so perfect? I haven't seen Kevin in weeks. I knew that relationship was going to end just as quickly as it started.

"You're too hard on Sloane," Momma says. "Hasn't Daddy proposed yet?"

I sigh and scratch an itch beneath my ass cheek where I'd been stung.

"You know, I was a single mother for a time," she says. "I guess I still am. It's been hard on Sloane. Now she's got someone. You're always a mother, regardless of what you do."

"I called for something else," I say. I move the phone away from my ear and wipe away oil that's collected on the screen. "Will you send me all my baby stuff? The blankets and my Boppy. You know, the stuffed dog I used to think was a rabbit."

"Was that a rabbit?" she asks. "You slept with that thing until you were twelve."

"I'm getting the nursery ready for the baby."

"In your tiny apartment?"

"In the corner of my bedroom," I say.

"Well, you can't do that, Dee-Dee."

I roll my eyes at her, although she can't see. "Newborns need to sleep in the same room as their parents for six months, Momma. Separating them is abuse now."

"No," she says. "You can't do that because I gave all that stuff to Sloane years ago, before she left. Didn't she tell you?"

At home, Daddy relaxes on the couch, drinking again. On the TV is another show about serial killers, but this one has dramatized flashbacks like a movie. I put my purse down by the door, slipping off my shoes. I don't mention his message to S, but as I walk to the couch, my eyes dart to the counter where the phone had been. I'm hoping I set it back exactly as I found it. I still wonder if he'd placed a hair on the screen or something to test me. His attention to detail makes our relationship both interesting and dangerous. At some level I wonder if he is as dangerous as I make him out to be, but that's the fun of it. He could kill me, or I could just think he was going to kill me; the relationship would feel the same regardless of the outcome.

I sit next to him and push my fingers through his hair, eager for his attention, knowing now there's someone else I have to compete with. I feel little bumps, like scabs, on his scalp. I itch them gently and feel them separate from his skin, pull my fingers away and flick them off. Hands back to the scalp, through his hair again. I hate feeling so insecure, but the fear excites me. I lean my face into his neck and kiss his jaw.

"The house smells like shit," he says into my ear. The trash can is overflowing, the dishes are stacked in the sink. Flies have gotten in; they congregate on congealed porridge in a bowl on the coffee table.

I fling myself into the seat next to him, splaying out. I can feel my stomach tumble me a little farther than I would normally go—the extra weight settling in.

"We'll take out the trash later," he says, patting my knee. "I don't want to get up."

He picks up a glass with melting ice and shakes it at me, a signal to get him a drink. I sigh and get up from the couch, which creaks from the release of my weight. I take the glass gingerly between two fingers, imagining myself as his housewife. In my mind I'm wearing a beautiful chintz dress, a gauzy linen apron with a delicate red line stitched along the border, my hair blond and rolled into victory curls. The baby is asleep in her vintage Edwardian crib in the bedroom, a magnificent darkly stained oak one that rocks gently with her movements. Daddy doesn't see it. He returns his attention to the show. The episode is about a killer who'd become infamous for the way he selected his victims: dark-haired, college-age women who looked like his mother, many lured to his car by gaining their sympathy for a fake injury.

"Don't all serial killers target women?" I ask. I drop three fresh ice cubes into his glass.

"Not necessarily," Daddy says. "There was the one who ate gay men. But you won't see any specials on that guy. Society doesn't care what happens to men. We're disposable."

I walk back over to the couch and set his drink on the table, thinking about Mike's, the field of stinking feathers in the huts. "It's people that are disposable," I say, sitting next to him. "Nobody cares about me at all, either, unless I'm pregnant. And even then it's questionable."

He puts his hand on my belly. It's warm. He makes circles with his palm. I breathe in deep and push my abdomen out as far as it will go, while trying to keep the muscles relaxed. It's a tricky move, but I've begun to master it.

"People only care about tradition and breeding a new life," I say. My abdominal muscles tremble, but I try to act casual. "Weddings, births, baptisms: people will be present then. But nobody cares about the after—they don't care about the marriage, about the children." I pause for a second, knowing if I say this, I'll get a lecture about it. "They don't care about women."

"It's different with men," Daddy says. His voice grows louder. "They work the most dangerous jobs, have the highest suicide rates. They're more often victims of violent crime. Men go to war, Daisy. Society doesn't see that as a problem." He takes his hand from my stomach, and suddenly a small sense of abandonment creeps in.

"Women go to war, too." It feels rebellious to disagree, even though I know I'll eventually cave.

"The most common cancer in the world is prostate cancer," he says, "but you don't see those plastic bracelets around everyone's wrist." He's now so loud, I glance at the popcorn ceiling littered with water stains, wondering if Sloane is home. I get indignant, rubbing my sore hands together, acutely aware of my back that never stops pulling my shoulders taut, the bone-deep pain in my lower spine.

"I work at a meat processing plant," I say. I put my hands in the air, frustrated. "It's dangerous there, too!"

"That's a class issue," he says. "I know that's something you don't quite understand. Men, especially men like me, are still more disposable than women in this world."

"Fuck you," I say. He wasn't going to win this game. I *know* I've suffered more, and somehow this granted me validation. I need that at the very least.

He smiles sarcastically and then points at my stomach. "*You're* more valuable," he says. "Get fucking used to it."

"Sleep on the couch tonight," I say. "I don't want you in my bed if you're going to treat me like this."

"Treat you like what?" He laughs bitterly. "You want me to treat you like a man, you'd better get used to higher standards."

"Sounds like you wish you were the one pregnant," I say. I massage the skin around my belly button and my chest relaxes.

Something in his demeanor changes. Challenge him all you want, but question his masculinity, and it's over.

"It's absolutely unacceptable for you to say something like that," he says. "As though I *want* to be some kind of victim who gets special treatment, as though I *want* to do or be something *feminine*. That is not me, and you know that. I have to be this way because it is my *duty*. It's my job to protect you from the harshness and violence and evil of the world, and I make great sacrifices for it."

When he gets like this, all I can do is sit and let the wave pass. He doesn't listen. He doesn't converse. He talks at you as though you'll understand him, as though all he wants is to be understood—and the truth is I do understand him, more deeply than anyone. I've heard it all so much before I can hardly care the way I used to, the way I did when we were younger, but the depth of that understanding is what keeps me tied. No one else will understand him like me, and really, it's my job to endure him, to love and care for him, to give him something good, because of all the sacrifices he's made. That's what a good woman does, a good wife, and I want to be his wife. But when he talks about the difference between good and evil, I get defensive. It feels like something I have to protect myself from. "You sound like Momma," I scoff, but I know this will just foment his response.

"Aristophanes talks about whether God is real, Daisy, and it's not relevant. Believing in those kinds of things makes better people and a better society. Liberals engage in moralizing—and all of it leads to subjective morality. If what is moral is subjectively decided upon—the idea, for example, that a pedo is just a 'minor-attracted person,' that they were, maybe, born that way or cannot help it—leads to the kind of thinking that they should no longer be subject to the rules of justice at play in our society. It's dangerous. People who kill and hurt for fun, society does what exactly? We go, 'Oh, there's nothing human left in them.' Society dehumanizes them. That's why we are morally able to put them to death. But, see, I don't think that's true. Those people are just mentally ill."

"So is society too forgiving of evil acts or is it not?" I cross my arms across my chest.

"Evil doesn't exist," he says. "Sociopaths aren't real. That's just a bogeyman that society creates because it can't accept people want to kill someone human. What it refuses to acknowledge is that a serial killer is not a healthy person and everyone can recognize they aren't. But it doesn't want to take responsibility for how the killer became unhealthy in the first place. The only reason they're able to operate is because society allows it."

Daddy takes the hem of my shirt, rubbing it in between his thumb and forefinger, pulling it slightly.

"Our society caters to individuals who punch down," he says, "to people who are immoral. That's American culture. And American culture is immoral. That's what's evil. It's the shirking of morality. It's wickedness by every definition. Violence isn't inherently evil, but using it for the purposes of coercion is. To defend one's self? That's not evil. It's the callousness to morality—that's what's evil. You can't reason with it. You can't convince it to do something different. That's the joke about Christianity. They think people like this can be forgiven, saved. I'm not like your mother, Daisy. Evil can't be fixed. It has to be burned out. They have to be completely destroyed."

It wasn't clear to me if he was talking about killers or pedos or liberals subject to moralizing their will. On-screen, photographs of three brunettes appear, all smiling in fuzzy senior photos from the 1970s. I adjust my seat and pull my shirt out of his grip.

He takes a sip from his glass and puts a hand on my knee, petting hard with his thumb until my patella burns, as though he's already forgotten our fight. I don't push him. On the TV, the killer, through a taped audio interview, talks about how he's always been seen as a pariah.My eyes move between Daddy and the TV. The serial killer is in a prison cell talking with an interviewer. The show has applied a filter to make the film look yellow, like old teeth. His voice is warm and rummy. Daddy turns the volume down and looks at me.

"Society tells you all the time that killing a person should be a gut-wrenching decision," he says. "I don't know. At times I've had to roll on someone's house because they owed me money. It's not like you're eager to break into someone's house and beat their head in with a baseball bat. You need to project power. If you don't, then they'll come do it to you."

His text message to S floats through me again. "You can't just do it once," Daddy once explained to me about stabbing. "It takes a lot of effort to kill a living thing with a knife. People who die from a stabbing have, like, thirty or forty knife wounds."

The TV cuts to a commercial about dish soap. A woman's hands dip into the sink, then the camera cuts to an underwater view of the dirty dishes. She wipes the sponge through a trail of meaty sauce and a clean line appears on the dish. She pulls her hands out of the water, and her skin sparkles, like a baptism.

XXXX

As soon as I step out of the car, the smell of winter-wet grass hits my nose, but it's followed by a kind of coppery, sharp rot—I can't trace the smell, if it's my breath, my body, or something else. Blake and Daddy are gone, but I don't know where. Bells twinkle on the collar of Sloane's cat, which scurries up the stairs. A puff of smoke ejects over the railing. It's Sloane's mother, Barb, smoking on the patio.

"Hey, Daisy," she calls, a little slow twang to her voice like she is on something. "How you doing, hon? How's the baby?"

"Hi, Barb."

Back in the day it seemed like she had everything—I remember the floral silk of her Sunday bests and a deep, healthy sheen to her hair. Now she wears cotton tees from Wal-Mart and ratty nylon shorts, flip-flops that reveal yellow fungal nails covered by chipped bright red polish. My feet brush past a few hardy spider plants potted in old tin cans on my way up. Sloane is home. I can hear her voice; it's soft, like the sound of air filling a latex party balloon. Steg shrieks in joy or terror. Sheer curtains billow in the window. Barb takes another drag and turns her head away as she exhales.

"I'm doing all right, Barb."

She flips her hand in front of her face. "Something fucking stinks," she says. "Shitty fucking landlord. Hope no one's died next door."

"Oh, haha—yeah," I say. The smell of death won't leave me. The filth has melted into the background.

"How far along now, sweetie?" she asks. She sticks her free hand out toward my belly and wiggles her lilac acrylic nails back and forth. The baby inside feels solid, like she's churning into butter.

"Twenty-two," I say. "Twenty-three weeks, maybe?"

"Damn," she says. "You're a big girl already, but I thought you'd be bigger by now, hon."

An ugly look washes across my face. She turns her head away to take a puff. I want to push her again, over the banister, watch her body flail backward and spin. But that wouldn't fix my problem. If she's not convinced, Daddy won't be, either. From the balcony, I see a glimpse of Sloane's apartment and it's clean. It smells like laundry.

"I'm showing," I say to Barb. I have to convince her so I don't push her down the stairs. The cigarettes will kill her anyway. I push my stomach out and rub my hands on my belly. "It's gonna be a little kicker," I say. Something a Christian mom would say, something wholesome. A good Christian mom would have her apartment clean and wouldn't have so much trouble keeping her husband around.

"Little early for kicking," Barb says.

I hate this woman, denying me the pleasure of this moment. I'm pregnant, for fuck's sake. Why do other mothers have to act like they know everything, just because they've had a child or two?

"Sloane was a damn demon when I was pregnant with her," she starts blathering. "Always keeping me up at night. She was like that even after she was born, I swear. Kept to the same schedule and everything. It's amazing how much you forget the difficult parts."

"Hey, Daisy," Sloane calls through the screen door. She's sitting on the floor, grooming a small, noodle-colored dog. Her hair's tied back with a tie-dyed handkerchief, and she's wearing an oversized black

T-shirt, the same Slayer shirt from twenty years ago, denim cargo shorts that reach to her knees, and white ankle socks with dirty white sneakers. The screen door creaks as I enter. Sloane grins wide and toothy, but the expression comes off as disingenuous. The noodle dog is belly up, getting her nails cut. The dog wags her tail and whimpers happily.

"That's Snack," Barb says through the screen door. "I've had her since Sloane was, oh, about fourteen, right, honey?"

"You got him long after I left," Sloane says.

"That's right," Barb says. "Shit. Anyway, Daisy, why don't you stay for lunch? I'm sure Sloane would love the company."

Sloane doesn't get up. I watch her drag a thin flea comb through the dog's pale fur. Two orange tabbies scurry around her, one whose tongue hangs out of a toothless mouth, its eyes cloudy.

"I've been making a list of words that Steg is saying now," Barb says through the door.

"Who?" I ask.

"Steg!" she says.

"*Diaper, pants, shoe, bug,*" Sloane says. "She knows them all."

"Oh," I say. "That's great."

Steg pulls on the playpen rail as if she might repeat the words now, but she just blinks at me.

I glance at Sloane's torso, tracing the outline of her prison tats. I think of the stabbing of the needle in her skin. *She makes me want to stab myself.* Stab. stab. The screen door creaks open again and Barb walks in and picks up Steg beneath the armpits.

"Take a seat, Daisy," she says. "I'll get lunch started."

"Anything I can do to help?" I ask. I lean on the kitchen counter, trying to relax, self-conscious of how pregnant I look, eager to eat whatever she offers, to be included. When Barb opens the fridge I see the name PETUNIA tattooed in cursive on her arm.

"I love flower names."

"What's that?" Barb lifts her head.

"Your tattoo."

"Oh, Petunia," Barb says. She pulls out American cheese slices and a tub of margarine and sets them on the counter. "Thank you. That's my baby's name. I got it after she left us."

"I'm sorry to hear that."

"Here we go again," says Sloane. She gets up from the floor and walks past me, close enough for me to smell her perfume. She still smells the same, like fruit mixed with sweat. Sloane pulls a pan out of the cupboard.

Barb rubs the tattoo with her thumb. "Petunia was one of the most precious things in my life. I got her when Todd was still around. Rick and I—Rick is Sloane's father—fostered my cousin's son Todd. He and Sloane were around the same age. He came to live with us when he was about sixteen."

"I don't want to hear about Todd," Sloane says.

"I remember Todd," I say.

She grabs a loaf of white bread and pulls out slices.

"He was crooked as a barrel of snakes," Barb says, "and my cousin was not a good mother. Not like I was. I loved that boy. But he never listened to me, ever. Conspiracy theories all the time, like a damn schizo. He needed medication. One day he started hitting me. The day we lost Petunia was the day Todd kicked me in the stomach—Sloane, you remember."

Sloane butters slice after slice of white bread. "Unfortunately, I do," she says.

"It wasn't easy for me," Barb says.

"It was even harder for me!" Sloane says.

"Don't piss on my back and call it rain, honey." Barb coats the frying pan with oil and turns on the burner.

"Is that how the baby died?"

Sloane laughs and throws the buttered bread into the pan, where it lands with a sizzle. She peels off paper-thin slices of processed cheese and places them on top. "Christ. My mom wasn't pregnant."

"Oh god, no," Barb says. "Petunia was a Cavalier King."

"I hated that dog," Sloane says.

"She was a *sweetheart* and I took real good care of her."

Barb's eyes go glassy. She takes the spatula from Sloane and flips the bread.

"Todd stormed out that day," Barb says. "I had done the only thing I could do to correct his behavior: I hit him. I slapped him. Petunia went chasin' after him, and that was when—" Barb chokes up, like she's trying to push the tears to the surface, and she peels back her bottom lip, exposing crooked teeth.

"When was this?" I ask.

"Just before Sloane left to stay with you," Barb says, wiping her eyes with a hooked index finger.

"So you do remember that," I say.

"Oh yes, it was probably best for all of us, what was best for Sloane."

"After I left, Todd left," Sloane says. Her voice is flat. She leans against the counter in front of the sink, the kitchen window open. Day sounds creep in, cars and birds. Sloane puts her head down and parts her lips like she's going to say something.

"The car came out of nowhere," Barb says. "I saw the whole thing—Todd running, and Petunia following, and the car hitting her. I ran to get her. Todd didn't even notice. He looked back once but kept going, running like an idiot, in those big jeans everyone wore back then."

"I hate thinking about Todd," Sloane says. She holds her arms across her chest, hands curled into fists, moving her thumbs over and under her index fingers.

"I carried Petunia back into the house," Barb says. "Her body was so broken up."

Somehow all this gore tickles me in a wild, uncontrollable way, like a laugh taking hold. I can't help but ask the question: "What did the dog look like after?"

"Awful," Barb says.

She flips the sandwiches over again and puts two of them on a plate. Sloane approaches with a giant knife. Her glare sends a spike of fear right through me.

"She died in my arms," Barb says.

Old mascara freckles the crescents of skin below her eyes. She turns back around to the stove, and Sloane rolls her eyes at me as Barb goes on. Sloane places the knife over one sandwich and presses down, cutting the thing in half in one go.

"You have to love your animals," Barb says. She wipes away more wetness, leaving small black streaks. "Really love them. You're responsible for them. Just like your kids. You're their shepherd."

It's odd listening to the details of Sloane's home life, like it's something I'm not supposed to know. How Sloane would hold my hand when we walked home, her never wanting to be there. I eat my sandwich of glittering fried bread and marbled orange cheese.

"Anyway," Barb says. She wipes her nose on her arm. "It's food-pantry day and the thrift store is open. Why don't you girls take Steg with you and go after lunch? They have maternity clothes, Daisy."

Sloane bites her grilled cheese just as Barb is asking, and she makes eye contact with me again. Her eyes soften.

"I don't mind," I say. I expect something in Sloane's eyes to change, but nothing happens. No annoyance or hesitation. No enthusiasm, either. Sloane nods at me.

"Sure," she says after swallowing. "We can talk about baby stuff."

She finishes her sandwich and watches as Barb gets Steg out of the playpen, changes her diaper, and dresses her, singing her a song about it. Barb cleans the baby's crusty nose with a wet wipe while Steg protests, swinging her head from side to side and screeching. I stuff the last of the bread in my mouth and wipe the crumbs from my face as we head down to Sloane's Volvo.

1998

After Sunday service I opened the door to our house to see Sloane lying on the couch in the light of a lamp with a faded paper shade on the side table. Momma bent over her, rubbing lotion into her large, pale belly. Sloane wore cotton shorts and her Slayer shirt as she reclined against a pillow. The house stank like burned bread. Momma nodded at me, her hair loose on her shoulders. She was like a different person, her eyes serene. Possessed. Her hands slid around Sloane's growing belly like she was shaping pottery. Momma made mesmerizing indentations in Sloane's skin with her fingers and hummed. Momma had never so much as hugged me in years except for the time I begged her to take in Sloane. I remained motionless, lingering in the smell of their failed breakfast. The wind pushed the screen door gently against its jamb.

"What?" Sloane said, making eye contact with me. "Jealous?"

A dark seam had formed from her belly button down to the bottom of her stomach. I tried to form a sentence, but nothing came. I could only think of the seam and a screaming fire opening her belly like a zipper. The harsh light on her cheeks revealed pockmarks and a few scars from hormonal acne. She'd stopped wearing foundation, and though her skin was dewy, her eyes were sallow and heavy. She wasn't that beautiful, I told myself. I didn't understand why I'd been so obsessed before. The film masking her imperfections had been pulled away.

"Are you going to stand there and keep letting the warm air out?" Momma said. "You'd think the church would teach you some respect for who pays your bills."

Sloane's mouth pulled tight like she wanted to laugh, but she smiled instead and took her feet off the coffee table. Momma stood up, massaging the remaining lotion into her hands and arms.

"How was church, Daisy?" Sloane asked. "How's the pastor?"

"You'd like to know," I said.

"Shut up," she said. Sloane pulled her shirt over her belly and patted it.

"Daisy doesn't retain anything from church," Momma said.

I wished my father were still at home to be a buffer between me and Momma. He'd gone to stay with a friend or brother—I couldn't be bothered to know which—in the Florida Keys, somewhere far away from here where the air would be good to him, because, he'd said, he couldn't handle the stress of the house with his upcoming chemo treatments. He'd call sometimes and have stilted conversations with me, one-syllable replies to my questions like "How's the weather?" "Good."

Sloane pulled her legs up beneath her and crossed them. I placed my purse at my feet and took a deep breath. Then I raised my hand and furrowed my brow.

"Flee from sexual immorality!" I shouted. "All other sins a person commits are outside the body, but twhoever sins sexually, sins against their own body!"

"Okay, Dee-Dee," Momma said. "Enough with Corinthians."

"Do you not know your bodies are a temples of the Holy Spirit, who is in you?" I opened my throat, fake crying. "You are not your own; you were bought at a price!"

"That's *enough*," Momma said.

Sloane slow-clapped, laughing. "Daisy is our little moral guidepost," she said.

"Back me up," I said.

"Sloane is a guest," Momma said. "Don't pressure her into doing something she doesn't want to."

"You're supposed to be my friend!" I shouted, my face crumpling. I grabbed my purse and stomped up the stairs to my room.

"I am your friend!" Sloane called back.

I closed the door and collapsed onto the bed. Dishes clinked in the kitchen. Momma and Sloane were cooking together. Energy collected at my crotch like a delicate string waiting to be tugged away, releasing its coil. Silently, I scooted out of my bottoms and grabbed a long candle from my dresser, stripping off stray wax. I closed my eyes, picturing Sloane in the closet, being fucked by the pastor. I teased myself, first with my fingers. It was weird to think of Sloane as the one being fucked rather than the one doing the fucking. In my fantasy, I became Sloane, and Sloane became the pastor in his sweat-stained white button-down. She took her tie off and slipped it around my neck, tightening it up like a dogcatcher's pole. Everything in my body clenched. She directed me, with the tie tightened, against the wall of the closet, mussing up my hair like hers. I reached my hand around behind me to touch her, remembering how her pussy had squeezed around my finger, and slipped inside her again. I stroked her swollen clit. It grew larger and larger until her throbbing clit was big enough to penetrate me. I slipped the candle inside myself and went mad, rubbing myself, pushing the candle in and out, until it felt like something was clawing its way out of me, descending from my stomach into my pelvis, pushing and pushing until, with a final burst, it bloomed.

XXXX

Sloane depresses the gas pedal, and the Volvo bumps along the edge of the highway, like we're four-wheeling. We pass a sign for the local fire station and she parks. When she gets out of the car she struggles. The way she tilts her hips forward looks familiar to me. Her hand is pressing at her back, her stomach juts out.

I walk around to her side of the car as she unbuckles Steg. "Are you pregnant?"

She hands Steg to me while she grabs her purse.

"That's why I wanted to come with you," she says, out of breath. "Mom doesn't know."

"What the fuck," I say. "This whole time? How far along are you?"

"The dad is in some trouble and not around a lot."

"It's not Kevin?" I say.

"Mom is disappointed." She nods, then looks down. She bends over, exhausted, and puts her hands on her knees. "She really liked Kevin. But he's a fucking prick. He started to get controlling with Steg, trying to parent her, step in when she wouldn't listen. And, like, she's a toddler? She's going to do toddler things."

"You're okay, though?"

When she speaks again, it's strained, as she lifts herself up again and stretches her arms to the sky. "I'm used to doing things on my own."

She says this dejectedly, not out of an excited sense of freedom, but something that's just a matter of fact. I track back the days in my head, to see if her baby's conception coincided with when Daddy and Blake started going out a lot more. I don't ask.

Sloane riffles through her bag and pulls out a pack of cigarettes. I watch in slow motion as she taps one out—a few are already missing— places the paper tip in her mouth, brings the lighter to the tobacco edge, and lights it. She sucks in deep, and a deep wave of disgust rolls down my throat to my core. I pull it out of her hand and throw it to the ground.

"You told me Aaron was born wrong," I say, hissing. "You want that to happen again?"

"I didn't want this baby," Sloane says, clenching her teeth. "But I didn't even know I was pregnant until a bit ago. Do you know how many clinics are in Missouri?" Her voice gets throaty and more urgent. "*One*, Daisy. Just one, and it's six hours away. I can't take time off work for this. I have another child to feed. I am just trying to cope."

I jut my hip out and Steg's legs clamp around me. She smells tender and pure, like vanilla soap. Anger grips me. I wonder if Sloane had wanted to abort her, too.

"Do you know how many women would die for a chance to have a baby?" I say. "Why can't you just give it up for adoption?"

"Spare me the theatrics," she says. "When you've lived this life, then you can lecture me."

"You're such a shitty friend," I say. "I can't believe you. Listen to me!" I pull Steg closer. Maybe I squeeze her a little too hard.

"I thought you'd be excited for me, us being pregnant together," she says. "You're being so jealous and insecure and right now."

The clouds part and the sun has a rare moment to shine. I am nauseated, sweating into my coat, and the stings on my thighs still hurt. I'm scratching them at night, it's endless. I'm overwhelmed with all I need to do. Steg squeezing around my waist doesn't help, and I need to get away from Sloane—suddenly everything, this fight, exhausts me.

"I'm sorry," I give in. "I just thought—never mind. Just go put your name in the line."

Sloane shakes her head. "Whatever," she says. The tension between us loosens, but it's still there. I hitch Steg up above my hip.

"I'll take this one inside to look at toys," I say.

The thrift shop is housed in a single-wide trailer. Boots are two dollars, and every piece of clothing is twenty-five cents. I walk toward the baby section, and Patti, the manager, walks by without a word. She knows me—she's known me for thirty-four years—and she says nothing. *That's fine, Patti. You'll die one day, too.* Another woman walks in and Patti says hello to her, and they discuss a velvet sofa set the shop's gotten in.

The baby section is full of overwashed, faded, pilled clothing. I sort through the racks with one hand, throwing what I want into a pile on a shelf. I'm pissed at Sloane for smoking. Steg reaches for clothes as I move them across the rack. She points at some of the onesies and repeats half-formed words. I grab onesies in yellow, gray, and powder blue. Even though I've always wanted a girl, I'm not sure of the sex yet. I grab a tiny puffer vest covered in gold sequins and put that in the pile, too.

Steg kicks her legs and points at a small, flea-bitten terrier in the shop. Bald patches on its head reveal scabby skin, and it has dull eyes. Steg reaches her hands toward the dog, who sniffs. She pats the dog's head in an exaggerated, clumsy way. It's not fair of Sloane to keep her. More often than not I come home from work and Barb is passed out in a prescription sleep on a lawn chair. I can hear Steg running back and forth in the playpen screaming, and Sloane's Volvo is gone. I know with certainty I'd be a better mother. Sloane must be the one who's jealous. That's why she found me after all these years, moved in above me, got pregnant. She's trying to copy my life—take my life, what little I've got. The way she placed her hand on Daddy's that night, when things had already been going south with Kevin. She hasn't even told her own mother about her pregnancy.

Steg pulls a shirt from the rack and a glass vase on the shelf above it falls and shatters.

When Patti turns around, I grab the bundle of baby clothes and grip Steg against me so she can't wiggle her legs free, and I rush to the exit. My hip knocks a table full of outdated bed linens and shelves full of games. A puzzle box falls to the floor, scattering pieces. I recover and push my backside against the door, my breath quick and shallow, and turn toward the parking lot as the door slams shut behind me. My armpits grease with sweat as I walk to the red Volvo, a welcome breeze on my face. We'd parked right in front of the glass doors of the food pantry. Sloane's still inside.

Something glints on the sun-bleached dash. Her keys. I put the pile of clothes on top of the car and open the door to Steg's car seat and buckle her in. I look at her for a long second, letting it sink in—all that I have lost, all the babies before this one. The hunger in me is an angry hunger, something Momma would never understand. What does she know of desperation? What does Sloane know?

"Ba-ba," Steg says.

"Yeah," I say in a singsong voice. "Bye-bye. We're going bye-bye. For just a bit."

My chest dampens my shirt. I fumble with the seat harness, and she struggles, kicking off a shoe.

"Shoe!" she shrieks. I attempt to twist it back on to her little socked foot, but my hands shake too much so I toss the shoe on the seat. I grab the pile of clothes and throw them in, get in the car, and slam the door. A gray sedan pulls into the lot when I start the Volvo up, and I push the seat back so I can work the pedals. The car roars to life, and I reverse blindly, then throw the transmission into drive and pull away. I speed past the fire station and the park and the lumber mill.

"Da-da-da," Steg rattles. She kicks and squirms around, hits her hands on the seat.

"You're okay!" I say.

I brake hard at the highway intersection. The Volvo skids on the ashy gravel, spewing up a cloud of dust. A semi is cruising toward us down the hill. My throat squeezes shut—really, where am I going? Steg shrieks, and my foot jams on the gas, swinging us ass-end first as I make a violent left. The clothes scatter across the back seat. The semi screams past, just missing us.

On the drive down the highway to my apartment, we pass the billboard with the newborn counter. Seven new babies. Steg cries and thumps her feet against the carrier.

"You're okay, you're okay," I keep saying. I turn the radio on, and Steg cries louder, so I turn the radio up. I'll decide what to do at the apartment. I'm hungry—so empty and disgusting—I can feel the baby shriveling up. In my purse I find my cell phone and a granola bar and pull both out and place them on the seat next to me. My phone buzzes and I pick it up, swerving the car. I have five missed calls. It's likely Sloane's already called Barb and Momma and told them I left. Daddy's been gone for a few days. I can hide out at the apartment and pretend I'm not home. Stock up on milk, fruit snacks, and chips at the Dollar General.

I fling my phone aside. My hands are stiff. The unfamiliar leather of the steering wheel sticks to my palms. Steg is quiet now. She bends her head down toward her chest, and a tangle of hair covers her face. She isn't moving, and I panic, thinking she's suffocated. She kicks the seat again and mumbles. Then she's back asleep, drooling. I take a right onto Old Exeter and pull into the harshly lit parking lot of the Dollar General.

Steg is unmoving when I open the back door of the car. Her eyes are closed, the long dark lashes like the very fine legs of insects. Waking her seems cruel. I consider the consequences of leaving her in the car. I'll be gone only a few minutes. The parking lot is empty. The day is cool but not freezing. I gently close the door. The store's glass doors slide open in front of me.

When my father left, part of me wasn't surprised. I didn't believe a man could successfully dedicate his entire life to another person, but I wanted to believe it was possible. Women could devote themselves to men. Or women to other women. Maybe only women could have relationships that didn't end. Men had expiration dates attached to their patience for women. There was only so much Daddy could put up with. Men's jobs, their duty, seemed to be putting up with women. I loved him like I loved a root canal: something painful but necessary. Like life was more painful without him.

My father got too sick and had to come back. Momma put him in hospice. Sloane got closer to her due date, and Momma became more invested in her pregnancy. I began to sleep on the itchy orange-and-brown couch in the living room. Momma made me fold and tuck away my bedding every morning when I woke. Then she'd casually order me to start the coffee. I rinsed out the coffee filter, still smelling of mildew. A tiny spite. Sloane sat at one end of the kitchen table and Momma at the other, smoking.

"Make some eggs, would you?" Momma said. "And don't shuffle your feet. Christ. What a horrible habit."

I grabbed the carton of eggs, slammed the fridge door shut.

"Scrambled or sunny-side up?" I asked.

"Scrambled," Sloane said.

"Sunny," Momma said, "but don't make the yolks too runny."

I made Momma's first. I grated pepper and sprinkled salt and slid them onto a plate. Then I made Sloane's, cracking two eggs into the pan. The toast popped, and I cut the two slices into triangles: one for Momma, one for Sloane.

"Don't scramble them in the pan!" Sloane said.

My back was to them. I slid her eggs onto a plate and handed them to her, sat down and sipped my black coffee.

"Aren't you hungry?" Momma asked.

I shook my head.

"Probably for the best," she said.

Momma held Sloane's hand and bent her head down.

"Bless us, O Lord, and these your gifts, which we are about to receive from your bounty," she said. "Through Christ our Lord, amen."

Sloane snickered. "Amen," she said.

Momma picked up the toast from Sloane's plate and buttered it for her. She held it toward Sloane's mouth. Sloane took a gingerly bite. Then Momma scooped up scrambled egg onto a fork and gave Sloane a mouthful.

"For the baby," Momma said. She fed her, bite by bite, until the eggs were gone.

"Why am I watching this?" I said.

"What's wrong?" Sloane asked. She laughed and wiped grease from her chin. "It's just for fun."

"You two are making me retch."

"Take a joke, Daisy," Sloane said.

I pushed myself away from the table and left the kitchen to go upstairs and change. Momma called after me. "Puking wouldn't be the worst thing in the world for you!"

I can't remember how it happened, but I was in my room and suddenly the mirror on my vanity broke. When I looked down at my hands, blood ran down my pinkie and the side of my palm. Momma and Sloane thudded up the stairs to ask what happened. "I don't know," I shouted back. I stared at my hand with morbid interest, at the blood and its formlessness leaking out of me. "The glass just broke," I said.

That night, I stayed up late watching an old black-and-white film. A bunch of handsome men vied for the love of the main character, a beautiful actress, who they believed was dead. I couldn't have imagined a better situation: to be immortalized and adored without any effort. The girl was found alive, though, when it was revealed that another body had been mistaken for hers. The search for the murderer continued. Eventually, they found the murder weapon in an old grandfather clock. A shotgun.

I remembered my father's old gun beneath my bed, an heirloom he'd gotten from his father but hadn't noticed I'd taken. He'd showed me how to load it, stood behind me at the edge of the backyard as I pointed the gun at the row of trees behind the house. He helped me steady the sight, cradle the wooden buttstock into my shoulder. With his finger over mine, he squeezed the trigger. The gun fired, exploding a squirrel into a burst of fur and guts.

I crept up the carpeted stairs, testing for creaks with my toes, and slid the gun out from under the bed while Sloane slept. The gun was cold to the touch and heavier than I remembered. I cradled it between my free hand and my chest as I opened the door to Momma's room. I cocked the gun and pointed it at her. Her face became clearer as my eyes adjusted to the dark: the shape of her nose, her hair undone and kissing her shoulders. This wasn't fair, I'd thought. I took a series of deep breaths. I didn't want to live according to the rules of good and evil anymore. All I wanted was for someone to love me, but I was always being replaced. Each breath hollowed me out further. The wind from the oscillating fan in the corner prickled the exposed skin of my arms. The house was always cold. The hair on my neck tingled in the artificial breeze. Momma stirred and the sheets rumpled as she rolled from one side of the bed to the other. I waited in the silence.

The house settled, wood creaking against wood, and the pop moved through me like a shock wave, leaving only the shadow of my body. I went back to the living room, taking the gun with me, and slid it beneath the couch. An ache filled my chest as I lay down and went to sleep.

Fruit snacks, milk, Vienna sausages. I pick up a shopping basket and rush through the Dollar General, repeating the list under my breath. Metal shelves full of canned food to my right, humming coolers full of soda to my left. I stop at the baby section first, scanning plastic containers of baby powder, boxes of diapers, and tubs of diaper cream. I hold my stomach with one hand, sticking it out as far as I can, and throw one of each into the basket. My phone buzzes again. I have three more missed calls and a bunch of texts from Momma.

momma
I'M CONCERNED, SLOANE HAS CALLED

momma
DEE-DEE, WHERE IS STEG?

momma
ARE YOU WITH HER?

momma
DON'T LET THIS BE ANOTHER ONE OF YOUR LIES, CHILD.

I don't know how I'm going to fix this, so instead I throw in three tins of Vienna sausages and grab some bags of frozen veggies from the freezer, my arms and neck stiff, my teeth grinding from urgency. Then I get a call that shoots the fear of God right into my heart: it's Daddy. I'm suddenly suffocating. I'm afraid of being abandoned, and I'm on the verge of it—everyone in my life colluding against me like this. I don't pick up. I should hurry back—explain everything to him, end it all. I want to be good. I do.

I just need to live through this one last lie and never lie again. I could do that. I could just hold on to this one secret. You can still be close with someone, even with a secret, can't you? It's not like you can ever fully know another human—about what lies in their heart like a grave.

Once it's over, Daddy and I can move on with our lives. He won't leave me. We'll have our family. And to what end? What comes after? I haven't thought that far and honestly can't. My stomach churns, it's so empty. I need to eat. I'm failing at this. I stop in front of a freezer full of ice cream pints and try to remember what I need. And something else bothers me, it's picking away at my resolution: that Daddy knows, which means I know for sure Sloane and he are talking. I throw three tubs of chocolate ice cream in my basket. I don't even like chocolate. I've forgotten the rest of my damn list. My phone vibrates again. Daddy's stern face flashes on the screen, a photo he sent when we first started dating. So much has happened since then. I'm afraid to answer, because he's the authority on how I live my life. Just like Momma, Daddy's always telling me what's best for me. And I listen. Because I'm afraid of being abandoned. I silence the call and remember: fruit snacks. I grab those in the snack aisle along with a couple of bags of chips.

I place all my items on the checkout counter, stretching my neck to check on the car through the storefront windows. A can of Vienna sausages drops, bouncing off my protruding stomach and hitting the floor.

"Uh-oh," I say, as if I'm talking to a child. I wait a moment to see if the cashier will pick it up for me.

"You see something out there?" she asks. "You keep looking out the windows."

She's wearing a yellow visor over braids. Her name tag says BELINDA.

"Just my car running," I say. A curl of exhaust billows from the back. I bend down to pick up the can.

"Brave," Belinda says. She rings the food up, stuffs everything in the same bag. "You hear about that baby that got snatched on accident a while back?"

The corner of my left eye twitches. "No," I say.

I hadn't considered that at all. Nor had I considered that if Sloane calls the cops, reporters might dig up my history, my permanent school records; they might interview people in town who'll talk. I imagine people saying, *She always was a weird one. One of those quiet types.* I imagine the pastor coming out on the news, ready to point fingers. No way in hell would Momma vouch for me. I scan the ceiling, searching for a security camera. There are none.

"Yeah," Belinda says. "Someone stole a car with the engine running right outside a 7-Eleven. But there was a baby in the back seat. Car got abandoned next to a park in Bella Vista, just over the state line. They left the car there with the door wide open, hazards blinking in the night, like they just ran off into the woods or something."

"What happened?"

"Cops found the baby in the back seat. She wasn't hurt. But damned if I don't leave my car running anymore."

"Thanks," I say. I grab the groceries and slide my debit card into my back pocket, the double doors dinging as I exit the building. Exhaust gently swirls from behind the trunk of the Volvo. I glance inside and Steg is sound asleep, a slight snore animating her rising and falling chest. The image draws me in like the intoxicating feeling of heat on a winter morning. I move closer to it, imagining a different route home. Instead of hiding out at the apartment, I could hop on I-70, sail through Kansas, go right on through Colorado. I try to think of the most depraved city west of Missouri, one where Momma or Sloane would never come looking. Probably Las Vegas. Steg and I could live in themed motels, rotate through them every week. I imagine making dinner in a little kitchenette, cooking up Hamburger Helper on a hot plate as she watches cartoons on the cable TV. I'd let Steg watch any TV show she wanted. I'd teach her to read using *Cosmopolitan* and *People* magazines. I'd throw away every Bible the Gideons had ever left. And at night, instead of watching the stars, we could walk the Strip, Steg in her stroller and me in tasteful khakis. Everyone on the street would stop and marvel at how beautiful and clever she was, and, by extension, me. I could—*we* could make a go of it there. I slide into the front seat and check the gas tank, which is a quarter full. Just would need some supplies first.

In the apartment parking lot, the buildings are familiar, but my adrenaline buzz makes them look strange and scary. I almost think I turned down the wrong street. Cars are parked in different spots, the grass has grown, the hedges have been trimmed. The trees had blown out with the fall, leaves skittering across pavement. Past Blake's car, a woman is talking to someone taller. As I pull into an empty spot, I see it's Sloane, already back and in a change of clothes. She's wearing a maternity dress. Her hair is braided into a rope. My legs feel as stiff as boards.

Steg whines. She's awake now and full of verve. "Eat, eat, eat," she says.

The other figure rushes toward the Volvo. I pull Sloane's keys out of the ignition and fumble in my purse for my apartment keys. I hear the familiar jingle and get out of the car, unbuckling Steg and lifting her out of the seat, all in a trembling rush. A few steps toward the apartment and my name is spoken as a demanding question. I turn around.

It's Officer Barclay. Sloane's not far behind him, scowling, her hand held beneath her belly, exaggerating her *condition*. I know this trick too well, how she manipulates everyone around her to make *herself* the victim. And I'm sure Daddy's pinhole eyes, his rage, and his rejection are all waiting for me behind the door.

"Labor is the easy part," Momma says. "It's the ring of fire when things get difficult."

"Ring of fire?" I ask.

"When the baby finally moves into position, your back feels like it's about to break apart. Your pelvis splits. The baby crowns," she says. "Looks like the sacred heart of Christ."

Officer Barclay stops short of my front steps with Sloane right behind him. I grip Steg close, but she reaches for Sloane and starts to cry. My cell phone vibrates in my pocket.

"What the fuck," Sloane says.

The officer puts his hand out to give me space. He moves his hand to his nose and sniffs. The smell of rot fills my mouth.

"Miss Daisy," the officer says.

"One second," I say.

The key makes a satisfying click in the doorknob, and I shove the door open and step inside, then immediately swing it shut behind me. The door bounces off the officer's boot in the threshold.

I drop the grocery bags and my purse. My next breath is cut with ammonia and metal. Pennies blooming green inside rotten meat. The apartment is a mess. It's unfit and I know it. Steg is wailing now. I put my hand up, shielding her from view.

"Daddy is out working," I say. "I'm sure you're here for him."

"We're not here to talk about your husband, Miss Daisy. This woman says you've taken her child."

"He's not my husband yet."

"This is serious. She also says you took her vehicle."

"Well, we have the same car. It's very confusing," I say. A gas flame is burning in my neck. "I—I'm sorry. I think there's been a misunderstanding."

"This is *ridiculous*," Sloane says.

"I went to get milk. Fruit snacks and cat food," I say to her.

Then I remember the baby is gone. Not gone but not alive. No, no. She's there. I run down the list in my mind again. I think about the Vegas Strip.

"Ma'am, I need you to hand over the child. Miss Dodson has agreed not to press charges if you hand over the child peacefully."

I look at Steg and her cherubic face. She's already mine, I deserve to keep her. My cheeks are cold with tears. The world wobbles. It moves one way, then the other. "It's a misunderstanding," I say again. "Sloane, you *told* me to take her, remember?"

"You can sort this disagreement out between yourselves, Miss Daisy, but for now we need you to safely hand over the child."

If Sloane says anything, I don't hear it. The baby's cries get more frantic. Or maybe I'm the one wailing. I hate conflict or the sense that

I've done something wrong. My lungs are tight and I steady myself against the wall, spots forming in my vision. The shape of Sloane's pregnant body burns into my mind like the ghostly images of a bare bulb shutting off. Steg disappears from my arms.

"No," I say. There it goes: my chance at starting a family. This is somehow worse than any miscarriage. It's over now. Sloane will replace me. Something moves behind me. Daddy's come out of the bedroom to talk to the officer, I presume, but whatever conversation they have, I'm long gone. "This is . . . Okay," I stutter between sobs. "I'll be okay. I'm going to be okay." I wipe tears from my eyes, my skin hot and burning.

"Mr. Mueller," the officer says, "I'm going to need you to step outside with me."

Daddy closes the door behind him, and I go into the bedroom to calm down. Plastic rustles from the living room. I run out, breathless, but nothing is there. Just the groceries beneath an air vent. I grab the bags and put them on the counter and pull out the pints of ice cream. I open one, peel back the seal. The ice cream is soupy. I swirl it with a spoon and take a lick. I hear footsteps upstairs. There's the muffled trickle of Sloane's laughter, then a man's voice. It could be the officer. I touch my belly, feeling for tautness, a human form stretched inside. There is nothing but squishy fat. I punch myself hard, until my guts feel like they are retreating into my lungs. From the cabinets above the stove I pull down a bottle of canola oil covered in dust and stove grit, pour some into my ice cream soup, and stir. Blobs of oil rise to the surface. I pick it up and drink as fast as I can, the oil and the sweet cream replacing the stench of hot garbage. I open up the back of my throat, sucking everything down. My stomach revolts, but I put my hand on my throat and that helps the retching.

Afterward I surf on my phone while cartoons play on the TV in the background. I'm reclined on the couch, hoping to fall asleep. I text Daddy, asking where he is, but he doesn't respond. The second pint of ice cream is sweating in my lap, and I spoon small bits into my mouth and scroll through discount maternity clothing online. My mind quiets once the sugar high recedes and exhausts me. Sugar is its own drug—the manic punch followed by the drop. A gentle lethargy. In my haze I hunger for Steg's toddler legs hugging the side of my waist. Muffled conversation floats down from the apartment above. Daddy still isn't home, and a sense of doom creeps over me. He has to be up there. He has taken the beetle to Sloane's and he's doing his sick little routine with her. I pick at the skin on my hands.

At half past two, the apartment above has been silent for a few hours. I pad to the bedroom and pick up the carved wooden box on my dresser. Inside it are pins from high school, a charm bracelet I'd gotten from my father, a hag rock. There's also the key to Sloane's apartment. I slip it into my palm, the irregular edges catching on my calluses.

I slip my sneakers on and pull on a jacket. My front door is heavy, and I twist the knob as slowly as I can, letting it swing open under its own weight.

The lot is quiet. Clouds cover the full moon, giving everything a gray sheen. I sneak up the stairs, careful not to make a sound. At Sloane's door, I close my eyes. The layout of her apartment is exactly like mine. I place my hand on the golden doorknob and blood pulses against my fingertips, as though the door were alive and not me. I have to know if Daddy is here. But if Kevin's the father of the baby, if he's back with Sloane, he could be home. I'm an intruder. He might kill me.

I have to know.

The cold numbs my fingers until I can no longer discern my hand from the doorknob. I take the tiny key and test the lock. A burp rises in my throat. My mouth opens as I slowly let out my breath, the taste of sour milk spreading across my tongue. My nose drips. I have an urge to sniff but fear any noise might give me away. I flex my neck muscles as if this might allow me to hear inside the apartment. There's only silence. The key slides in farther, tooth by tooth. The blood in my ears speaks in violent whispers, the overused tendons in my hand shrieking, my shoulders seizing from the cold. I tremble as the highway rumbles, and the key nestles into the slot. The deepest of breaths escapes my body. I grip the doorknob and turn it delicately and give it a silent push. Just like that, the door to Sloane's apartment is open. A portal to another world, both familiar and strange.

"The first answer is Proverbs 8:21," the pastor said. "I'm gonna lay hands on someone right now."

Someone pushed me to the front, and I pushed back in fear. Adults swarmed around me, reaching for the pastor's trousers. He looked down at me with dull recognition. I looked away, to his wife on the organ.

"I wanna pray," he sang. "Jesus will reach on through and touch your life. Jesus will give me the praise."

Two, three pairs of hands pressed me forward. Fingers at my shoulders, my neck, and the open space of my back. Tongues trilled above me. I squeezed my eyes shut, letting their hands touch me all over. My body felt like a bag of maggots.

Onstage, Pastor Anderson moved toward me. He swung his hands back, and as he threw his hands forward, someone grabbed my shoulders and pulled me to the floor. I collapsed as if an invisible ball of energy had hit me. The faces of Momma and my father and Sloane appeared before me, their features dark against the overhead lights.

Sloane's face looked almost concerned. The congregation's chanting merged into one long drone.

A humidifier hums somewhere inside Sloane's apartment. Blue luster emanates from the bedroom, like from an aquarium or a night-light. A cat jumps from a table, making a small thud and sending a swell of adrenaline through me. The cat comes to inspect me. I leave the front door ajar and approach the blue, standing in the bedroom doorframe for some time, letting my eyes adjust. The cat rubs against my leg, her purr vibrating in the bones of my ankle, and I hold my breath. After my eyes adjust, the scene reveals itself. Sloane lies in the middle of a queen-sized bed with a wicker headboard. Steg is asleep next to her. An alarm clock glows red on the nightstand, a humidifier glowing blue. I take a single step, and Sloane shifts but doesn't wake. With each step, greed rises in me. Sloane is beneath a big comforter and a tangled top sheet, her head cradled by a thick, fluffy pillow. I smell a hint of sweat, as if it's seeped into the carpet. The stench of cigarettes, too, like a wet ashtray. On the other side of the bed is a crib filled with laundry and toys. Next to it are boxes of diapers and a basket of more laundry.

Back in her kitchen, the air changes. Footsteps ring the iron steps outside. A man calls Sloane's name. I shift my feet and duck into the open doors of the pantry. The doors slide closed, and I crouch between inset shelves and a mop and broom.

"Sloane?" the voice says again, low and deep. Between the slats of the doors I see a man enter the apartment. I hold my breath. The figure stops in the living room, just as I did, then he moves into the bedroom. My humid breath settles on my face. I slide open one door and place a hand onto the cold linoleum. The man continues his whispering. I make for the door as fast as I can, my feet hit the stairs, the parking lot; my breath is sharp as the streetlights bounce off passing cars. Once inside, I lean against my door, my chest heaving, and rub my hands against my sweating forehead. Then I smile. That was better than sex.

The footsteps continue above me.

I go into the kitchen and open a drawer full of knives. My warped reflection looks back at me from their perspective. I see Momma's face in them, the same terseness. I am mirrored in her, and perhaps that is why she has always hated me. I'm an expression of her, and in that way I'm an expression of her dedication to God, and if I don't comply, then she has failed God and, most of all, failed herself. Her hair is gray at the roots and mine has not changed too much yet, just a few sparse hairs at my temples. I pretend I am going blond. Daddy loves blondes. The door bursts open.

"Daddy?" I ask. I slam the drawer shut. "Where were you?"

He's breathing hard, holding a plastic insect carrier the size of a toaster at his side.

"At the station," he says.

XXXX

Daddy closes the front door and drops his backpack to the floor, places the insect carrier next to it, dozens of spiky white caterpillars inside. I go over to him and rest my hand on the crown of his head, twirling little curlicues of hair, imagine ripping them from his head one by one. Without a word he steps away and I wring my hands.

"You *know* Blake didn't want the cops coming around," he says. "What the fuck are you doing?" He taps the carrier with his foot and the caterpillars jump a little. "I could've lost a thousand dollars of goods."

"I'm sorry I scared you." His beachy blue eyes examine mine. Another urge to laugh takes hold, like a thread being pulled through some loose stitching.

"I've tried to keep you away from this as much as possible," Daddy says, "but I can't do it anymore."

"I only took her home," I say. "Sloane asked me."

"You're not listening, Daisy. The cops cannot come around here. Do you want me to go to prison? Wildlife smuggling is twenty-five years easy. In *federal* prison. Then I'd be gone, and you'd be alone with *your* baby."

I hear more movement upstairs. "Our baby," I whisper. I take Daddy's hands and direct him into the kitchen. "She *said* I could take Steg for the night."

"Blake has too much riding on this next trip," he says. "I don't care what you did, at this point we're gonna lose money."

I stroke the scar on his cheek, adjust a strand of hair away from his forehead. "I understand why you're angry, but nothing bad happened. I just want to be a good mother for you. I wanted to know what it was like to hold a kid, to be a mom."

He grabs my hand from his cheek. "This is insanity," he says.

"We're gonna have a good life," I say. I stroke his face again and drag my finger to his lip. "Why are you getting mad at me for that? I'm doing this for us."

He doesn't push me away this time. I've won.

"I'm doing this because I love you," I say. I lean forward to kiss him and slide a hand into the top of his jeans. The harder I kiss, the more he pushes back against me. I slip my hand in farther, and he rises against my palm, pulling in breath through his nose.

I lead him into the bedroom, and he pushes me onto the bed. My mouth is at his throat, my hands unbuckling his belt. Daddy removes my shirt. I release my bra, and he muscles his palms around my breasts. His eyes are gentle but sharp. My hips shiver against him and I wet both of us. My thighs are sore, stinging still, and hurt when I sit against him. The heady perfume of his crotch wafts up. He glances at the terrariums. The moths dance toward the low-lit lamps. There's nothing else for me to do but please him. Daddy puts his hands on my waist and taps his fingers there. He does that tongue-flicky thing against his teeth, caught in a thought.

"What can I do for you?" I ask.

A hand leaves my waist and a finger points to the cages. My arms go weak. I'd forgotten about the beetle. I imagine his anger, and my face primes itself for the slapping. But the lid to Jeff's enclosure is closed and he's pointing to the praying mantis.

"Meredith," he says.

He slaps my side, his way of saying, *Get her.* I move off the bed toward the cage, and his eyes alight, his mood elevating. I lay my hand flat against the branch where the mantis is perched and tap behind her to encourage her onto my palm. She crawls forward, one scratchy leg on my wrist followed by another, and I fight the deep-in-my-flank impulse to fling her alien physical form off. The impulse reminds me of an earlier miscarriage, when parts of the fetus didn't leave my uterus all the way, and all I'd wanted was for them to get out. The hospital had me come in to do a dilation and curettage, using only local anesthesia. Medicaid wouldn't cover general. On the examination table my legs were in stirrups, and I feared pain from the instruments. I'd had to will myself still. I closed my eyes, while the doctor's tools tumbled around inside me. But instead of pain, there was only a strange, dull cramping and a few sharp pokes. I wanted to see the remains and bury them and grieve on my own. The doctor pulled the sheet out from under me and balled it up before stuffing it in a biohazard container. He was out the door before I was even aware the procedure was over. For weeks after I'd been a tender blister ready to burst.

Daddy looks like he has a double chin from this angle. I return to the bed and crawl between his naked thighs, Meredith perched on my wrist, and bend my arm to place her on his chest. She takes a few cautious steps, her toes seeking branches where they don't exist.

"I must be the weirdest person you've ever met," Daddy says. He stretches his mouth taut as Meredith makes her way onto his chest, her hooks furling into his chest hair.

I shake my head. "No," I say. I'm intent on keeping eye contact. "You're very normal."

I squeeze his thighs and he flexes, his naked cock bouncing up.

"I like it this way," I say. I feel empty as I say this, going through the motions, and consider what compels me. Loneliness. I spit in my hands and go back to stroking him with my eyes closed, trying not to think of the bug on his face or the leftover stings on my thighs, which don't seem to be getting better. Some deep part of me loves the darkness. That he has a secret only I know, though a stray thought of the women before me creeps in, then I wonder about Sloane, too, and I swipe it away. He rocks his hips and he slips in easily. I open my eyes for a moment and watch the mantis crawl toward one of his tiny, inverted man nipples. The areola is oval, with small raised dots around it. A useless thing. Daddy thickens inside me, the only part of this I like. My ploy has worked. I undulate my hips and his eyes roll back. With my eyes closed, I am in a different place—in my childhood fantasy with Sloane. Daddy rubs my breasts and my imagination falters, because his hands are heavy and callused and not delicate at all. But something in me feels different. My breasts are sore, swollen. Heavy with milk. With each thrust, my belly expands. There is no conversion without conviction.

I push faster, breathing hard, making tiny yelps. The further I draw Daddy inside of me, the larger my belly swells. I rest my hands against the wall and look at Daddy's face. When we first met, he told me the scar was from a bottle in a bar fight. A few months later, while drunk, he'd told me he'd been cut with a knife trying to break into someone's home. The man was in bed, and a fistfight had ensued. Daddy said he tried to pull a gun, but the man dragged a serrated knife from beneath his mattress and sliced it across his cheek. "Sometimes it is advantageous to bring a knife to a gun fight," Daddy had said. He said the guy was lucky he didn't lose any teeth.

Meredith rests on his chest. His eyes are closed in ecstasy, mouth slack like a fool's. The insect seems interested in something, like she is smelling him. But that doesn't make sense. I look closer. Her mandibles work like little scoops, pulling strings of flesh into her mouth. Meredith is eating his nipple. She pulls her head back to swallow. I want to look away, but a button of blood swells from the spot and drips down his chest, bright and red as a candied cherry. Daddy notices our rhythm has slowed, and he grips my neck, hammering his hips into me. My thighs slap wet against his, his wiry fur chafing my skin. It's growing— the pain, the baby, my purpose in life—I'm getting close.

Daddy's back arches—I imagine myself tearing the legs off the mantis, ripping her in half; I imagine Sloane, her belly bursting. The baby must be real—I want it—want it now—I'll have it—she will be mine—"Oh god," he cries, his voice an octave higher than I've ever heard, as a throbbing rhythm fills me with his come. A million possibilities draw closer to my heart. I clutch my belly and we split apart, both making sharp breaths as we lie on our backs.

Daddy says nothing. He puts a hand on his forehead, wiping away sweat. Meredith continues to chew.

"Do you want a tissue?" I ask.

He shrugs.

"It feels nice, actually," he says. "It feels like something."

I can't look. I touch the stings on my thighs in response. I find a large bump and push it down inside myself. When I press, there's something hard, and pain roars down my femur.

Daddy pulls his phone out and scrolls through the news. Our breathing softens, and I drift off, feeling a little bit blissful. I'm ten weeks away now. I walk into the kitchen, dreamlike, opening up the fridge and cabinets.

Daddy shouts from the bedroom, "What are you looking for?"

"Dunno," I say. I massage my distended belly. An object is there beneath the fat and muscle, sensitive to the touch. It hurts. I'm growing

194 / ELLE NASH

it now. I pour a glass of whole milk. I pull down a box of saltines and dip them into a tub of sour cream. I take a bite of the cracker, a sip of the milk. Wet clumps travel down my throat and hit my stomach. At church they taught us that transubstantiation—the eucharist's essence changing into the body of Jesus once eaten—was an empty, unconscionable sacrament. Conviction is what mattered most, not some blind act of faith. This baby will come only if I participate in its arrival. I picture those paintings of a newborn Jesus: *Body of Christ, my body of Christ.*

XXXX

A faint light pierces my eyelids. Daddy's shining his phone into my face, likely. He does that when I've fallen asleep before him, annoyed I've left him alone. I open one eye, then the other, drugged by dreams. I don't want to wake up. I stretch out my arms and feel my belly, larger now. The bed is empty. On the nightstand, my phone buzzes until it goes to voicemail.

Two missed calls from Momma. Another call comes through on my way to work. I tear along the highway, barely keeping the Volvo on the road. The baby billboard with its giant newborn in forever peaceful sleep taunts me. The bright red numbers burn ghosts into my vision, 58,666 of them.

The parking lot is full when I arrive. I walk across the gravel, anxiety scrubbing my gut, then I get dressed and sanitized and hurry to the floor, passing the first section of the line. Three men shuffle back and forth between the loading dock and the line. Giant crates of chickens are being stacked near the loader. One man thrusts his gloved hand into the swarming mass and pulls out a chicken by the ankles. He hangs the bird upside down and locks its feet into the mechanical fork, where it joins the chain of chickens being pulled to the stun station. The newest chicken arches its back, flapping its wings, trying to right itself. I'd forgotten what the other sections of the line were like.

A hiccup occurs. This happens sometimes: a carcass falls and jams the machinery or a part breaks. The men turn and notice my presence. The towering pallets squawk and cluck, shedding feathers. I rub my eyes; they're weary from the drive. A number of the chickens at the stun station revive, flapping their wings, twisting their bodies, and one writhes a few feet from a row of chickens with bleeding necks and bloody heads at the next station. One hundred and forty per minute, eight hours a day, five days a week, over the past five years. Not counting the culling from quarantine. I don't do the math. It doesn't matter. I'm no longer capable of any sympathy for the birds.

The stench of excrement lingers in my sinuses as I approach my section, hoping to slip in unnoticed. When I get there, the way the light hits the walls is different, like this isn't my section at all. Everything has become strange like that, lately. There's a floater in my spot. Blond, short, thick-bodied. Workers look up as I walk in, eyes moving from their tasks to me, their mouths beneath paper masks. Number Three pulls hers down.

"Boss is pissed. No call, no show?" She rubs her lower face with the back of her arm. "Girl, you're so fucked," she says, sharpness in her tone, almost happy to be telling me it.

"Morning sickness," I say, but my words are muffled by the mask. I pull it down. "He can't be *that* mad."

Number Three rubs one gloved hand with the other. The floater glares at me as I cross the floor to my spot. I push her out of the way and inspect my station.

"I'll tell the manager you're here," the floater says. Peachy chicken bits are flecked all over my station, and the tenders in the vat are cut unevenly. I rearrange them, from smallest to largest, thinnest to fattest, throwing out the irregular blobs.

Number Three continues to rub circles in her palm.

"How is your hand doing?" I say, monotone.

"I'm thanking Jesus for this break," she says.

If Jesus gave her the break, he's also the one that put her here in the first place.

"Something's pulling," she says. She holds her hand out straight and relaxes it. Her middle and ring finger pull inward toward the palm. Carpal tunnel. I take her hand and press into the skin, which gives like a wet sack. Her fingers are stiff when I pull them open.

"That fuckin' hurts," Number Three says. She yanks her hand back and shakes it out.

"Just trying to help."

The alarm reverberates against the walls, tiled in gypsum covered with white paint, which has gray and yellow stains collected in the corners. The sound feels sharper than it should, because everything in this place is sharp. The stainless steel of the machines, all cheap brushed metal that suggests, if you swiped your bare finger across it, it might splinter into your skin. The room feels heavy because of the clay-red tile floors, always wet with sanitizer; the air razored with a chemical cleanness, but you never feel clean inside. A loud hiss begins at one end as the machine kicks on again and resumes grasping each spine and stretching it apart with a snap to behead them, revived chickens included.

Once, in the 1940s, a headless chicken lived for two years. The owner took him out to a university in Salt Lake City to prove it wasn't a hoax. The headless chicken traveled on sideshow tours across the country, was featured in magazines and newspapers. The owner became rich. Prosperity rich. They called the chicken Miracle Mike.

Chickens run and flap their wings after they've been beheaded because, when you chop the head off, the brain stem remains intact.

The stem continues pulsing messages through the spine to the muscles in the legs and heart. What kills the bird is not the lack of a proper brain but bleeding out. After Miracle Mike's neck healed, he tried to preen himself and even crow. But all he could do was gurgle from his throat. A brain stem can send signals for a scream, even if there's no mouth to eject the call.

The death number hits oddly today because of the breakdown. I'm not sure what time it is until the line manager comes and pulls me from the floor. He tells me to take off my scrubs and clean up and meet him in the office. In the bathroom my hands shake as I remove my shoe wraps, my gloves, my arm wraps, and my paper mask, which I'd tied too tight. I rub the indentations on my cheeks that form a disturbing joker's smile. I change into jeans and sneakers and a lavender-print maternity top. The fabric bunches up around my stomach, but not enough. The butterfly sleeves reveal my faded Ugly Duckling tattoo on my upper arm, just a black outline, where the black has faded to a kind of mottled green. I squeeze the tattoo, and the skin inside the outline turns a sickly yellow, then softens back to pink.

The floor manager tells me to sit. He rests his chin on his palms, massaging the wrinkles around his mouth. He was a good line leader and is a fair manager. Once, there was a reporter who came to investigate the plant's business practices, and he protected the identity of any line workers who'd spoken to out about how Mike's wasn't supplying the workers with enough PPE, that the cost came out of our paychecks, that anyone caught attempting to unionize was fired or threatened with deportation or cancellation of their work visa, that we weren't allowed bathroom trips apart from our lunch break. Ownership questioned him and a few other shift managers about who might've talked. The night manager gave up everyone he knew almost immediately, but our line manager wouldn't budge. He didn't tell them anything. Ironically, ownership found out that the night manager, too, had spoken with the press. They fired him and put the line manager on double shifts. When the article came out, it caused a national scandal. The story reflected so poorly on Mike's that the company gave us all a 1 percent raise. In return, we had to meet 10 percent higher productivity.

He opens his mouth to speak, but I interrupt.

"It won't happen again!" I say. "I spent all morning puking up my breakfast."

He lays his hand flat on the desk, smoothing out a folded corner of paper. "There's no easy way to put this," he says, looking at the paper. "There's been too many infractions."

"I need the money. David's not working regular hours." I hold my belly, rub it dramatically, waiting for the familiar softening of his face.

"I have to let you go."

Pressure builds behind my face. It's going to happen again—the urge to laugh is going to split me open, and my entrails are going to spill all over his desk. I press my stomach in hard.

"It's not fair," I say. "We can't work as fast as you make us. All day you sit in your office, and you go home. You don't remember what it's like to stink like chicken shit and death."

He stands up and looks me in the eye for the first time. It's disturbing, the way his demeanor can go from one of friendliness and care to only thinking about what is best for the company. The way that money and desperation turn people cutthroat. It's always about me and mine, not me and ours. What about when he held out, unlike the night manager? That was different, of course, because everyone stood to benefit at once. Now, it is just me. And it is obvious. One person doesn't stand a chance in the machine. The line manager raises his hand, rough and worn, and motions to the door.

"Leave the premises now or be escorted off," he says. His face is completely stoic. "I'm sorry."

"You're killing us on the line, and now you're killing me. And maybe even *this baby*," I say. "I'm glad to be leaving this shithole behind."

"Don't make this harder on yourself," he says with a pleading look. "You'll find other work. It's better for you out there."

I shoot from the chair and run back down the hallway, my duffel bag banging at my knees. When I show up at my section, there's someone else in my spot, and Number Three is showing her how to use the air-powered scissors. She'd known all along.

The Volvo howls down the highway, past hills with scrawled trees and dilapidated farmhouses. I drive into the rain, an oncoming mist. I fantasize about another life—wearing my baby in one of those baby wraps, gently stirring vegetables around a pan, steaming rice. The baby nestled between my breasts, her nose pressed against my sternum. I'm tired of pining. I think of my conviction, a small nugget of coal inside my chest. The prospect of losing her almost makes me black out. All the times I've gotten news of friends' pregnancies, I congratulate them and disappear, rotten with envy, as I watch their lives play out from a distance, at the grocery store, in line at the post office, even seeing them drive around town.

I pass my apartment and head to the cemetery. I walk past the wet gravestones of Confederate soldiers jutting out from the grass, the signs noting historical battles, to a small, wooded area uphill from the graves. There, a small clearing is canopied by a large, ancient magnolia, with little waxy buds already beginning to form. The magnolia is majestic.

In bloom it will look bridal. I kick around a few stones, checking for signs in the earth of what happened here. No evidence, none at all. I take a small stone and put it in my pocket, again imagining myself with the baby in the kitchen. Like revisiting an early-morning dream, I have trouble conjuring it. In my daydream, Daddy isn't there, and neither is Momma. But a voice from the bedroom calls my name. Sloane's.

I don't get back home until late afternoon. The rain has picked up a little. Blake's car is in the lot, as is Sloane's, and there's some flooding, dark brown puddles that look endlessly deep, like they could swallow an entire person. My foot catches on the concrete steps up to my door and I almost fall.

In the apartment I find Daddy sitting at the table while Blake is in the kitchen puttering around bacon in a frying pan. Fat and salt scent the air. Blake looks up from his spatula, then scrapes the bacon onto a plate and adds hash brown patties to the pan, an unlit joint in his mouth.

"Hey, crazy," Blake says. "Steal any kids today?"

"Fuck off," I say. My pulse beats through my ears, erratic. I take a bite of overcooked bacon, but the dry crunch reminds me of the mutilator crunching up all the chicken carcasses, and I return the strip to the plate and get a glass of water.

"That was a misunderstanding," Daddy says, explaining to Blake like I'm a child he cares for. He looks at me, then down at the floor, as though he doesn't believe his own words. For the first time, he's the one avoiding conflict. He fingers a small cardboard box on the table.

"What is that?" I ask.

"Larvae," says Blake, flipping a cake of burned hash browns. "Super-rare larvae."

"I don't even want to know."

"Then don't ask," Daddy says.

"Why are y'all such dicks today?" I flip over the plate, spilling bacon into the kitchen sink. "No one else would ever treat a pregnant woman this way." I start to cry. The cries turn into sobs. I wipe the tears from my face, and Daddy gets up from the table. He looks a little concerned. I'm surprised, because this hardly works with him. He reaches for my stomach.

"What's up with you?" he says.

"I'm fine," I say. "I'm fine—I got fired."

He drops his hands to his sides. It's hard to tell if he's annoyed with me or in shock.

"Yeah," I say. I sniff, wipe more tears away. "I had a doctor's appointment today, and my manager wouldn't let me go. I pushed back and he fired me. I explained the whole situation, but he didn't care."

Blake stares into the frying pan, smoke rising to the ceiling. "Timing's right for it," he says. Daddy holds his hand out, as if to silence him.

"It's gonna be fine," he says. "Things are gonna be okay, money-wise."

My phone rings in my back pocket. It's Momma.

"You gonna get that?" Blake asks.

"It's the doctor," I say. "I'll call back later."

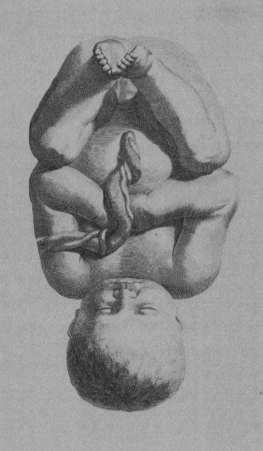

Third
Trimester

XXXX

Momma exhorts me through my voicemail.

"What do you hope to gain by ignoring me?" she asks. "Dee-Dee, pick up the phone."

The thought of listening to her mention God is overwhelming. I don't want to have to think about my past, especially the last few months. The approaching months feel like a wall before me, a sucking death. A knock on the door wakes me up. I roll over in bed, hands searching for Daddy, my eyes burning and wanting to stay shut. He's gone. The comforter is airy and soft. The sun is already too bright. I pull a loose T-shirt and shorts on and go to answer the door. A brown package is on the stoop. I take it inside and knife open the taped-up side. Then my phone dings from the bedside table.

From Sloane: We have to talk about this. Don't ignore me.

I'm not ignoring, I type out, but my text is interrupted by a call from her. I cancel it and go back to typing. She calls again. I cancel it and stare at my phone, hands shaking. Again, her name flashes on the screen. I give in. My head fills with boiling water.

"Look," she says, "I'm really not cool with what happened."

"It was a miscommunication," I say, "a misunderstanding." The knife slides beneath the last slat of taped cardboard. "I would never do anything to hurt you or your daughter. You know me."

208 / ELLE NASH

"When we were kids," she says, "it's like you didn't bother to notice what was going on with people around you. Maybe your mom sheltered you too much, or because your dad died. I mean it wasn't until after he died, really, that you closed yourself off. Then there was that death threat on Frank—Mr. Anderson."

"That shook everyone up," I say. I set the knife down on the table. "Everyone."

"You watched the news like a zombie."

"Momma never let me watch TV," I say. "I savored every chance I got to watch, even if it was the local news."

The truth wasn't that, though. The truth was I was obsessed with death. It blotted out any other hobby or interest I had at the time. That was the year we read *Of Mice and Men* in school, and though it was uncool to be into the books assigned in class, I became obsessed with the imagery of Lennie holding the woman's mouth shut, running his hand through her pretty hair, Steinbeck wanting to demonstrate the ways the world is cruel and unfair. It was my first taste of death, Lennie killing that woman, whose name I don't even remember—many firsts: first taste of danger, of recognizing the world is something other than what is taught to us, than what is represented to us. It was a world outside the cage, where little girls could disappear, their screams could even be muffled, the force of men could hold them down while their manicured hands squeezed the muscles of their bare ass. Saying no, asking for more.

"I just don't know how I feel about this," Sloane says. "I've been staying in Monett."

"Monett? What is even up there?"

"I met a guy, he's a doctor. Well, he's a psychologist. He works out of the hospital up there, and he's been real nice, and he's letting me stay with him. We talk all the time about my past, about my daddy's illness, about my trauma. He's been so kind."

"He doesn't care about the pregnancy?"

"No. He's into it actually—"

"Your dad?"

"The last time I saw him, all he did was complain about how his daughter doesn't come see him. I don't want to deal with that. I want to focus on my future, not what I left behind, anymore. This guy's smart, Daisy," she says, talking a bit faster than usual. "I'm sure he is the one. He wants you and David to come up for dinner sometime, but I told him that probably wasn't a good idea. He thinks it would be good for us, though, and that I should be confronting my fears head-on, to develop my self-esteem."

As I open the package, my voice cracks. Peeking out of the package is a prosthetic belly. I don't remember ordering it, but no one else knows I'm a barren piece of shit, or else Sloane is playing a trick on me. The receipt includes a note:

> *To Future Daisy,*
> *The more you embody your desires, the more likely your*
> *dreams will come true.*
> *Love,*
> *Daisy*

"Your fears?" I ask, trying to stay focused. "The thought that I might have ruined our friendship . . . it hurts, Sloane."

The prosthetic is Hollywood-grade quality. It looks like a comically large chicken breast. Whatever guilt I feel about Sloane unspools. The prosthetic even has a little nub to simulate a belly button. I unwrap it and squeeze it a few times. The material is silicone, but it feels almost real. I place the belly on the dining table.

"Why don't I throw a baby shower for you?"

"I don't want one," she says.

"Wouldn't Mr. Psychologist think it's a good idea? If you're resistant to it, we should do it. We could even throw a party together. Save on costs."

"No one threw me a baby shower before. Certainly not getting one now."

"Please let me in," I beg. "Let me make it up to you."

"I don't know," she says. "Maybe we can talk this out when I come back to the apartment next week."

"Don't shut me out like this."

"I'll think about it," she says.

XXXX

At my third pregnancy class, I meet a woman named Payton with a face like Momma's, only hers is young and has a healthy tan. She's wearing a soothing gray-and-white maternity dress. Her body is so big it looks like a bed, like I could lie in her lap and fall asleep while she played with my hair.

"I'm about seven months," she says after we introduce ourselves. She smiles at me, wide, with big, pretty teeth. They look like veneers; the curve at the bottom of each tooth is almost too symmetrical.

"Do you know the gender?" I ask.

"Oh yes," her husband whispers. He has slicked-back hair and a jaw like a paperweight. His baby-blue button-down wrinkles as he leans over, and I smell faint notes of department store cologne. Middle class. I swoon.

"A girl," he says. "Augusta."

He's already picked out a name. Daddy hasn't so much as brought up the subject. I entertain a split-second fantasy of being married to a man like this stranger, someone with a job, who shaves every day, who is cleaner and gentler and has better posture.

"I lived there for a while," I say.

"What?" Payton asks.

"Augusta, Georgia. I lived there for a while as a child. My dad was in the army. Then he got out and we moved to Cassville. We lived there ever since—but then he died of cancer. My mom is still around, but she's a few towns over. I'm alone now. It's just me here, but I'm soldiering on, and I'm happy to give my child a better life than my parents gave me, you know? Besides, I've got great community around. That's what I love so much about small towns. There's a real sense of community here. I don't have any contact with my childhood friends on account of moving around so much, but once we settled here, I did make some friends, and it's been good. I don't think I'll ever leave. I want her to grow up in the same place, have that stability. You know?"

I pat my stomach, waiting for Payton to reciprocate with the same line of questioning. She smiles at me with her teeth that are too symmetrical. She doesn't say anything about herself. But now that I've got the prosthetic, I fear nothing. I am just like every woman here.

"And how far along are you?" she asks. She is still smiling.

The instructor enters the room and taps the table for us to be silent.

"Also seven months!" I say.

The lights dim and the projector turns on. I want to make friends with Payton so our future babies could theoretically one day be friends. My confidence begins to fade. I start to think I've said too much and exposed myself as different. Every mother here seems so much more put together. I slip my hand beneath my thigh, pressing the cystic bumps left over from the bee stings, which have only seemed to grow. The markers of my class always betray me; they're present in how I talk, the way I see the world, the way my skin and teeth look. Even the way I'm aging is different, caused by the strain that Mike's has inflicted on my body. I understand now that aging comes from stress. These women attend polite churches every Sunday and have husbands who work in oil and gas, but in offices. They have rotating friend groups with hobbies like watching devotional cinema, knitting hats for the homeless, or cuddling drug-addicted newborns in the hospital. They have families that make an effort on special occasions, that give more than they take. They have money for whiter teeth, laser hair removal, new clothes. And all that would be rubber-stamped right onto their offspring. The kind of mothers who post dozens of filtered photos on their mommy blogs and social media, their children dressed like little adults in designer clothing more expensive than my rent: *Sally is eight months old today. She hates carrots but loves peas. She says, "Da-da-da-da-da." She loves her daddy. We go to the park every day.* I want to emulate them because it's an easy way to get validation, but I'm disgusted by people who farm their children out for validation. I wonder in which ways I will imprint onto my baby. Will she feel alone like I do? Will she struggle with the same compulsions? Will she fall in love and hate her mother? On a scale of one to ten, if she had all the money in the world, how lost would she feel without a father?

"Seven months," Payton says. "A-*may*-zing. Never would have guessed."

Had she seen my wild-eyed look when I entered the room, taking in all the other women with fresh blowouts and dewy skin? How had she determined I was approachable? I keep my swollen red hands beneath my thighs, which are twice the size of Payton's. My body is a bloated corpse.

The instructor, a nurse in purple scrubs with a silver name tag that says MEEGAN, stands at the front of the room. She sets up a PowerPoint and guides us through the basics of childbirth preparation—all stuff I've already learned. A slide on Lamaze, a slide on the Bradley method and hypnobirthing. These methods frustrate me. They all require the support of a partner. None assume a person will give birth alone. I scowl. Payton leans into her husband, tousling his brown hair and whispering to him. Then she leans over to me.

"That's what I'm doing," she says. "Hypnobirth. The whole medical thing is terrifying. C-sections, epidurals. It'll *fuck* your baby up. You need to research it."

The instructor stops talking and shines her laser pointer at Payton's chest. "Would you like to share something with the group?" Meegan asks.

"Oh, nothing," Payton says. She waves her hand at the laser.

Meegan discusses how a birth coach can help a woman assume certain positions during labor or push on her lower back to relieve pressure or pain.

If I go into labor with Daddy there, he'll probably end up criticizing me. I can see him telling me to move my legs this way or that, and me moving my legs this way and that, and him telling me it's not right. We never cook meals together for this reason, never take part in team sports, never build things together or work on projects. No matter the situation, he always takes charge and tells me what to do, or tells me what I'm doing is not as good as his way. He never lets me learn to do something on my own. I even hate driving if he's in the car. But isn't his taking charge what I loved about him in the first place? We haven't had to worry about rent in months. I'm eating whatever I want, ordering baby items online.

Meegan reads us a story about a woman who has to ask for help to learn to breastfeed. She explains that there's no shame in hiring a lactation consultant. Payton leans over to me again. Meegan stops speaking and taps her foot.

"Ma'am, if you have a question, please ask the class so as to minimize interruptions."

Payton clears her throat. "Mercy Hospital is considered baby-friendly," Payton says, "but is it mom-friendly?"

Meegan walks to the other side of the screen in white leather sneakers. "Mercy sees the baby's life as having the utmost urgency," she says. "Studies show keeping the baby in the room—eliminating the nursery—

has a beneficial effect on the first few days of development and on the mother's healing—"

"My sister had a major surgical complication and was woken up every couple hours by the baby," Payton says, interrupting. "It took her weeks to recover, and the ward refused to give the baby formula because they were so breast focused."

"That said," Meegan continues, "we have a nursery on-site for women who choose not to have such a, well, baby-friendly birth experience. We are aware that we cannot satisfy everyone in their desire for a perfect to-plan childbirth, and we maintain flexibility for this reason. Now let's move on."

She points her laser at footage of a wriggling newborn moving toward a nipple on a fat, blue-veined breast. All I think about is Meredith. Meegan whispers, as if the newborn were here and she might disturb its feeding. "The newborn will root naturally," she says. "But if you have trouble, there's a lactation consultant available at the hospital. It's crucial to meet with them before leaving for home if you want to breastfeed successfully."

Later, there's a tutorial with a doll to demonstrate how to give a newborn a bath. Meegan walks around the room with a bubble machine as we pretend to bathe our plastic dolls in a small tub with a dry cloth and an empty bottle of soap. Meegan stops at Payton and me, the bubbles floating down around us. Payton laughs, reaching up to pop the bubbles. Each one looks new and exciting, but every bubble is the same.

I leave the hospital when class is over, fidgeting with the stolen security bracelet in my hands, too afraid of what I might do if I try to get into the nursery. My mouth waters when I imagine myself holding a baby swaddled in gauzy cloth. It's only a matter of time. I force myself to walk toward the manicured lawn in front of the ER and sit beneath a large, sparse magnolia. "You prune a branch so that the tree bears more fruit," the pastor had said. "God perfects your faith through His pruning."

"The brain segments, too," Momma said. "All those little neurons are branches in the tree of God. Science doesn't know shit about faith. Science is just another cult. Religion already knows what science is just discovering. And even then, science keeps changing. God never changes."

I pick up a seed pod and rattle it. Magnolia flowers start as a tiny cone, then bulb outward like a small cabbage. When it gets warm enough, the flowers explode into bloom, white petals like papyrus and silk woven together. The thick stamen juts out, erect. Daddy told me in some cultures, white is an omen of death, a symbol of the spirit passing through the earthly realm. Death: the only thing that can't end. Even a God can die if you crucify Him.

By the time the baby is here, the magnolias will have budded, ready to reproduce. Now that I no longer have the soothing repetition of the pneumatic scissors, the due date thumps through my head like the beat of a song.

XXXX

"Lay up his *words* in your heart, Dee-Dee. God blessed David, God blessed Solomon, and when he got into sin, he lost everything, not just the ten tribes. Dee-Dee, he lost so much when the Babylonians came."

Momma sounds tense in her voicemail.

"And do you know why?" she rasps. "Because of sin. Sin brings poverty."

I wince.

I lost my job.

I'm losing Daddy.

Lost the—the real baby. But the baby's spirit is still here.

"Get it into your head, Dee-Dee. Prosperity comes only by the power of God. Call me."

Waiting in the car for Daddy to grab his stuff and lock the door, I squeeze the prosthetic belly, amused at the continued newness. Daddy wanted to have sex the other night, so I kept my cami on, telling him the doctor said we could only fuck from behind. If I lay on my back, I said, a big nerve got pinched and it got hard to breathe. I stretched my arms out onto the bed, the prosthetic jiggling with each thrust. Now the adhesive is starting to pill. I'm wearing a white maternity dress, ruched at the stomach and hitting at my knees. In the mirror, before I got in the car, I held my hands around my belly without pressing my stomach. I'm glowing, my skin the color of a Christmas ham. Beneath the jersey of the dress, beneath the prosthetic, my stomach gurgles, which my heart registers as a baby's kick. Goose bumps rise on my arms up to my pits, the cool air on them a deep swoon thick in my chest, and I press my hands into the prosthetic. The hair on my arms rises in a pure surrender to desire, to everything she is . . . and how I could have her, my babe. Under a wide-open expanse, sea salt in the air, I see her face: loose waves through her soft hair, the mottling of freckles on her skin, the look of flush in her cheeks . . . I press hard through the prosthetic down to my gut, which gives in to the pressure. Nothing. *Don't kid yourself. There's nothing there.*

The window to our apartment opens with a screech. Daddy waves at me through the window, then comes out of the apartment.

"Just airing the place out," he says. On the way to Monett, we pass the baby billboard again and I avert my eyes, wishing the number I last saw to remain the same.

The psychologist's house is a three-bedroom ranch like every other house on the street, big green elephant ears in the yard, the exterior an elegant gray cobblestone with large, vaulted ceilings inside. It looks nice-rich. Sloane gives me a reluctant hug. She shakes Daddy's hand and takes my coat and purse and places them on a chair next to the door. She's being more formal with us, in this delicate way that feels like acting. The foyer opens up into a living room with a white brick fireplace and inset bookshelves on either side. Behind that is the kitchen with a farmhouse-style table and stylish black-and-white tile. Vinelike plants with wide, flat tropical leaves decorate the windows. This is the lifestyle I always assumed Sloane would have.

The psychologist walks out of the hallway. His graying hair is slicked back in what looks like an attempt to cover some balding, but the gel makes the hair clump together, revealing his scalp. He has thin eyebrows and gentle-looking eyes, a squarish face with lined, aging cheeks.

"Steg is taking a nap," the psychologist says. "I'm Niall." Right up close, he's at least a head shorter than Daddy, who puts out a hand for him to shake. Niall's skin is tan but leathered. He's wearing a crisp white shirt and a pair of khakis with black socks. I wondered why someone like a psychologist would be so eager to take Sloane in, someone without a stable job, with baggage, children, a criminal history. But seeing him now, with his age and stature, it all clicks. He's old enough to be a father to both of us. He must be divorced. His children are likely in college, which he is paying for; he's bitter about alimony, and most of all, he's lonely.

After Daddy and I remove our shoes in the foyer, Niall quietly offers Daddy a beer, and the men walk away into the kitchen while I follow Sloane into the living room. Spices and garlic warm the house as the sun sets pleasantly through large bay windows.

Over the mantel is a large porcelain Christ hanging from a crucifix. Droplets of blood are painted at each of the nails in his hands and feet and on the skin of his knees and his injured side. Jesus is emaciated, his head tilted upward, his eyes rolled back in permanent agony. Such naked representations of suffering were not allowed in our church.

"Niall is Catholic," Sloane says.

"Honestly, I'm in awe," I say.

"I know, it's kinda odd."

"You were always so against the church."

"Just ours, really," she says.

"After Frank," I say.

She looks hurt when I mention him. But the truth is we've been friends for twenty years—at least I say that to her when she brings up Steg again, and I reiterate how it was all a mix-up—but she still hasn't told me directly about what happened. I tell her the time between our last moments together as teens and now has slowly stitched together, as though we'd never been apart. "I feel close to you," I say, "like I can confide in you. And I want you to be able to confide in me. In a way, I've always looked up to you," I tell her, though I'm not really sure I believe it myself. I've never looked up to anyone, but instead cowered in fear, ready to wash someone's feet with my hair for a gentle scratch of the head. "When you left—"

"It's fine," she says. "I understand why you might still be mad about that." She maintains eye contact with me, but I look away.

On the bookshelves are various figurines of Mary in all sizes and colors, styles of halo. Both Momma and the church vehemently asserted that Mary was not holy and that reverence of Jesus's mother would cast a shadow on one's reverence of Christ. In short, they feared her.

Sloane tells me she met Niall online. She rests her hand on her belly. Attuned to the quickening of my breath, I nod and add small ohs and yeses between her sentences, completely lost in my jealousy, until the conversation turns to how I've been doing.

"Oh, good, good," I say. "I've been going to my appointments every other week and the baby is growing well."

She pulls out her phone and scrolls through pictures of Steg when she'd just been born. "Are you going to get an epidural?" she asks.

"Maybe," I say. "But I'm worried about a C-section or the baby getting stuck and whatever else that could happen. I want to be prepared for anything."

Sloane puts her hands in her lap. "Don't worry. The doctors know what they're doing. I had a C-section with Steg. You don't feel a thing."

"Isn't it after birth that it's hard?"

"Honestly, it wasn't that hard for me," Sloane said. "I did have one friend whose pelvic floor gave out. She said her organs had just fallen down, through her uterus, into her bladder. And she felt like she had to pee all the time. But then they fixed it, with some surgery. You just have to put your faith in the doctors."

Sloane moves back from the window into the shadow with a serene look on her face. She doesn't know me at all, I think.

Earlier in the month, I'd rolled out of bed, careful not to wake Daddy. I tiptoed over to his phone on the stool next to the bed and slipped into the bathroom with it. His password hadn't changed, so either he wanted me to see his texts or he had no idea. My hands shook as I unlocked the screen.

s

hey, u never told me what

your scar was from

> I don't like to talk about it

s

you can trust me

> When i was a kid. mY mom tried to kill
> me

s

oh, shit,

explains a lot.

> About?

I placed the phone back on his nightstand, blood pounding, and peeked through the front window. Sloane's Volvo was in the lot. I grabbed the old tenant's key and crept up there, not knowing exactly what I was looking for. I wanted to watch her sleep again. I had been dreaming about it, like an astral body projecting myself from above directly into her apartment. She had Steg in bed with her. The cat was no less curious about me. I imagined Daddy sneaking out at night and watching her like I was. A more elaborate scene came to life: a faint knock at her door, Daddy running his hands tenderly through his hair as she answers, and the two of them lying in bed, her ass in his crotch.

With each step, my foot remembered where the give in the floor was, which made me feel a particular kind of power. I made my way to the bed and kneeled. A small snore caught in her throat. I imagined her caressing Daddy's scar. My hand passed over the bee stings and pain shot up my spine. A delicate hair hung in front of Sloane's mouth and I pushed it away. I pressed my lips softly against the bottom of her open mouth. A scale of dry skin from her parched lips caught on my tongue, and the sensation sent shivers through me.

I spent two hours like that, leaning over Sloane, my hands rubbing my prosthetic to comfort me. Steg had crawled to the edge of the bed. I picture myself sleeping between them, Sloane's buoyant stomach pressing into the curve of my spine. Even when she stirred, I did not move. My back ached and my legs burned. I licked salt from my lips and palmed her arm, petting her downy hair with my thumb and forefinger. Steg rolled over, and my legs buckled at the whine leaking from her mouth.

I caught myself and left the bedroom. I stopped at the breakfast bar to catch my breath and found some papers from the hospital and some spiral-bound books for parenting and childbirth classes. I flipped one open. On the inside front cover was her last name: Dodson. Her birthday: August 23, 1981. Her phone number and address below that. At the very bottom, scrawled in blue ink, was the due date and sex of her baby: *April 12; Female.*

Niall comes into the living room and asks if we need anything. He has a half-full beer in his hand and leans against the bookcase. His face reminds me of the pastor's. Slightly sunken cheeks, as though he's melting with age. Stubble growing in the sallow-looking space where a mustache would be, a darker gray. Not even money can fix that.

"We're good, thanks," Sloane says, and Niall disappears back into the kitchen, where I hear the hiss and clink of two bottles opening.

"Anyway," Sloane says, "with the caesarian they had to cut all the way through the muscle of my abdomen." She speaks in a low voice, as if the gory details might offend.

"How do they know not to cut too deep to hurt the child?" I ask.

"I don't know," Sloane says. "Maybe they cut in layers?"

"Did they use a scalpel?"

"I didn't see that part," Sloane says. She puts her hands in her lap. There's a peal of laughter from the kitchen. "Sounds like they're getting along."

I nod and glance toward the other end of the living room, to the dark hallway that leads to Steg's bedroom. I look back at Sloane, imagining a C-section scar as brown as a worm from hipbone to hipbone. "Did you bleed a lot?"

She's quiet for a second, as though she has to work to recall the experience. "There was a lot of blood," she says, "but they put up this large blue sheet to block everything. The sheets soaked up everything, they turned purple."

I can't think of anything else to ask and stare blankly at Jesus on the mantel. Momma would hate Niall and his obsession with Catholic Mary. I slip my hand into my purse and pull out a small black-and-white print. It's another ultrasound. I can't remember where I got this one, either. Another memory hole. If I try hard enough, the exam room comes back to me, the soapy smell of the technician's skin and her soft, clean hands. The glow of the machine, the glittering cold jelly on my abdomen, and the pressure of the ultrasound wand.

"Twenty-eight weeks," I say. I study Sloane's face for a reaction.

She coos over the grainy shape.

"The baby already looks like you," Sloane says. "I can see the nose. Do you know the sex?"

I shake my head. "I want to be surprised," I say, "though I have an inkling it's a girl."

Sloane covers her smile with her hands. "Girls really are the best," she says. "They walk and talk earlier, they're not as rowdy. We're having a girl, too. I'm thinking of naming her Matilda." Sloane lowers her voice. "How is David doing with all of this?"

I swallow and glance down at my feet. I wonder if she's invited me over here so she can see him. A part of me wants to bring it out into the open. I want to tell her everything.

"He's doing fine," I say, faking a smile. "Is there anything I can help you with for dinner?"

"Oh god," she says. She puts a hand on my knee. "You're further along than I am. Please don't think you have to do anything in my house."

I follow her into the kitchen. Niall and Daddy are seated across from each other at the dining room table drinking beer. Niall has a wet shine in his eyes, like he'd been drinking for a while before we arrived.

"The hardest thing," Sloane says, "was not having my mom there with me." Sloane grabs a serving dish from a cabinet by the stove. "But you know Agatha came to see me, right?"

This stuns me. "No," I say. "Momma never tells me anything about you."

I smooth out the front of my dress and excuse myself to the restroom. All those times I picked up the phone, expecting Momma somehow to accept me, to love me. But she is the same every time— the same nagging, confrontational stance; the same hacking, phlegmy lungs; the same put-downs; the same threats to my eternal soul. As if it's up to me whether Momma and I will end up in the same afterlife.

I splash water on my face and acknowledge that I stopped picking up the phone because I have accepted that Momma is not concerned with my life. She just doesn't want to be alone, even in the kingdom of Heaven. She's afraid.

There's a knock on the door.

"You all right?" Sloane asks.

I cup my hands under the water and drink. It bothers me that Sloane pretends to care about how I'm doing. I know she doesn't; her real interest is in whether Daddy and I are going to break up.

I turn around and try to examine the cystic lumps on my thighs. Something white and hard is growing inside of them. I touch the head, and pain shoots through my hips so hard it feels like something's squirming inside it.

"I have ginger if you're nauseous," Sloane says.

"I'm fine," I call, pushing down my panic. I hear another voice, one with more bass. I hear Sloane say, "David." I flick off the light and pull the door open a few inches. Daddy stands behind Sloane, close. His mouth is at her ear, and her face is turned toward him, her eyes down, her bottom lip sucked under her teeth. But their interaction is over the moment I open the door. His head snaps up and Sloane turns toward me, smiling wide.

"Everything all right?" Daddy asks. His face is softer after a few beers.

"I'm too sick to eat," I say. "Can we do this some other time?"

Sloane brushes a hand across my face, removing a stray hair. Together, they treat me like I'm a child and they're my parents.

"It's fine," Sloane says.

I'm sure she'd spent hours preparing dinner and cleaning the house—this house that isn't even hers. I was starting to see a pattern in her now that I hadn't noticed as a teenager, adapting to be whatever men needed in the moment, clinging to them as her way of surviving in the world. I stroke my thumb along the corner of the doorjamb. She is so perfect I want to hit her.

The time my father skinned a wild hog, he'd still had weight on his body, his cheeks pink. I was nine. He'd hung the hog up by its back legs from a rafter on the back porch. The carcass swayed gently. My father crouched in front, placed his hand on the back of my neck, and brought his forehead to mine, our noses touching.

"You need to watch this," he whispered. "Skinning and gutting are basic survival tools."

He placed a hand beneath me, in between my legs. He patted for a second, and my ears got hot. Then he traced his pointer finger right up to my sternum like a knife.

"You start at the anus and make your way up, right through the middle." He clicked his tongue. In seconds, he had sliced down the center of the hog in a single line from asshole to chin.

When my father died, Momma said life was "like a flower." This phrase was stupid, for flowers can live for a while after they've been cut. He'd been in hospice so long by that point, it was like he was already dead. But she made me read all the Bible verses about flowers she could remember. I had to recite them at his funeral. I hated this so much, had spent so much time dwelling on the stupidity, that I had inadvertently committed them all to memory.

All flesh is grass and all the goodliness thereof is as the flower of the field.

As for man, his days are as grass; as a flower of the field, so he flourisheth. For the wind passeth over it, and it is gone, and the place thereof shall know it no more.

He cometh forth like a flower, and is cut down: he fleeth also as a shadow, and continueth not.

Man, who is born of woman, is short-lived and full of turmoil.

Momma was the one who found him dead. She was down in the lunchroom, licking her thumb and turning the waxy pages of her Bible, eating sweet coleslaw from a Styrofoam cup. After an hour she went back to check on him, had brought him some hot tea, and found he'd passed. He'd asphyxiated on his own vomit.

At his funeral, flowers were all I could picture. Violent flowers, blooming bloodily from every one of his orifices; vines stringing his body up. I walked by the open casket behind Momma, stopping to say goodbye as I was expected to. The pale matte powder on his skin looked like the texture of lilies. I wondered how his insides had been removed, if he'd been cut anus to throat like a hog. His buttoned suit and knotted tie hid the mortician's work.

I pause at the front door and tell Sloane I'll stay and try to eat. She walks me to the kitchen with a hand on the small of my back and pours me a glass of lemonade. Niall emerges from the bedroom with a sleepy Steg in his arms. I pick the skin at my lips, eyes moving between Steg's angelic face and the disgusting sense of smugness on Niall's, like he's reliving his former glory days as a family man. But what does he gain? Sloane will stay until the relationship starts feeling like a trap to her, until she moves on to the next, and the next. She doesn't have the staying power I do. He pats Steg's back, and an unremarkable jealousy fills me up, making me heady. I could have been in his place—be the one to care for Steg—and here Sloane is trusting her with some strange old man. She channels the same energy as every Christian mother from church group, an apron tied around her waist, her manicured, sanitized hands transferring perfectly cooked food from pots and casserole pans into white crocks decorated with little mushrooms and flowers.

"Sloane tells me you're having a girl. It's unfortunate"—Niall clears his throat from all the way across the kitchen—"that she can't hand off Steg's baby clothes. We'll be needing them ourselves."

"Daisy must have shown you the sonogram then," Daddy says.

"Can't tell an asshole from a nose." Niall laughs.

The room seems unfazed by Sloane's immaculate conception, that it's obvious we all know this new man is not the father. Still, Daddy's not going to say anything; I'm certainly not, either. A quiet moment reveals the awkwardness of it all.

"We need to figure out who to invite to our baby shower," I say. Sloane sets a bowl of beige noodles in the middle of the table next to roast pork loin, sliced, with chunks of fat slightly toasted along the top.

"I don't want a baby shower," she says. "I have nobody to invite."

"Sweetheart," Niall says. He sounds like Dr. Phil. "Try to focus on the positive—your friend is trying to do something generous for you."

"It might be your last chance," Daddy says.

"Fine. What about Agatha?" Sloane asks.

"Um, that's not a good idea," I say.

"You should invite her," Daddy says. I'm shocked to hear this from him. He hates Momma. He places his hand on mine, rubbing my knuckles with his callused fingers, and suddenly I regret offering to throw the shower at all. I want him to drive me out of Monett, right past the apartment complex, all the way to the clearing in the woods. Somewhere secluded and dark where I can hold his hand and listen to '80s metal on the radio with the cold wind blowing, while we talk about the places we could live instead. The room is humid from the cooking, and the smell of the pork and the vegetables sickens me. I close my eyes and rub my forehead.

"Maybe we can talk about this later," I say.

"Daisy, if it's too stressful, don't even worry about it," says Sloane.

Niall pulls a chair out, Steg still in his arms, and sits down. Sloane serves Niall, then Daddy, then the baby, then herself. She motions the serving spoon at me. I shake my head. I lean back and pull the maternity dress tight over the prosthetic; glee rushes through me at the sight of the nubby belly button poking the fabric.

"Damn," Sloane says. She takes me by the elbow, her eyes on my stomach. "How far along are you again?"

I squirm away from her, slipping my elbow from her palm.

"I keep telling Daisy to eat more," Daddy says. "But the doctors say she's fine."

"I'm bigger than you," I say. "The doctors said I'm just carrying high."

"Did you get to hear the heartbeat yet?" Sloane asks.

"Nah," Daddy says, all casual. He takes a swig of beer, stuffs a piece of pork into his mouth. He wipes the dripping juices from his chin with a napkin.

"Weird," she says.

Every time Daddy has tried to come to a doctor's appointment, I've made up a lie or started a fight. About how they wouldn't let him in the room because we aren't married yet, or it was something more personal than an ultrasound. I shrug, as though Daddy couldn't care less. I place my hand back on my stomach and rest it there.

"Really," Sloane says, resting her fork on her plate. "That's kinda weird. You should go with her to those appointments. It's hard doing it alone."

"I'm fine," I say.

"There's no need to pretend to be so independent," Sloane says. "I learned that the hard way. Lean on the people who love you."

Daddy looks at me. "Maybe Sloane is right," he says.

"I'm tired," I say. "Honestly, I think I need to leave." I push myself up from the table and pull at Daddy's shoulder.

"We just started eating," Sloane says.

"Yeah, well." I shrug again. "I said I was feeling sick."

Sloane rolls her eyes. "Uh, okay then."

Niall laughs. "You fight like sisters, the way you two bicker." Daddy laughs, too, neither of the men catching the sharpness of our glares. Neither of them takes our anger seriously.

"Are you going to be back at the apartment this week?" I ask.

"Maybe," Sloane says, getting up.

At the door, she kisses me on the cheek and tells me to feel better, but I can tell she's hurt. Before she turns away, I put my hands on her stomach. Something tugs inside my throat when I caress the line where her belly meets her waist. As I merge onto the highway back to the apartment, I envision Sloane's stomach growing and growing, like the eye of the one-eyed cat, until it bursts, and a tiny girl climbs out, wet and dripping, and curls into my arms. Sloane's stomach opens like the petals of a tiger lily, red and pulsing on the inside, palest white where the flesh meets the muscle.

XXXX

The light shifts evening blue as I park the car in our lot, the streetlamp casting stripes across Daddy's figure. We get out, the car doors slam. It's quiet in the neighborhood. As Daddy puts the key in the dead bolt, the sound of twigs shifting in the shrubbery by the door stops me. He leaves me outside as I go to crouch, using my phone to illuminate the dark. Curled beneath the mass of leaves is One-Eye. I reach out to pet him softly, the cat's lips curled back. His gums are anemic, pale pink. His bulging, blind eye is crusted around the edges, like it's the only thing holding it in place.

"Fuck."

A shadow from behind eclipses the light. "You have to take care of this," Daddy says.

I gently stroke the cat's flank, full of hairy knots as thick as knuckles. "What?"

"You didn't throw him in the way I told you to," he says, "and now he's suffering."

Shock poles through my spine. "You were the one that threw him," I say.

"Because *you* couldn't do it," he said.

I don't feel remorse for this, but no sense of duty comes to me, either. All I feel is the inescapable pull of Daddy's power mixed with my fear. The sense that, if I don't do what he says, I might lose him or lose my life. I cower as one might prostrate before a god. I'd fucked it up, fucked up my penance to him. He strokes the cat's cheek and spit foam spills from its mouth. I look back at Daddy. His eyes contain no answers.

"Why do I have to do it?" I ask. I don't know why I ask, but it comes out like a whine.

"You wanted this animal," Daddy says. "So handle it."

I search around the apartment for a blanket or a box, something I'm willing to throw away. Already the fear of disease settles in me—where had the cat been, and why had no one seen him in weeks, and why today of all days, when I am rattled and full of wanting and etched raw. This seems like a cruel joke, or a test from Daddy. He might do that— see how far I'm willing to go to do the things he tells me. I wonder if I'll always be too afraid to act on my own behalf.

By the window is a large potted fern, dried out from neglect, with a few still-green strands. I grab the pot and bring it into the kitchen. Daddy brings the cat to me like it's a baby. I press my hand against its forehead and pull the skin back, separating the crusted lid from the bulging eye. The cat is silent, but his breathing quickens. I sit on the floor, Daddy looming above me, and he places the cat in my arms. His hands are shaking.

"Do it quick," he says. "Grab the base of the head with one hand and then grab above the shoulders. Just pull as hard as you can and snap back."

"This isn't like the chickens," I say.

"It'll be easy," he says. "I promise you."

"I don't want to be responsible."

"Daisy," he says, "you are already responsible."

I pull the cat in closer to my chest, cradling his skull, and he curls against the warmth of my body.

"You'll see," Daddy says. "Most of the time, when you kill something, you don't feel nothing. TV depicts people feeling guilty for killing—murder, whatever. But when you do it, when you finally pull the trigger, killing ain't shit. That's what tears people up inside. That they should be sorry, but they're not."

I don't know how to react, so I push my fingers through the cat's mossy fur, deeper now, massaging his bony ribs. I imagine bleeding him out like the hens from the abattoir, hanging him by his feet in the tub, slashing open the throat. To do that we'd have to stun the thing first. Daddy doesn't know, but I understand what he means when he describes the nothing-feel of killing. Humans don't care. We've been killing for thousands of years. And Daddy talks to me as if I'm dumb. He's so distant from the life I've lived, concerned with only what I can do for him, rather than what I am.

Daddy sets a hammer next to my feet.

"Jesus," I say.

He stands there without saying a word. I do wonder if, in his experience, he's killed only animals before or if he's done worse. In Missouri, almost every man has at least killed a deer or put down a rabid dog. But his fascination with death leads me to think, *What else?* I place my other hand on the base of One-Eye's neck and ready myself. My mind creeps up against a block, some resistance, and my nerves fray. I stare at the cat, at his cloudy, bulbous eye rolling, and steady my hands.

I decide to try the chicken method—take a deep breath, pull the neck, and snap back quickly—and nothing happens. He doesn't even wince. I can't determine if he's in pain but unable to express it. My chest gets tight—I'm fucking this up—and I close my trembling hands over his neck and squeeze. I wring and wring, but my hands are reluctant to tighten. I have to will my mind to go over the wall—*Kill! Kill him!* I think—and suddenly a pressure releases, like water over a dike. The cat's neck goes rubbery as small bones pop and break loose. His good eye rolls back, but he is still, after all that violence, alive. I squeeze harder, grind my teeth, push through any remaining reluctance, and finally, finally, the cat's body jerks and twitches, and I hold the dead thing close as the last throes rumble through him. When I lay his limp body onto the linoleum floor, a rusty stain colors my palms. I've torn his skin open—it's blood. The stain is the same temperature as my skin and hadn't felt like liquid at all as it seeped into the prints of my hands, a red burnt orange. The bright red dries to matte in seconds.

I turn to Daddy to show him my palms, and he's suddenly pale, his skin like a corpse's. He lurches over—it's so fast—and orange spew erupts from his mouth, forcefully, splatting all over the linoleum. I hop up, and he puts a hand out to stop me from touching him. Then he falls to the floor unconscious, his legs straightening out, stiff. Panicked, I push at the meaty part of his back, trying to roll him over in case he vomits again. I'm feeling for a pulse in the soft part of his neck but can't tell if I just can't find one or I don't know where it's at. Once he's on his side I place his free arm under his cheek, to hold up his face, slick with spit and sick. I put my cheek to his mouth, feel soft breath puffs against my skin. So he is alive. I try to adjust his legs in a more comfortable position, but he's too heavy to move, and his jeans are damp and warm between his legs.

I never told Daddy about the times I'd cleaned hogs with my father, filled buckets with crimson organs and meat covered in bone-colored fat. I'm drawn to him because of this lingering ferocity I see in men— the possibility of violence. The kind of man I prayed for all those years ago, I didn't consider the other side of it, what the roots of loving someone like that would be, what it would grow into. And now, seeing this, I'm perplexed, but my fear has snarled itself so thick into my life I am suspended within it.

He blinks his eyes and looks around, and it's almost like there isn't even a person inside there for a second, like in his passing out, everything had been reduced to the smallest functioning portion of his brain, trying to understand where it was in the world and in that moment.

"Are you okay?" I shout. "Are you okay?" The blankness in his face is still there. "Do you know where you are? Do you know your name?" I want to bring back the Daddy that I knew, the one who's strong, the dangerous one.

He presses his fingers into his forehead, squeezes his eyes shut hard like he's trying to understand. "Sorry," he says. "That's . . . never happened before."

"I don't understand," I say.

"The blood—I've never—I don't know, I don't want to talk about it."

He grabs his glass and fills it with ice, pours three fingers of whiskey, and looks down at me, with One-Eye's body near my lap, curled in on itself like the neck of a fiddle. He looks wild-eyed and embarrassed, and suddenly pride swells inside me that I'd had the strength to withstand something he couldn't.

"Need to figure out what the fuck you're gonna do with that cat," he says. "Throw it in the trash, bury it, I don't care. Just get it out of here. It's gonna stink." He clenches his jaw, the muscles hardening the curve in his cheeks. He walks toward the couch in the living room, sits down, and sighs. On the TV goes.

I dig the fern carefully out of the pot. The leaves crackle and break into a fine dust on the tiles. I take One-Eye and place him inside the pot, set the root ball on top, and scoop the remaining dirt with both hands around the fern, patting the topsoil.

The adrenaline is gone, but my stomach burns. The animal is still with me. A weight is on my hands, like a pair of gloves. I never experienced this at the abattoir, or maybe I was always too distracted by the shit and my aching muscles and the clucking to notice. Serial killers and soldiers must endure their victims like this, too. The lives they take must shroud them. Daddy pushed me to experience this to understand him better, I tell myself. I tamp the pot, then sweep the remaining soil, and I put the pot back in front of the window. Just for now, I think, until we can dump him. I walk into the kitchen, pour water into a pitcher, and water the fern until it bleeds through the holes in the bottom, making small pats onto the carpet. The whole thing takes only a few minutes. I brush my hands against my pants, but the gloves stay.

Daddy was right, though. There was no guilt or sadness or mourning. Only the silky cloy of the cat's end against my palms, the same filter of death clouding everything I touched.

XXXX

Payton asks me to lunch and I say yes in a desperate attempt to push yesterday out of my mind. I look for something to wear. Nothing fits right—without the prosthetic, I look like donuts squeezed into a plastic tube, round in the wrong places. I wash and dry my new stomach, and peel off the shiny paper backing to reveal an adhesive layer of goo. I match the center of the belly with my own and press it down. The flat edges fall flush against my skin. I put on a light gray maternity shirt with butterfly shoulders and an empire waist. I peek down the front of my shirt and the belly looks real.

Relief smooths my anxious brain like molasses over shit. *Embody your desires to make your dreams come true.* This perfect orb is jutting out from me. I suddenly understand what it's like to be in love. It's everything I need. The belly itself is just temporary—a stop gap in case anyone starts asking questions. I mean, I'm pregnant. But now I'm not as far along as I've been saying I am. All I need is everyone else to believe I am until the time is right. I pull on a pair of white leggings and red sneakers, grab my faux crocodile skin purse, and head out the door.

A Golden Corral server hands me a plastic tray and walks me up to the dingy kiosk to prepay. I see Payton sitting in the cafeteria already, waving at me in another of her neutral-colored, flowy maternity dresses.

"Can I come back and fill my drink once I sit down?" I ask the cashier.

"Honey, your server can do that for you," the cashier says. She sets her teeth gently on her bottom lip in an open smile, her gums glinting like plastic. Her eyes move toward the belly.

That's right. My eyes are up here, but you can stare all you want.

"Boy or girl?" she asks.

"I want to be surprised," I say. I rub my belly in wide circles, marveling at the gentle give of the silicone. The cashier hands my debit card back and gives me a cheery thanks. I get a sudden rush through my center—almost sexual—as I realize I'm getting away with the deception.

It's early for lunch. Elderly are scattered in small groups throughout the restaurant. An old woman with cropped hair and a pastel purple blazer nods politely, her glasses hanging on beads around her neck. At another table, two construction workers in yellow vests eat heaping plates of eggs and toast. When I set my tray down at the table, one worker, his cheeks flecked with dried paint, jumps up from his seat and pulls mine out for me. I laugh flirtatiously and nod a thank you.

"No problem," he says. I watch him return to his table, and they both smile at me. I imagine fucking them both at once, a pair of daddies for my unborn child.

"Oh my *goshh*," Payton says, drawing out the *shh* in that almost Valley girl way that southern women take on. "You look so *gooood*." She reaches a French manicured hand out to touch my shirt, and I skirt away and laugh, sitting down. We make idle chitchat while I steal glances toward the buffet stands. She's probably saying some more stuff about how Mercy Hospital is bad, but I'm thinking about the vanilla-chocolate swirl soft serve at the ice cream station. I see hot fudge and caramel, too.

On my first trip to the buffet I drift by it. The handles are dirty and the dispensers are dripping, but the thought of dessert makes my breath ragged. I want it now, but I should eat proper food first, I tell myself. I pile roast beef, macaroni and cheese, and cheddar biscuits onto my plate, then visit the brunch station and grab some mini-waffles and top them with baked apple and pecans and fluffy whipped cream. When I take my tray back to my table and sit, the prosthetic bunches up, pulling away from my hips. The adhesive pops off one side, and I press my hand against it, pushing the seal back onto my skin. No one seems to have noticed.

"What are we drinking today?" a server asks. She's heavyset, with almond skin, brassy yellow hair with dark black roots, red lips, and black-lined eyes. Her name tag says JUDY.

"Just a Coke, Judy," I say.

"With ice?" she asks.

I don't want ice, but I don't want to appear picky, so I say yes. She takes my glass and flashes her customer-service smile, and I also order milk. Payton asks for water because Coke is unnatural, she says, and has bad energy. Judy nods and leaves. I look down at my plate. The beef juice has bled into the macaroni and cheese and the waffles. Payton is eating a salad with split tomatoes and shredded carrots in it. There's not even any salad dressing on her plate. A grilled chicken breast, as small and dry as a hockey puck that probably came from Mike's, is on another plate next to it. She leans over the table and smiles at me.

"I brought you something," she says. She reaches into her linen hobo bag and pulls out a small brown resin pyramid that looks like it has garbage cast inside it—little bits of metal screws and flakes of foil. "Have you ever heard of orgone energy?"

I shake my head and put my fork down, examining the paperweight.

The server comes back and sets down a water glass but not a Coke, and I raise my hand. "Miss?" I say. She doesn't hear me and walks away.

"I carry these with me everywhere," Payton says. "It basically protects you from all the inorganic frequencies bouncing about— Wi-Fi, 5G, electromagnetic waves—these things aren't good for our brains or the babies, either. Did you know they've done studies that prove that Wi-Fi actually keeps us from being able to sleep? It's a potent hormone disrupter. I don't even keep a Wi-Fi router in my home anymore. We just plug into the ethernet to get our internet."

I nod and dig my fork into the macaroni and take three bites, followed by a bite of cheddar biscuit. Her enthusiasm reminds me of Momma, but at least she isn't talking about God. The tender roast beef spreads in my mouth. The gravy has seeped further into the waffles, so I scrape the apples off and put the soggy waffle on my tray.

Payton pulls her lips back in a look of disgust. "Oh god. Red meat, huh? Look, don't worry about it, I'm sure a little exposure is okay, but you'd be better off without. Anyway, I don't want to alarm you. In fact, I think any fear is really, really bad for the baby. That's why I wanted to meet with you!"

"Can you tell me more about hypnobirthing?" I ask. I pretend to be interested while she talks, demolishing the mac and cheese, which I mix with the roast beef. Each bite fills me with a woozy warmth. I'm afraid of being rejected, and I don't mind the company. I need to learn everything I can. Payton talks about relaxation techniques and the power of the mind. In some ways, I think she's right. She says that pain doesn't have to be part of the birth process and that you can make your body work with you. I think about my own pain—it's not physical, it's emotional. I could move past it if I wanted, look toward the future like Sloane wants to. Instead of fear, there's my baby, waiting for me.

242 / ELLE NASH

Fear is what causes you to lose what you want before you've even had a chance to grasp it.

"It's about the mindset," Payton says, and I agree.

I adorn my second plate with two heavy spoonfuls of Frito pie. At the baked potato bar I slap a hunk of butter on a potato, then a spoonful of sour cream, crunchy bacon bits, and shredded cheese. Another serving of macaroni, this time with the bacon. At the brunch bar I put ten pieces of bacon on my plate along with a slab of French toast. I get two more cheddar biscuits. Back at the table, I cut up the potato and alternate bites of food for a while. I swirl the baked macaroni with my spoon. Some old women stare, soup dripping from their spoons. I stir the Frito pie, but it's cooled and the cheese has hardened. I eat three large spoonfuls, finish off the macaroni, and eat both cheddar biscuits, which melt like cotton candy in my mouth. I cut the crusts off the French toast like a child and add some melted butter from my potato onto it, taking two bites. I drink half a glass of water, damning the server who forgot my milk.

I push the half-finished plate to the edge of the table. The old woman in the purple blazer who acknowledged me earlier is staring now, her lip upturned in a sneer. I maintain eye contact, drowning the last slice of French toast in the sour cream of my potato, and then stuff it into my mouth. She turns her head to look out into the parking lot. The construction workers are drinking sweet tea and talking. They look over at my table, but when I smile they give no response.

Payton doesn't seem to notice or care how much I eat. She's focused on preaching the gospel of natural birth. She talks about all the enemies women have now that we live in the modern world: chemicals in food, liberal men, abortion, feminist hospital centers that force C-sections and unnatural births, cell phones, social media, cancel culture. It's all part of one grand plan to separate and divide us, she says. That's when she starts talking about her church.

"It's apostolic," she says, "not like other churches."

I can hear Daddy's voice in my head: *But what makes it different?* I already know what makes it different. It's all just another way to be baptized. Someone a hundred years ago disapproved with how someone else was teaching the Word and decided that this wanton desire to disagree was actually a message from God to start his own church. Too intimately familiar.

"How does orgonite fit into this?" I ask.

"Because it protects you from the utter depravity of human nature, Daisy. I have tested them at home, and they deflect enough electromagnetic junk without screwing your energy."

I put the pyramid in my bag.

"It's all about frequencies. No matter which side you lie on, Jesus is coming back for his Millennial Reign upon earth. And I'm just doing my part to protect the people I love from sin. I could tell you had a good heart when I met you, Daisy. I can feel it in your energy. That's why I want to invite you to our congregation."

"I . . . I've had a bad experience with the church before."

"Not this one," she says. "The people are wonderful—the community is good. Those people you dealt with before, they've just lost the path."

More people enter the buffet for lunch, and through the crowd, I see Sloane slip in with Niall and Steg. She looks so put-together, and I get up from the table immediately and go to the dessert bar. I pull the handle for the vanilla soft serve, which pours out faster than expected. I head to the fudge and caramel machines and the hot toppings bar to melt the ice cream in my bowl. I sprinkle peanuts and M&Ms on top and spoon the soupy ice cream and toppings into my mouth as I walk back to the table. Sloane and Niall make their way to a table on the other side of the restaurant. As I go to sit down, she looks behind her and sees me right as I'm stuffing a spoonful into my mouth. The ice cream itself is bland, and once I've finished the fudge and caramel I realize how much I dislike the rest of it. She turns back around and sits down without acknowledging me. I get up again, my bowl still two-thirds full of ice cream, and put more caramel and fudge on top. On my way back to my table I notice that the old woman in the purple blazer is gone and has left four dollars as a tip. I pick up the dirty bills and stuff them in my purse. Payton tells me more about the church, and I tell her I have to go, that I'll be late for a doctor's appointment. I finish as quickly as I can, leaving four empty plates and an empty bowl. I don't leave a tip. Payton and I get up, and in the lobby, the walls are stained with spilled soda.

"So how does it sound?" Payton asks.

I stick my hand in my bag, wrapping it around the pyramid. Something about its weight feels comforting. "When is service?" I ask.

XXXX

I find another ultrasound. The text on the bottom says thirty-two weeks. I crumple and return it to my purse. I stay in bed for days and watch Benny Hinn on the laptop, or I sleep, or I pretend to sleep. In bed, I daydream of worlds where I'm no longer connected to Momma. In one, I chew off my umbilical cord and push myself through her cervix, swimming madly, like a dying fish twisting on a sandy bank. In another, Momma brags about how quick her labor was, only three hours. I tell her mine will be so easy I won't even have to give birth.

Suddenly my lower back begins to ache. It's the baby kicking my spine. I groan with pain and annoyance as my water breaks, drenching my inner thighs. I run to the bathroom, peeling off my sweatpants, smelling the crotch. It's just pee.

The bumps on my thighs have multiplied. A fourth has appeared. I'm sure it's hormonal. The original has grown to the size of a quarter. When I touch it, searing pain travels across my thigh into the new bump. This part is not a dream.

If I share my dreams with Momma, she'll interpret them. I already know, as the Bible makes its followers predictable, that Momma will refer to the story of Joseph in prison, when he interprets the dreams of prisoners and the king of Egypt. She'll tell me about God giving me the dreams to hone my spiritual understanding. I don't need God to understand. I know what is to come. Momma hasn't left me a voicemail in a week. As the gap between us widens, so grows my clarity. I'm able to muse on the verses Momma has drilled into me.

Out of his belly shall flow rivers of living water.

One more pregnancy class is left, covering C-sections and newborn aftercare. I roll out of bed around noon and Daddy's asleep on the couch. He wakes, pulls on a pair of black Dickies from the floor near the coffee table, and rubs his hairy belly. Daddy fastens his belt and walks over to me, kisses the top of my head, audibly smelling my scalp. I dress in the closet, with the door closed. I've been wearing the belly nonstop, keeping my cami on at all times around Daddy, only showering and changing the adhesive when he's gone. I've gained weight; none of my jeans fit. I pull on a pink maternity top and a pair of jeans with the wide elastic band at the top. Piss echoes into the toilet bowl. When he's done, I brush my teeth while he finishes getting dressed in the bedroom. We move from room to room without speaking. Like with everything, I feel alone in this. I spit the foamy toothpaste into the sink. Half stays, sticking to the crust in the dirty sink. Curly black hairs coat the porcelain.

Daddy walks up behind me as I bend over to rinse my mouth. He gets his hands around my belly, but before he squeezes I jump, headbutting him in the chin.

"What are you doing?" I ask.

"All right, Jesus," he says. He puts his hands in the air. "I'm sorry. Just wanted to feel the baby."

"Ask first," I say. "I'm sore everywhere. My back hurts, my tits hurt. I'm basically a swollen pimple, ready to pop."

"It's been weeks since I've seen you naked," Daddy says.

"Just because I don't want you to touch me doesn't mean I don't love you," I say. I follow him to the living room. His hounding has become impossible—every day I'm wondering if a random touch on my shoulder or hand on my lower back will lead to an attempt to get me undressed or touch my stomach.

He doesn't respond. He pours some coffee and sits at the table. His cell phone and keys are lined up next to the same cardboard box as before, the super-rare larvae, as though he's waiting on a call. I make a point not to look at the box as I walk to the coffee machine, hoping the larvae suffocate inside it.

"Breakfast?" I ask.

"No," he says.

I pour myself a cup of coffee, stir in sugar. "What you got going on today?"

"Job."

I turn, lean back against the counter, twirling the spoon in my cup. My eyes float to the keys, to his feet where he has a small duffel bag.

"How long?" I ask.

"Don't know."

"Will you ever know?" I snap.

Daddy taps his foot on the linoleum. "I wish you understood me more," he says.

I sip from my cup and burn my tongue.

"Do you need money for your class?"

I smile a big fake smile and shake my head no, hoping this expression will reassure him. He pulls a wad of cash from his wallet, peels back a fifty. He places it on the counter. He looks at me, mimics my smile. The distance grows and grows and I don't want it to. I wait, coffee in hand, hoping the atmosphere will change. But it doesn't.

Two months before Sloane's first baby was due, I crossed the highway and walked into the local pet supply store. An old woman approached me, asking if I needed help, and I told her I was looking for a gift. A puppy, I said.

"We don't sell puppies here." She leaned over the counter and pointed to the back of the store. "We have supplies, though."

"Thanks," I said. I inspected a number of leashes that hung on the wall. I settled on a medium-length bright pink one with a harness. At the checkout, I bought a bag of duck jerky.

The bell for second period rang. From a distance, I watched kids scramble off the front steps. Smokers lining the road put out their cigarettes and walked with reluctance toward the school. When everyone was inside, I cut through the football field and entered the subdivision where Pastor Anderson's house was, kicking pebbles along the way. His driveway was empty, and I snuck around the back to peek into the living room. His white mutt lay on the painted deck and poked his head up languidly. I tore open the plastic bag of jerky. He jumped at the sound of crinkling plastic, jingled the chain that confined him to the deck. I climbed the steps one by one, jerky in hand, and he approached me warily. He was no bigger than the light-up baby Jesus in my neighbor's yard.

"It's all right," I whispered. "It's okay."

He took a few uncertain steps and looked back at the house, for either approval or acknowledgment that I wasn't an enemy.

"It's okay, see, it tastes good," I said. I held the dry treat out in my fingers and tossed it next to him. The dog sniffed. Then he took the jerky in his mouth and retreated to the sliding glass door. I watched him awhile, at first crouching on my toes. My feet grew numb, so I sat with my legs crossed. I laid out another piece of jerky, luring the mutt closer. I got him into my lap and stroked the bristly fur on his head and he licked my face. I clamped my lips to keep him from licking them. His breath was sour, like he'd eaten something dead. I slipped the harness on and attached the leash, removing his chain.

I pour another cup of coffee and a box of baby clothes taunts me from the corner. I decide to unbox a few onesies and a toy or two and put them in the crib Daddy set up last week. He let me buy it from the internet. I put a small sheet with a star pattern on the crib mat and tie pink bumpers with embroidered smiling teddy bears to it, visualizing my new life. *Believe to receive.* Attached to the crib is a mobile with stuffed felt stars that plays "Twinkle, Twinkle, Little Star." My phone chimes and it's Sloane. She's asking if I'm attending my prenatal class today.

I text back yes.

Do you want to get dinner after? she asks. I can come get you.

It would be good to have someone pick me up from the hospital— to see me come from class. It would make everything seem more real. I tell Sloane to show up after class ends.

In class, we put diapers on fake dolls. The seats next to me—Payton's and her husband's—are empty. I spend most of the class lost in the fantasy of giving birth, palming the security bracelet I lifted off the nurse from my tour. When it's over, I wait in one of the bathroom stalls. A few women come in and pee, stay at the mirror for a few minutes as they chat. I'm reminded of high school. I remember hiding with my feet on the toilet, as I heard a few girls talking about Sloane's pregnancy. "At least we know she's not a lesbian," one of them had said.

When I'm sure everyone's gone, I leave the bathroom and take a right toward the elevator, where I follow the hallway to the maternity ward. I walk with my back to the reception desk in front of the ward's double door and make a quick left down another hallway where I find a break room with a snack machine and a few white coats on hooks. I consider grabbing one but stop, feeling superstitious. A nurse wouldn't be looking for her own baby in the hospital where she works, but looking after the babies of others. I'm going to check up on *my* newborn. I keep going, my chest getting tighter as I make right turn after right turn, until I loop back around to the double doors, this time cutting behind the reception desk. My thumb rubs the bracelet in my pocket. To the left and right of the doors is a small white box with two little lights on it: red for stop, green for go. I pull the bracelet out and wave it at a white box. Nothing happens. I wave it again, and again nothing happens. My shirt sticks to my damp skin. Sneakers squeak from behind the double doors. I take a deep breath and this time press the bracelet against the white box. I hold it in place for a count of two. The green light flashes, followed by a heavy mechanical clicking. The doors open.

Every section of the ward has the same white boxes to buzz people in, but after the first set of doors, the rest are propped open. I make a series of turns, looking for the nursery, but can't find it. A ward walks by, eyeing me, and I smile, touching my belly. I take another turn and arrive at a room with large panes of darkened glass. I press my face against one and see two rows of tiny beds rimmed in clear plastic walls. Inside the beds are four swaddled newborns. Three of them are asleep and one of them fusses. A nurse picks up and rocks the fourth, patting its bottom. My heart feels like a cotton ball soaked in water. I lean in closer, and my forehead bumps the glass. The nurse looks up. She makes a curious face, then comes to the window.

"Can I help you?" she asks, muffled.

"I'm looking for room number four?" I say.

"Room number four?"

"My friend just had a baby," I say. "I got lost."

I hide my hands behind my back, showing my belly. The baby in her arms begins to cry, its mouth a gummy maw. The strangely familiar urge to laugh builds within me, reaching all the way to my fingertips. I want to reach through the glass and grab the baby. I squeeze the bracelet in my fist. The nurse sighs.

"I'll page someone to help you," she says, and turns away.

"Oh no, that's all right."

"It's fine," she says over her shoulder. "Wait here."

She holds the newborn in one arm while she dials a phone on the wall. I hear her through the glass. "I don't know how she got in. Are the doors open?"

I check the time—6:30—and dash for the elevator.

I step out of the glass lobby and Sloane pulls up in her Volvo. I bend over, trying to catch my breath. Sweat gathers at my chest and armpits. She parks and puts on her hazards, getting out to open my door. Her belly sticks out of her khaki trench. Only Sloane could make a baby bump look like a seasonal accessory. Her hair is in a low ponytail, and when she waves at me, her large hoop earrings swing.

"You look good," I say.

"I know," she says, opening the passenger door.

"Charming, too. Where are we going for dinner?"

"It's a surprise," she says.

We drive into a gray evening on the way back to Cassville, passing double-wides with tin siding set up on cement blocks. Sloane takes a

252 / ELLE NASH

right down Old Exeter, the way I'd go if I were going to Mike's. We pass the cemetery on the way, a few streets past the Wal-Mart. The gravestones stick out like jagged teeth. Behind the cemetery is the clearing and the old magnolia tree.

I sometimes wonder if I'll ever tell anyone about the dog. Every time Daddy shares stories of his past, the violence he's inflicted, I want him to know we have more in common than he thinks. It's this secret that first separated me from everyone in my life—the amount of space it takes up inside varies, but its presence is constant. I relive it in some way every day.

Do you know what it's like to live with a secret? I want to ask Sloane. Maybe that's why I need a child. Someone who is too much like me to reject me. I look over at her, the epitome of everything I am not. Outgoing, a mother, a person with strong family ties. My secret's taken everything away from me. Or rather, it's kept me from everything I want.

We pull into the shaded lot. Sloane pulls the e-brake and leans back in her seat to take a breath.

"I thought we were going out," I say.

"I got takeout," she says. "It was delivered."

"While we were gone?"

Something seems off. I think back to the maternity ward and the newborns in the nursery, like porcelain dolls with little bean-bag bodies. The tiny plastic bracelets on their tender wrists. The urge to grab one still fires through me like a piston. I'm terrified of what compels me. The nurse catching me, her phone call, then Sloane pulling into the hospital parking lot—it was all too close for comfort. What would I have done had the nurse not been there? I ease myself out of the car and hold my belly like Sloane does. My shirt lifts when I sling my purse strap over my shoulder, revealing the prosthetic. I pull the shirt down and close my arms around it, painfully wishing it were real, then denigrating myself for the negative thoughts. It'll never happen if I don't act like it's real. Sloane doesn't seem to notice. She guides me to my apartment, not hers, and fixes her eyes on my front door. Then she pushes me out of the way and opens it. I fumble for the light switch, confused. Streamers, tufts of pink crepe paper, and balloons pop into view. I feel jarred.

"Surprise!" Sloane laughs. "I got you, you fucker."

A half dozen people jump out from hiding places in the kitchen and living room.

"Happy baby shower. This is for us."

Stunned, I scan the faces of the people squeezed into my small apartment. Daddy is in the kitchen. Niall is in the living room with Steg on the couch. My cheeks bloom with heat. Sloane picks up Steg, revealing her round, pale stomach when she bends over. I hitch up my maternity pants, as the elastic band keeps slipping down the prosthetic, and hug the belly to my frame. The adhesive loosens each time I move. Sloane looks impossibly large, like she might go into labor at any moment. Steg blows on a tiny paper harmonica and throws confetti. At the far end of the kitchen table, an older woman sits with her hair tied up in a painfully tight brunette-and-gray bun, wearing neat khakis and a sea-green button-down blouse. It's Momma.

XXXX

A wave of nausea roils my gut and persists so long it brings to mind the morning sickness of my first pregnancies. By some hope I pray that a living embryo has replaced the spirit of this dead baby that has possessed my life. But maybe, at this point, it's too late for miracles.

Sloane hands me a turquoise gift bag with gold tissue paper sprouting from the top. I look inside, and it's a Wal-Mart brand wash set for the baby, lavender with embroidered yellow stars. I place it on the table with a scatter of other gifts. On the breakfast bar is a hand-frosted pink cake next to a tray of finger sandwiches in a checkered white-and-wheat pattern. Sloane tails me to the kitchen, where I try to pour a drink of water, but my hands are shaking.

"Sit down," she says, and directs me to the table next to Momma. I avoid eye contact. Sloane takes off her coat and puts it on the back of my chair, then pats me on the back and brings me a glass. "I know you wanted to throw one for me, but I wanted to surprise you. I made cake!"

"This . . . is a hell of a surprise," I say.

I smooth the hem of my shirt and tuck it up under my stomach to accentuate the roundness, mimicking Sloane's. On the living room wall near the door is a series of party-game posters, one with a silhouette of a pregnant woman and space for people to write their names, another with the header PIN THE DIAPER ON THE BABY. Sloane takes a seat next to me.

"I'm glad we're doing this," she says. "I regret not doing more when we were kids. I regret not being kinder to you."

Her candor catches me off guard and I get emotional. "When you got pregnant, I just figured that was it for me," I say.

"It wasn't like that at all, Daisy. I wanted you in my life more than ever. I was afraid of what might happen to me, of my parents."

I give a placating smile.

"Imagine if we give birth on the same day."

"It would be everything I've ever wanted," I say.

Sloane laughs, thinking it's a joke. She says something about her back and how well she's been sleeping lately, but I stop listening. Daddy and Niall chat, swigging beers and eating finger sandwiches, while Sloane and Momma catch up. I'm losing clarity, distracted by Momma's eyes burning into me. I observe the way Sloane's hands float along her stomach, smoothing out her shirt, and am reminded of that dishwashing commercial on TV. How the hands represent something more than cleanliness: they represent labor without the physical work; a magazine-clean house. I rest my head in my hands and press the heels of my palms into my tired eyes. That's what Sloane's baby is to me: all the good parts of living, with none of the struggle.

"Can I feel your baby?" I ask.

Sloane puts down her glass. "Of course!" she says.

I put a hand on Sloane's stomach, and for a brief, blissful moment, I'm touching my own pregnant belly. The baby migrates to the very spot I touch, as if seeking my warmth, my assurance. Seeking the love of its mother. Heat coats my hands and forearms, like on a chilly day when the sun's light still provides some measure of protection. How glorious it is that we can create this. The responsibility and the curse. This power that belongs to only your body. This love that is unlike the love you have for your partner. It is a love that comes from within you, that you alone create. Unconditional. A word so overused it's lost its true meaning. Without condition, endless, Christ-like. What a terrible grief it is to love even when you do not want to love; a hole is carved within you, and you become emptied of everything you have to give. Loving this child becomes your singular focus. You deaden against everything else.

An immeasurable guilt hits me. I do not want to be reminded of what I've done for Sloane. But nothing else would have delivered me from the pain of wanting her. I had taken the pastor's dog to the county cemetery, just past the path, beyond the wooden fence that separated the graves from the brush. His white fur caught the wheat-like blades of grass as we walked. With a hand spade, I dug a hole in the small clearing beneath the magnolia tree, chopping at the roots and grass with the sharp end. By the time I'd finished, the hole was as wide as it was deep, a grave big enough for a baby. My palms were blistered. A pile of red and dark brown dirt had grown next to the hole. I wiped new and dried sweat from my forehead. I was hungry and parched, thought I might get myself a candy bar and a soda from the gas station after. School would just be letting out. I unhooked the dog's leash from a sapling, and he pulled back against me. My limbs burned from the digging, but he was small, and although I was hesitant to force him, I knew what had to be done. I hogtied his legs with twine, removed the harness, and pushed his little body into the hole. He kicked and barked and I panicked, pushing the pile of dirt back into the hole, packing it in as hard as I could. I dropped the trowel, snapped his little snout shut with a forceful pop, and wrapped duct tape around his mouth like a muzzle. I pushed more dirt in until only his head was uncovered. It sat aboveground like a stone in a garden. Then I formed a mound around his neck. His eyes were wide and pleading. He was as desperate as I was. I bit my lip and looked around. No one had passed through the cemetery while I'd been here. No one would come, either, I was sure, as the cemetery housed only unknown soldiers from some forgotten battle in some war no one cared about anymore.

I'm lost in the bliss of feeling the baby's kick. I remove my hand and place it on my prosthetic. My belly isn't warm like Sloane's. She gets up and walks over to the cake. Momma leans over to me before I can follow her, the smell of her breath against my cheek.

"I hope I'm not bothering you," she says. Vertical wrinkles crease her lips when she forms the word *you*. The flash of yellow teeth. "I had to come. Sloane said you needed the support." Momma squeezes my shoulder with her bony fingers.

"Why are you here?" I push her hand off me. "Can't you take the hint?"

"I'm worried, Dee-Dee. Worried for you." She occupies her fingers by messing with a seam on her khakis. "I thought you could use the company of your mother, someone who has some experience with childbirth."

I notice a floral overnight bag parked at the foot of the couch.

"I know Sloane's been a great mentor to you," she says.

She can't even look me in the eye when she speaks. She nods at Sloane, who's watching us as she serves cake on paper plates. When I make eye contact, she looks away.

"Momma, I don't want this."

"You need the support, Dee-Dee." Momma adjusts her collar, pulls a pack of cigarettes from her purse. "You are due in less than a month. The baby could come at any moment."

She laughs a little, slides out a cigarette.

"You came early, didn't you know?"

She never spares an opportunity to remind me how I arrived three hours into her labor and spent days in the NICU in an incubator, a false womb, to strengthen my lungs. My transition into this world was so quick I hadn't been able to adjust.

"That's because you smoked," I say.

"Things were different in the eighties," she says. She brings a cigarette to her mouth, lights it, then sucks in deep. "You don't mind, do you?"

"Actually," I say, "I mind very much."

She ashes into an empty coffee cup on the table, the butt already stained pink with lipstick, and shrugs her shoulders. I want to travel back to the moment of my birth, the first breath I took, and hold it in forever.

Daddy sits on the couch with Niall and sips beer, watching Steg play with a lump of purple Play-Doh. She tries to stick it through a noodle machine, gets frustrated, cries, and hands the device to Niall.

"Spaghet," she says.

I lock eyes with Daddy, and he turns his attention to his phone, petting the scar on his cheek. Sloane hands out pieces of cake on paper plates. A sense of fear comes with her; something unpredictable in her behavior. Does she know my secret? Is she going to tell everyone?

"David," she says, suddenly smirking, "you know, you're going to be a parent, too. You should also get a gift." The suggestion sets me on edge.

She picks up a red medium-sized gift bag with ribbons tied to the handles and leans over the couch, placing it on his lap, directly on the crotch of his jeans. Right above his cock. Then her hands rest on his shoulders, squeezing them a few times. Niall's eyes go to her hands.

"Well, this is unusual," Daddy says. "No one ever cares about the fathers-to-be."

Daddy gingerly picks out the sparkled tissue paper and hands it to Steg, who promptly rips it up.

"I wanted to get you something really special," she says.

He pulls out what looks like a framed photo. He flips it around for everyone to see. It's a shadowbox. Inside the box is a preserved black male stag beetle, frozen in flight, against a shock-white background. It's pristine. It's Jeff. A part of me thinks for a split second that Daddy will be devastated, and this makes me happy to see. Something to wedge them apart. Daddy touches the glass, pulls the whole thing closer to his face.

"Wow," he says. "The legs, they're perfectly articulated. The sheen to the shell, and the wings are splayed without any damage at all—how did you preserve it so well? Sloane, I'm touched."

"Fuck's sake," I say.

"What's wrong, Daisy?" Sloane says.

Her tone takes me back to our teen years, to the smugness in knowing something bothers me, but she persists, to get a reaction.

"You can't tell me this is innocent." I stand up and back my way into a corner of the kitchen. Daddy and Niall both chuckle, chalking it up to hysterics. My vision glitters with flashes, then narrows into nothing.

It wasn't the dog's fault. I knew that, even as I was burying him, but it was cathartic to focus my rage on him. My chest loosened once it was done.

Once I left the dog to die, I mean.

I imagine his desperation as he starved, the sun beating down on his skull, sucking the moisture from him. How severely the animal must have wanted to be free, and how baffled, how terrified, he must have been to be denied mercy. How the earth pushed against his ribs, making it hard to breathe. It filled me with a bitter satisfaction to know he craved the way I did. To see my suffering manifested outside of myself was almost beyond comprehension. At night I snuck out to check on the dog. In the three days it took for him to die, the person I was had transformed. There was no going back. I had to accept it. Embrace it. Desire is just the idea that free will is false.

I come to when Momma grips my shoulder.

"Please don't curse," she says.

"Christ," I say. I get up and go to the bathroom and sink to the floor. I hear Momma speaking, dishes clinking, the rustle of paper. Sloane and Daddy whispering, conspiring. I fear Sloane will tell him about me, about everything, though I'm not sure if she knows about the dog. This is it. This will be the night. There's a soft knock on the door, and I hear Momma's voice again, clearer.

"What?" I say.

"Please come out, dear," she says. "I know I said I would stay, but I have somewhere to be tonight. You could come. Sloane and Niall have already left."

At one of the prenatal classes, Meegan set out dummy babies for us to practice infant CPR. Diapers and a small bag of sample-sized newborn care products were handed out. I had no idea newborns needed their own laundry detergent.

If I raised my hand the instructor looked at me with an expression of sympathy reserved for single mothers. I preferred to entertain a fantasy of myself as a pregnant widow roughing it alone, like an old-time homesteader. My husband was away fighting some far-off war never to return while Momma was dying of tuberculosis. I got to spend my days mourning the deaths of everyone around me. In my fantasy, even the children died. I gave birth to three of them, all beautiful and pink during the first days of their lives, but then gone in just as many. In this way, I never had to take care of them. I only got to bask in the glory of having achieved motherhood.

I wash my face in the sink and scrub my skin with an old, threadbare hand towel. I pull down the stretchy hem of my maternity pants and bend over backward to look at my backside in the mirror. The largest cyst has multiplied into several other, smaller cysts and has formed a white head. I grab a pair of tweezers to try to pop it, squeezing at the white head at the tip. Instead, it seems to wiggle beneath the pressure. My eyes are wet from the hurt, making it look like I've been crying. Momma knocks again, and suddenly a new kind of rage curls through me. I swing open the door and push past Momma into the bedroom. On the left wall are all the shadowboxes Daddy has made from his dead insects and the cages for Meredith, the feeder moths, the crickets, the roaches. There are dozens of closed containers full of whatever he's been smuggling: rare moths, walking sticks, more mantis nymphs. I pull Meredith's cage down and open the top, throwing the dirt all over the room. It hits the floor with a flop, and Meredith bounces off somewhere into the mess. I grab the next cage and open it, too. A hundred tiny moths scatter satisfyingly toward the light. The more I destroy, the more I want to. I open a container of fruit flies, the smell of sweet rot, letting the whole tiny flock out, swatting them away from my face. Every tiny container on the shelf, I rip open the top, one after the other, flinging soil and wood shavings across the floor, some caterpillar or larva flying out like a tiny prize.

"The fuck?" Daddy says. "Why? Why are you doing this?" He walks over the mess and puts a hand out.

"Don't touch me," I say. I grab the shelving unit and look at him. It's tall enough that if I tip it, it will hit him if he doesn't move. *She makes me want to stab myself.* I pull my hand against the back of it, sending it to the ground with a crash, and Momma shrieks, Daddy steps back. They're both calling my name, but I'm too angry. I place my foot on the hard edge of the back of the shelves and hoist myself nearer the wall and pull off one of the shadowboxes, one with a brown cicada in it. I throw it at Daddy, and he raises his forearms to cover his head. My breath catches as the corner hits the top of his head, bouncing off. It hits the floor and glass shatters. I'm not conscious of anything anymore. It's automatic. What Daddy and I have isn't true love. It never will be. We'll never get what we truly want, in this life or the next. We'll spend the rest of our lives in a limbo reserved for the worst kinds of people—those who envy. People who thrive on the constant fantasy of a better life, even when the ones they have aren't that bad to begin with.

"Here!" I shout, throwing a stick insect.

"Are!" A gem-blue swallowtail butterfly hits the ground near him.

"Your fucking bugs!" A brown tarantula with red knees now joins the spoils.

For one gleaming second, I have power. Like a cock on his roost, I look down on Daddy and Momma and feel like I am the one in control, I'm the one ruling in fear. I'm wet between my thighs, tingling everywhere, biting my lip to hide my nerves. The soil on the carpet looks like crumbled brownies, shredded wheat. I take a step down, right into the glass and the dirt, and set my toe atop a bright green caterpillar with strange fractal-like appendages over its entire form. I press down, goo squishing out of it. And it feels so good. I step on another, a beetle larva this time, which is as big as a summer hot dog. A disgusting black ooze squirts from a seam in its pale, gummy side. Momma looks stunned.

This is the moment everything turns, like a cant in the road. I should ask Momma to leave and hold Daddy's hand and put it close to my chest. I should sit him down, explain how much I love him, and tell him everything. How much we're alike, how we're not alone in the world, while I still have power. I should tell him about Sloane—about the baby, about the dog.

But I don't do that.

"You're fucking her!" I yell. "Just admit it."

Daddy puts a hand to his mouth. When he catches my scowl I stare directly at the spot between his eyes. Daddy told me once that liars will look away or to the left when they lie. I let my eyes lose focus. If he knew just how much I've endured to be here, maintaining this stoic look on my face for years, and how I've subdued my fear of facing him, he would be proud of me. But he'll never know what I'm capable of or how well I've learned from him.

Daddy turns away. He takes a step toward the bedroom door. My blood pressure bottoms out. "You're fucking insane" is all he says. He takes another step.

I'm me again. Miss Nobody. I wipe tears from my face with the back of my arm, my eyes raw like a skinned grape. "Please don't be mad," I beg.

He shakes his head and walks through the living room, toward the front door, swings it open. Then he is gone.

Meredith is gone. Sloane is gone, now. And all I have is this baby.

The fluorescent light in the bathroom flickers; the moths are all bouncing off the light cover. I suck in my cheeks and close my eyes. I walk to the bedroom door and, for a second, look over my shoulder at the crib and the small dresser in the corner. Someone has taken the clothes and toys out of the crib and organized them. Whoever it was had strung up a tiny sliding curtain to make a little room for the baby inside the bedroom. I feel uneasy, spooled with queasy yearning. Momma's silhouette appears before me in the bedroom doorway.

"Dee-Dee," she says, "you shouldn't be alone right now."

XXXX

Momma drives against my protestations. She's a terrible, nervous driver. Once, we took a trip out to Branson when I was seven, and my father made her drive a shift. She jerked the wheel to avoid a turtle in the road and took us into the ditch when she confused the gas for the brake. No one was hurt, but we popped a tire. My father changed it out, comforting her the entire time, telling her the crash wasn't her fault. Since then, she's never left town unless she was in the passenger seat. I'm surprised Momma drove on the highway to see me.

The inside of her car smells like a nursing home: baby powder and old wet cigarette butts. The ashtray is full, and there's faint dust on every surface. I want to wipe my hands on my pants but roll down the window instead. Rain splatters inside the car.

"Roll it up," she says.

"Where are we going?" I ask.

"The only place that will make you feel better."

The entire ride, I turn the events of the party around and around in my head, assessing the damage. Does Sloane know I've been faking the entire time? Is she playing tricks on me? Maybe she'd been the one to send the belly, to plant the ultrasounds in my purse. It'd been almost seven months to the day since she moved in. Does everyone around me know and they're all indulging the lie because they pity me?

It's not implausible. Sloane kissed me all those years ago not because she loved me but because I loved her. She is the only woman I've ever loved. She let me believe in the possibility of closeness with her by egging me on. But why?

The car pulls into a gravel lot. We park a few rows behind a large white tent. Momma turns off the engine. She grabs the door handle and turns her head toward me. She looks at my lap, at my fake stomach. Maybe she knows, too. Her eyes move up to mine.

"I miss when your hair was longer," she says, "like Sloane's."

She smooths a lock of hair behind my ear. Then we get out of the car. Organ music blares from the tent. It's revival season.

On the fourth night after the dog burial, I'd snuck out of the house. While walking to the cemetery I imagined it like a hog that my father would butcher. *Their pain is necessary for our survival,* he would have said.

In the clearing beneath the magnolia I got on my knees and brushed away the dirt. The dog's mouth was open, his bloated black tongue lolling to the side. His gums were no longer shiny. I tried to move his head around, but his neck was stiff and cold. I pulled a long hunting knife, one of my father's, from my bag, and placed it at the base of the dog's neck. I began to saw at the spine, the toughest spot, and worked my way through the bone. Flecks of flesh and fur collected on the blade, a few stray hairs catching in the wind.

Miasma, like shit or death, filled my mouth and nose. My father told me when you smell the dead, one of two things can happen. If the death is new, you get hungry. You inhale the hulk of meat, the float of blood, and your brain signals for you to eat it. If the death is old, the stench makes you want to vomit. My father said there's nothing like the smell of old death; its unique purity is known immediately. But when he butchered wild hogs and deer, he'd split them open and the guts would slip from their open slits and I'd get hungry. For steak, for the sweet sizzle of flesh on a fire.

The dog had been dead awhile. I gagged. But with that neck sawed open and the muscle of its shoulders exposed, I thought immediately of a ham hock, of Momma's split pea soup, the smell of roasted ham and stock filling the house.

Once I cut through the spine, the rest was easy. Its head flopped to one side, congealed blood collecting around its gums. A car parked in the distance, the door latching shut. I dumped out the contents of my backpack, spraying pencils and paper everywhere. I picked the head up by its ear—it was as light as a small gourd—and put it in my bag. Bits of fur caught in the zipper.

Momma leads me through the tent to a middle row with about a dozen people. I sit next to women with hair pulled into intricate buns who fan their faces with long-sleeved arms, their legs crossed beneath floor-length skirts. The men are in suits and ties, their hair faded on the sides and slicked back on top. An electric organ is set up in front of a familiar older woman, her white bangs teased above her forehead. Pastor Anderson's wife. At the pulpit stands the pastor, a good forty pounds heavier, balding, even sweatier than twenty years ago. The lines in his face are deeper, the flesh around his eyes looser, his lips thin. He is an old man.

"Through His name," the pastor says, "miracles happen. Healing is yours. No other name can save and heal. No other name gives you peace. Hope. Joy. Darkness vanishes and bondage breaks when you speak His name. Sickness is gone when you mention His name. Jesus is Lord. The Lord of God the Father in His wonderful presence is here, right now. Lift your hands. Forget your troubles. Forget your diseases. Forget the problems of life. Love Him now.

"Kings," the pastor sings, "and kingdoms . . . they all pass away."

The crowd joins him, off-tune, to no melody in particular.

"But there's something in . . ."

My heart rises in anticipation, but I don't want to hear it.

"Jesus once again," the pastor says. "Jesus . . . Jesus . . . Jesus . . . There is something about . . . Him. Master, Savior, Jesus. Like the perfume after a rain."

The women clap, a few glancing at me. Momma takes me by the hand and leads me down the aisle. She sits me in the second row, and as Pastor Anderson raises his hands, Momma raises hers, too. I look behind me and everyone is raising their hands. Palms up, to the Lord.

"I am saved," they sing. "I am saved, I am saved."

The music is buoyant, and I fight a growing euphoria. The vibration of the organ and the boom of the pastor's voice are everywhere at once. The people clap, a rhythmic pulse in my chest I can't resist.

Pastor Anderson says, "Let's welcome any newcomers tonight."

The congregation responds the way I remember: sounds of sadness and desperation, dozens of mouths crying. "O Lord," the mouths say. "O Lord, thank you," the mouths say. Their sadness fills my head. It bounces off the tent walls and churns in my chest. The words are repetitive; they lose shape and transform into belief.

"Pray with me, children," the pastor says, his cheeks like bruised apples.

Amid the noise, he glares at me. The light in the tent is the same dull yellow glare of the church of my childhood.

Pastor Anderson quiets everyone and begins his sermon. It doesn't matter what the sermon is. He says something about lost sheep. About foster children and good Christian parents and special people.

"Somebody loved those children," he says, "born in a home that didn't want them. Where there was no love. But God found a special person and led them to those children. That special person had a holy mission. That is a lot like why we are here today. You may have come here because a special person brought you here today. That special person had a holy mission, too. That, ladies and gentlemen, is the history of tent revival in this great country. We want to welcome anyone who has recently committed their lives to God."

I hear a man from the back: "Ye!"

"We want to welcome anyone who is considering committing their lives to God."

An old woman: "Amen!"

"We are here for you."

Two people at once: "Hallelujah!"

The local news had reported live from the pastor's house. As lights flashed, the news ticker rolled: "Local Preacher's Dog Beheaded." Pastor Anderson looked into the camera, wearing his white collar, the black shirt. Never off-duty. His eyes burned into me. "When someone threatens the army of God," he said, "our fight is a righteous one."

I closed my eyes that night and had a deep, nothing kind of sleep. I woke up with someone standing over me. I thought it was the pastor, and my heart shrieked in fear, but it was Momma. She put a hand over my mouth, the lace cuff of her nightgown scraping my cheek, and lifted me out of my bed gripping painfully beneath my ribs.

Terror glimmered in her eyes. She lowered me to my feet, and I steadied myself, untangling my pajama pants from the bedsheets. The news had descended on the congregation like a rolling storm.

"Now it's more important than ever to stand firm against Satan by reflecting Christ's characteristics in our lives," Momma said urgently. "I can no longer trust you to guide yourself."

She ran up the stairs, two at a time, into my bedroom, where Sloane slept.

"Momma—"

"Satan cannot be reasoned with," she said. She guided Sloane down the stairs by her arm. Sloane covered her belly with the Slayer shirt. "It's only a matter of time before more attacks come. The congregation may already be at risk. Both of you—and I—must resist Satan and his demons."

Momma glanced at the shirt. "This must be burned," she said, and pulled it off Sloane, who was stupefied.

"We cannot take these risks anymore. Only strength matters now." She handed Sloane my blanket from the couch to cover herself, then pulled us to our knees with her in prayer. I felt as though I were in a painting of my life and not my actual life. Momma gripping my hands so tight the bones hurt. For years she had prepared for a situation like this—a satanic attack—and now it was here and it was because of me.

"There will be more," Momma hummed, "in time. Pray, children."

But there was no Satan. Or maybe I was Satan and never realized it. As I lowered my head to pray, life suddenly came into transparent view. I could see my actions as plainly amoral, something done out of survival. I could see Momma's actions the same, and Sloane's. We were all just animals functioning much the way animals do, which is to stay true to their nature. And somehow that clarity had been lost to me.

The organ music crescendos. I try to hide behind other women, sway without raising my hands. I'm the only one not clapping or praying. The pastor asks if anyone would like to come up to the altar to repent.

"God brings us together for a specific purpose," he says.

I swallow, my dry throat sticking together. I scan the congregation to see if anyone's going, but they keep singing, their hands raised, their voices trilling. I close my eyes, arms crossed at my waist. I fumble with the edges of the prosthetic, pick the skin at my thumbs. I'm nervous. There's no way to hide it. My feet propel me into the aisle. The song's changed now, but it's my own pulse in my ears. "You better make a change," the congregation sings. "You better make a change"—they clap—"a change, a change."

I'm mobbed by women when I get to the altar. All of them have serene, dopey smiles, and each, one at a time, touches me: one places her soft hands in my own, one palms my shoulder, another places her hands on my waist. I see Momma in the second row, hands clasped and pressed to her mouth. Her eyes are wet with hope. Then the pastor points a finger to my chest.

He thanks Jesus for the opportunity to save me. He moves his finger to my forehead as the organ gets louder. As it rises, my pulse quickens. The laugh feeling inside me rises, but it also feels like I might cry. I once read that we tend to mistake emotion for God. I can no longer discern the beat of my heart from the deep bellow of the organ, nor the organ from the chorus of voices. It's one long, formless sound. The pastor shouts, I can't be sure. A throbbing hits my chest, vibrating up to the open spaces in my head, clattering my teeth. "Where you go when God gets in." That's what Momma is fond of saying. The space I went to, half in the physical world, half in the world of my pregnancy. My eyes roll toward the back of my head. My vision goes blue then black, then a thousand bright sparkles bounce behind my eyelids and

I am gently guided to the floor. For a moment my body is weightless. My hips and back and shoulders touch the cold dirt. Countless hands slide out from under me.

XXXX

"Pastor says that God's perfection doesn't allow Him to experience sin," Sloane said, the summer before her pregnancy.

We sat surrounded by tall grass in a field near the cemetery.

"He can't," she said. "His nature won't allow it."

She'd braided flower crowns all day and put them on my wrists, the pulpy yellows feathering color onto my arms, staining random patterns. We lay together on a shared blanket, taking sips of a hard cider she'd swiped from her father.

"But Todd says God's incapable of understanding the condition of being human," she went on. "He exists outside His creation. He is unable to have empathy for it, for us."

"Wasn't that the purpose of sending Jesus to us?" I asked.

"Todd says even Jesus's last words were 'My God, my God, why have you forsaken me?'"

She leaned up on her elbow, her body shielding my face from the sun.

"Todd says God let His only son die because He was incapable of understanding the sacrifice humans endure for faith."

"Do you believe this?" I said.

"Lucifer understands, Todd says. He was God's first creation, after all."

She caressed my face, making the peach fuzz on my cheek tingle. I thought for a second she might kiss me, but she continued talking.

"Sin, the so-called rejection of God's love, started with the angel Lucifer."

"You really do believe in this," I said.

"I'm telling you it's no use loving a god that has betrayed you," she said. "God told Adam from the outset to avoid the tree of knowledge. But if God was truly omniscient He would have already known the outcome. And if He had already known this, He would have already known that man would be tainted. He would have known that His project would end in failure, and yet He let man fail anyway. How could God be just if He knew from the beginning that His creation was born to suffer, separated from His holiness and favor for all of their insignificant lives on this earth?"

She leaned and placed her lips lightly on my mouth. She kept her mouth there for a moment, her face pressing into me, and pulled away. Her hair was a frizzy ring filled with sunlight.

"Todd says we were never given a choice," Sloane said. "Don't you wonder why?"

Momma and I step out of the tent. My eyes burn as they adjust to the darkened sky. We begin to pull out of the parking space, but Momma waits, letting three other cars pass by. On the highway she lights a cigarette, takes a drag, and sighs.

"That was nice," she says. "You're coming around again."

I stare at the night outside my window, the stray farmhouse light in the distance, the navy sky. My head bumps against the glass when she hits a pothole in the road.

"Can we take a pit stop at Mike's?" I ask.

"Your old job? What do you want there?"

"I left something in my locker," I say. "I need to see if it's still there."

Mike's lot is empty when we arrive, except for a single car. Third shift has just cleared out. Momma turns off the car, and we fall into silence except for the night sounds of crickets.

"Is it even open?" she asks. She pulls the keys from the ignition and places them on the dash.

"Well, someone's here," I tell her. I point at the sedan.

She follows me into the unlocked building. Rows of emergency lighting glow along the freckled drop ceiling. I lead her through the labyrinthine hallways until we get to the manager's office, which is locked.

"This is where you worked?" she asks, looking around.

I nod.

"It's so clean," she says. She runs a hand along a painted yellow wall.

"You haven't seen the floor," I say.

We reach the door to the processing line, and I place my ear against it and hear nothing. Someone from third shift probably got a ride home and left their car. I ask Momma to wait in the hall, and I enter. I turn on my phone's flashlight. I walk along the beginning of the line with the large garage doors, the killing wall, and through the windows I see the long rows of chicken huts. I turn the corner to the deboning line. Five empty tubs shiny with sanitizing fluid sit in a corner. At night, the machine is clean of ground flesh: the chrome sparkles, the sanitized tools are all hung on hooks. When I reach my old station, I follow the air hose to the pneumatic scissors and pick them up, unscrewing the hose from the handle. I've missed their weight, the rubberized grip. Without air to power them, opening and shutting them takes a lot more muscle. I try it once and hear the satisfying sound of metal sliding against metal. We sharpened them every day at the end of shift for the next crew. I unscrew the other end of the hose from the air machine, wrap it around the scissors, and stuff them in the back pocket of my jeans.

A month before Sloane's due date, she left to go live with her uncle. He drove west from Kentucky in his black BMW and picked her up at our house. I watched from my window as she walked down the driveway. Her uncle threw her duffel bag and a box of belongings into his trunk. Momma ran down to the car and shook his hand. It was all very formal. Then Sloane opened her arms for a hug, and the two embraced. She patted Momma's back, looked up at my bedroom window, then looked away. She got in the car and left.

The last moment I remember at my pregnancy class, the instructor asked if anyone's doctor had mentioned the risks of a C-section. I raised my hand. A few other hands went up, too. One of the other hands belonged to a woman with short blond hair tied into a sleek ponytail. I studied her face and, for a second, her lips and cheeks reminded me of Sloane. Every woman since she'd reentered my life seemed to take on the shape of her. I judged them all by Sloane's actions, by the way she treated me, and punished them in my mind for their betrayal.

The instructor tapped at the screen.

"Some women will schedule their C-sections," the instructor said. "Some of you will have emergency C-sections, so it's important for you ladies to be prepared for anything, you may go into labor without being induced. Warning signs for fetal distress include sudden change in the movements of the baby, swelling of the hands and feet, and seeing spots."

I checked my pulse and squeezed my wrists and hands. Everything checked out normal. The instructor said C-sections at times are performed because of problems with the placenta, fetal distress, or the position of the baby. The baby may move down the birth canal feetfirst instead of headfirst, in which case they'll need to be pulled out as quickly as possible, ass-first. The instructor called it a breach birth.

What did mothers do before C-sections? And how would they know if the baby's head was positioned properly? I was most curious about the placement of the incision, which the instructor said was done at the bikini line. She said the actual delivery took only five minutes. The baby is pulled from the uterus, and a surgical nurse suctions the baby's nose and mouth, cleans it, and clamps the umbilical cord.

"The baby's first cry is the most important one," said the instructor. "A strong cry helps fill the baby's lungs with air and discharge fluid."

I raised my hand again. "Can the mother die during a C-section?" I asked.

"It's rare, but complications do occur," she said.

"What happens if the mother dies before the baby is born?" I asked. "Does the baby die, too?"

She cleared her throat. "Theoretically," she said, "the baby would have a few minutes before dying, as the body would still circulate blood, and that blood would make its way into the umbilical cord. But it would depend on how the mother had died, to determine how long the fetus has before it expires."

"You mean like if the mother is bleeding out?" I asked. "Could the mother bleed out from—"

"Not if done correctly," she said, interrupting me. The energy in the room had turned. A brunette girl near me went pale.

My shoes squeak against the linoleum in the hallway. Some ways down, a toilet flushes—I think it's Momma, but then I hear a masculine cough. I double back to the factory floor toward the garage doors.

Next to them a smaller door opens into the parking lot. I slip through it outside and run to Momma's car.

The sound of flesh being cut by a pair of scissors is different from that of paper or cardboard or even the stems of flowers. Flesh sliced by scissors has a certain give, the insides are wet. When you butcher a hog, you make two diagonal cuts behind the right and left shoulders, then at the top of the spine you cut right through the vertebrae to behead it. Next, you make a long, lean line down the spine on both sides. From those lines, you make horizontal cuts as close to the ribs as you can. After you've removed the spine and move on to filleting, something weird happens. The flesh is smooth where you expect it to be tough. You can't put too much pressure on the animal or you'll bruise the muscle. You'll damage it. We forget that the meat we see plastic-wrapped in the supermarket refrigerator was once part of a larger animal.

It's the same for chicken. You spend so much time picturing it in a certain way. The most popular part of the chicken is the breast. It happens to be the least moist, least flavorful, least nutritious muscle in the chicken. If you see it on the shelf, pear-shaped, fat on one end, you don't think of them as breasts. I say *breast* and your mind goes someplace sexual, or maternal. You think of your own breasts, or the breasts of your girlfriend, your wife, or your mistress. Maybe even your mother's breasts. But you don't picture a chicken's, because you don't have to raise it, feed it, kill it, skin it, gut it, and cut it into pieces. You assume the chicken breast comes from a larger structure much in the way that apples come from trees.

And if it's your job to slice through them every day, you don't pay any mind to what those breasts were attached to seconds earlier. Instead, your focus is to maintain a delicate control to keep the fragile flesh from bruising and splitting beneath your fingers. You know exactly how to do it, the same way you know how to take a familiar curve in the road.

I move Momma's seat back to work the pedals and speed out of the parking lot. My phone is in my back pocket, buzzing from a phone call. The scissors are on the seat next to me. When I park the car in front of my apartment, I glance up, straining my eyes through the haze of streetlights to see what I know is there in the sky: Cygnus, the Northern Cross, the swan in flight.

Light shines through my front window, but I bypass my apartment. I see myself from up above, like I'm watching myself from Cygnus's perspective. Up the stairs, my heavy footsteps clang the wrought iron like a bell.

I reach Sloane's door and knock. Sloane falls backward to the floor when she opens the door. Do I see myself push her? The orgone pyramid is in my hands, it's heavy, and it hits her head. She begins to scream, and Steg wakes up. Now I have no one. I will have to fundamentally let go and be beholden only to myself. I will take care of my own heart. I will compress my own wounds. I disappear inside. I look through Sloane's bathroom window and see me pulling Sloane into the bathtub by her hair. Steg's small hands thud against the locked door.

She stops screaming. It takes much longer to choke her than Daddy told me. Sloane kicks and kicks and a shoe flies off. My fingers are raw from pulling the air hose tight, but finally her legs straighten, her toes, too. My hand on her chest wills the death throes to stop.

She jerks, seizes, and I panic that she is still alive, that I've fucked it up. A blood vessel has burst in her left eye. Grief and fear rip through me. Her body stark against the porcelain, blood pools around her like a gloriole. I brush a greasy streak of hair from her face, now calm. Her fingers splay open, muscles loose. I have only minutes now. I pull the pneumatic scissors from my jeans.

The moment Pastor Anderson allowed my deliverance in the tent will stay with me forever. The long, steady drone in my ears: everything is like that now. The flesh gives easily. Sloane's body gives off the familiar smell of rust. Her energy passes on to me, formless. And out of the formlessness comes an opalescent shape, a shimmer of life. I hold her in my arms and wrap her purple form in a white towel, her thin limbs moving dumbly like an upside-down insect. I see myself whole for the first and last time. The words from the sermon detonate in my mind. I begin to weep. She sucks a hard gasp of air in her lungs and breathes. Then my baby cries. Like the crack of an egg, the wet sound breaks against the walls. I can hear Momma's voice in it, screaming, *I am saved, I am saved, I am saved.*

2015

BABY IN CRITICAL CONDITION AFTER BEING RIPPED FROM MOTHER'S WOMB

A baby girl who was ripped from her mother's womb in what Cassville authorities have called a fetal abduction case remains hospitalized in serious condition, according to the mother of the slain victim.

The family of Sloane Dodson, 34, who police say was strangled and then had her baby cut from her womb, released photos of the baby with her grandmother, Barbara Dodson. The baby is suffering from jaundice and exposure but is expected to recover.

Police say Dodson went missing on March 19, a month before she was due to give birth. Her cause of death was ligature strangulation, authorities said.

Daisy Adams, 34, was found at the scene of the crime a week ago in critical condition with severe injuries to her abdomen. Authorities rushed her to the hospital when they found the missing baby had been placed inside Adams's torso in a self-made wound, half sewn shut. Adams is charged with two counts of felony kidnapping, capital murder, and tampering with a human corpse, Barry County jail records show.

Mutual friends of the two women told authorities that Adams and Dodson had been close friends for more than two decades. They met at a religious compound, the friends said, and Adams reportedly told her boyfriend, David Mueller, she was also expecting a child in April.

Police officials have not said if they believe Mueller is involved in the kidnapping or Dodson's slaying. Mueller has not been found; according to officials, he has a history of drug possession with intent to distribute and is considered dangerous and armed. Anyone with information is requested to come forward. Mueller is 6'5", white, with chin-length brown hair and a large pink scar on his right cheek.

Acknowledgments

This book would not have been possible without the help and support, firstly, of my husband, whose constant encouragement took me through every stage of the writing process, even when I struggled to believe in myself. Thank you.

Thank you to the wonderful writers whom I am lucky enough to know, who read this novel before its publication and gave the best feedback and support: Genevieve Jagger, Juliet Escoria, Amanda McNeil, Mesha Maren, Shy Watson, B. R. Yeager, Sarah Gerard, and Brian Allen Carr.

Thank you to Tony Tulathimutte for his editorial insight.

Thank you to Hannah Maureen Holden, who published an excerpt of this novel in *Columbia Journal*.

Thank you to my agent, Kent Wolf, who helped this novel find its place.

Thank you to Olivia Taylor Smith, who cemented the idea that it takes just one person to believe in your work for doorways to open.

Thank you to the team at Unnamed Press, including Chris Heiser, for their clear vision in the final version of this novel.

Thank you to my friends whose support in motherhood buoyed me during the years of writing this: Jessica Nickel, Erin Poor, Emerald Tune, Mila Jaroneic, Lindsay Lerman, Geneva Souders, Leza Cantoral, Heather McDaid, Autumn Christian, Siobhan Lewing, and Jessica Fuller.

Thank you to my child, who is my unyielding source of inspiration. You are my why.

For anyone I have failed to mention, please forgive me. Know that I am forever grateful for the way you have brought inspiration to my life.